THEODOR STORM

Hans and Heinz Kirch

with
Immensee

and
Journey to a Hallig

Translated by
DENIS JACKSON *and* ANJA NAUCK

Introduction and notes by Denis Jackson

ANGEL BOOKS
London

First published in 1999 by
Angel Books, 3 Kelross Road, London N5 2QS
1 3 5 7 9 10 8 6 4 2

British Library Cataloguing in Publication Data:
A catalogue record for this book is available from the British Library

ISBN 0 946162 60 3

This book is printed on acid free paper conforming to the British Library
recommendations and to the full American standard

Typeset in Great Britain by Ray Perry
Printed and bound by Redwood Books, Trowbridge, Wiltshire

Contents

Translators' Preface

CLIFFORD BERND's description of Theodor Storm as 'primarily a poet for the ear' not only precisely describes his work, but also affirms the difficult task of translating it. Sound was as important to Storm as meaning, and the poet's natural precision and economy of language were central features of his style. Each therefore needs equal attention in translation if the reader is to experience anything of the richness and beauty of Storm's writing. No amount of care, however, can bridge the natural tonal differences between the languages, nor always match the economy of Storm's German.

We have often been asked: To which nineteenth-century English writer can Theodor Storm be most closely compared? Our answer has always been: Thomas Hardy. Theodor Storm was to his native North Friesland as Thomas Hardy was to his West Country. Both were prose writers and poets passionately devoted to their local regions, absorbed in their folklores, cultures and natural environments, and both conveyed their regions' natural beauties and rural rhythms in their writings, at the same time exposing their often harsh realities in human terms. Where they differ significantly, however, is in foreign dissemination of their works.

Through long absence of English translations, the works of Theodor Storm have not enjoyed the popularity in the English-speaking world that those of Thomas Hardy or other classic English writers have in Germany and elsewhere. Of Storm's fifty or so Novellen only ten have ever been translated into English, and virtually all these translations have been out of print for some time. My own new translation of *Der Schimmelreiter* published by Angel Books in 1996 under the title *The Dykemaster* was the first in thirty years. The present volume, in which two of the three works it contains appear in English for the first time, is part of a continuing programme aiming to win Storm his rightful place among the classic European authors in translation.

A thorough understanding of the nature and culture of Storm's homeland, which so deeply inform his poetry and prose, is essential for adequate translation. Our researches in preparing our translations of *Hans and Heinz Kirch* and *A Journey to a Hallig* therefore took us to the town of Heiligenhafen on the Baltic coast with its church, harbour and offshore island known as the Warder, and to the remote islands of the North Sea tidal flats, the Wattenmeer, respectively. The setting for *Immensee* is fictional, although various views have been expressed as to the location that could possibly have been in Storm's mind.

Heiligenhafen, a location unusual for Storm, is less remote today than during his lifetime. The single track railway along the coast has long since been closed, but road access over the hills to the town has improved. The church at the heart of the story, the Heiligenhafener Stadtkirche, remains as it was at the centre of the town, and the sloping cobbled lanes leading down to the shore and harbour from the market-square are much as they were. The fish's tail with the humorous verse still hangs over the town hall door, and the Shipmasters' Gallery in the church, the Schifferstuhl, continues to provide a view across the nave towards the marble bust of the naval commander Moritz Hartmann, exactly as described in the Novelle. The Warder, too, which as a rock and sand spit creates an inner harbour for the town, although much changed over the years by wind, tide and local construction, remains a feature of the coastal region today. Ships of all kinds still frequent the small harbour, unloading their cargoes from various parts of the world, and as one walks down the narrow lanes towards it, one can almost hear the resolute steps of Hans Adam Kirch as he strides past about his business. Such are the powerful impressions left by Storm's prose. A monument to him stands today in the town near the church.

There is nowhere in the world comparable to the Wattenmeer, with its immense tidal flats and small scattered undyked islands, the Halligen, that 'like dreams . . . lie in fog upon the sea.' To visit these islands, surrounded by a seemingly limitless stretch of water, is to visit another world; windswept and completely isolated from everyday events with just the noise of the wind, the birds and the sea for company. Hallig Süderoog, with its large isolated hallig-house on an earthwork that Storm describes in precise detail, is one of the furthest islands from the mainland. For the tale Storm had to tell there could not have been a more perfect setting, both realistically and symbolically, and the experience of a visit to any one of these small islands is precisely as described by him: the houses on lonely high earthworks, the deep watercourses that need to be crossed, the reservoirs, the quietly grazing animals, the constant noise of the sea, wind and screeching of gulls. Today Hallig Süderoog is a nature reserve.

Given the diversity of styles and language among the narratives in this volume translation has not been easy, but it has been a collaborative task of immense pleasure and satisfaction, each of us contributing our own particular experience and knowledge. We hope that readers will enjoy reading these Novellen as much as we have enjoyed translating them.

The texts used for our translations are from the four-volume collected edition *Theodor Storm: Sämtliche Werke*, edited by Karl Ernst Laage and Dieter Lohmeier (Deutscher Klassiker Verlag, Frankfurt am Main, 1987–8): *Immensee* – volume 1, *Gedichte, Novellen. 1848–1867*, edited by D. Lohmeier, pp. 295–328; *Eine Halligfahrt* – volume 2, *Novellen. 1867–1880*, edited by Karl Ernst Laage, pp. 40–68; and *Hans und Heinz Kirch* – volume 3, *Novellen 1881–1888*, edited by Karl Ernst Laage, pp. 58–130.

Denis Jackson   *Anja Nauck*
Cowes, Isle of Wight   *Müden, Germany*

March 1999

Acknowledgements

TRANSLATING literary texts is never an isolated task, but involves the assistance of many. Our thanks therefore go to Professor David Artiss, Memorial University of Newfoundland, for his troubles in researching and supplying us with valuable material; to Frau Petra Mischke, Museumsleiterin, Heimatmuseum Heiligenhafen, for her kindness in providing historical information; to the Württembergische Landes-bibliothek, Stuttgart, for providing maps of the Baltic and the Wattenmeer (c. 1860) from *Reymann's Special-Karte von Deutschland;* to Mrs Ruth Knight for her painstaking work in preparing maps based on them; to Frau Ingrid Schmeck for her permission to use her fine etching of old Heiligenhafen for the book's cover; to Herr Udo and Frau Helga Wiedersich for historical material concerning Heiligenhafen and for the great trouble they took in tracing and acquiring old chronicles of the town, without which our task would have been immeasurably more difficult; and to Frau Silke Vierck, Frau Sylviane Capell and Mrs Anna Sherwell for their helpful critical readings. The valuable assistance of our editor and publisher, Antony Wood, on numerous problems of translation and presentation is also gratefully acknowledged. Finally we should like to thank our respective partners, Janet and Christopher, for their valuable criticisms of the texts and constant and patient support during the project.

Denis Jackson and Anja Nauck

Introduction

THE NOVELLE was the dominant fictional form in German literature throughout the nineteenth and well into the twentieth century.[1] Its freedoms, in contrast to those of the novel, are limited, yet its concentrated structure admits a huge variety of narrative strategies. Theodor Storm (1817-88) was one of the German Novelle's greatest exponents. His style and treatment of the form changed considerably during his lifetime, but the reminiscence tale (*Erinnerungsnovelle*) remained a favourite underlying structure for him. He considered the Novelle a genre of the highest importance.

> The Novelle of today is the sister of drama and the strictest form of prose fiction. Like the drama it treats of the profoundest problems of human life; like the drama it demands for the perfections of its form a central conflict from which the whole is organised and in consequence the most succinct form and the exclusion of all that is unessential. It not only accepts but actually makes the highest demands on art.[2]

But Theodor Storm was first and foremost a lyric poet, and his poetry not only reflected his deep affinity with his local region but also greatly influenced his prose. Clifford Bernd's description of Storm as 'primarily a poet for the ear' could equally well apply to his Novellen.[3] His lyric poetry is the key to his prose work. Words are chosen as much for the quality of their sounds as for their meanings. The lyrical attitude of mind is apparent in all his works: as he said to a friend towards the end of his life, 'My craft of fiction grew out of my lyric verse.'[4] His writing embodies not only a literary transition from late Romanticism to Poetic Realism, but also the socio-political transformation that Germany underwent in its development from a loose confederation of independent principalities to a unified nation.

Storm is a writer characteristic in every respect of the movement known as 'Poetic Realism', marking the broad period of literature written in the German language from the 1840s to the 1880s, which aimed at portraying life, but only as far as life was seen as artistically significant and appeared to possess intrinsic value. Classicism of the Goethe era firmly subordinated reality to ideas; Naturalism, nearly a century later, claimed to render reality 'as it was'. Between these two movements, to quote Walter Silz's analysis, 'What naturally resulted was a compromise between pure Romanticism at the one extreme and Naturalism at the other, between the poeticisation of the world and the stark reflection of things as things, without symbolical valuation or interpretation. This compromise was called Poetic Realism.'[5] It tended

> to have the colouring of a particular region to which its persons are attached. It tends towards provincialism rather than nationalism. It deals by prefer- ence with the 'Kleinstadt' or 'Dorf', whereas Naturalism was to turn to the metropolis and its masses. The social matrix of Poetic Realism is the liber- ated middle class, the 'Bürgertum' . . . [It] has a strong leaning towards sym- bolism, for it believes that things have deeper meaning than appear on the surfaces.[6]

Storm's particular form of Poetic Realism is a product of his reminiscence technique, which places the reader within the minds of his characters, giving an almost Proustian living experience of past time; it is a central characteristic of his writing. The lives of ordinary, unexceptional people are precisely observed. 'The world of external nature and domestic existence are palpably there, yet the overall effect is one of transfigured, poeticised reality.' The narrative technique in addition is one of suggestion and 'the artistic principle one of silence'.[7]

Storm wrote more than fifty Novellen. The three selected here reflect the two broad stages of his development seen by his friend Paul Heyse, the first being when he 'painted in watercolours', and the second when he 'began to paint in oils'.[8] The 'watercolour' Novellen, from *Immensee* (1850) to the pivotal *Eine Halligfahrt* (*Journey to a Hallig*, 1871), are reminiscence tales dwelling with elegiac resignation on the vanished happiness of youth and the past. The 'oil' Novellen, from the early 1870s onwards, such as *Draußen im Heidedorf* (*A Village in the Heathland*, 1871) and *Viola tricolor* (1873), take a more realistic and dramatic direction. With *Aquis submersus* (1876) Storm turned to historical Novellen (*Chroniknovellen*), and in *Renate* (1878), *Eekenhof* (1879) and *Zur Chronik von Grieshuus* (*The Grieshuus Chronicle*, 1884) he made the past live, often skilfully simulating the language and style of old chronicles. In his last years Storm became more and more a Realist in Novellen dealing with modern problems, such as hereditary madness in *Schweigen* (*Silence*, 1883) and euthanasia in *Ein Bekenntnis* (*A Confession*, 1887).[9] Of ever-increasing complexity of narrative technique and scale, his fiction culminated in the masterpieces *Carsten Curator (1877)* and *Hans und Heinz Kirch* (1882), his most concentrated Realist achievements, portraying social reality in the harshest terms, and *Der Schimmelreiter* (*The Dykemaster* in my translation, 1888), which combines all the elements of Storm's art – the cyclic frame (*Rahmen*), poetic use of mood and atmosphere (*Stimmung*), reminiscence (*Erinnerung*), historical perspective, and Realism – to affirm his pre-eminence in the Novelle.

Hans Theodor Woldsen Storm was born on 14 September 1817 in the German-speaking coastal town of Husum, North Friesland, in the then Danish duchy of Schleswig. His father, Johann Casimir Storm (1790–1874), after studying at Heidelberg, had opened his own law practice in Husum in 1815 and set the seal on his position in the town by marrying into the patrician Woldsen family. The Woldsens had been prosperous merchants in Husum since the early seventeenth century and their large patrician houses were well-known as centres of social activity. Johann's family were Low Saxon, for generations hereditary owners of wind and water mills at Westermühlen near Rendsburg in the duchy of Schleswig, although he himself had followed the traditions of his mother's side, which produced clergymen and members of other learned professions. He was a rationalist who never attended church, adopting, however, the life-style of a Protestant ascetic.[10] Young Reinhardt's remarks to Elisabeth in *Immensee* that 'it's just a story' and 'there are no such things as angels' might well be echoes of this non-religious household.

Husum had changed little in the century before Theodor Storm's birth; its development was arrested by the silting up of the small harbour and the continental blockade of the Napoleonic Wars. The only street lamp was by the harbour and Theodor and his friends relied on their lanterns to guide them about the streets on winter evenings. Until the middle of the nineteenth century the harbour had no sea-lock to protect it, and the sea dykes protecting the town from the North Sea were also inadequate. Not a year passed without the low-lying houses being flooded in stormy weather, and many frightful memories of severe storms during his childhood are recalled in Storm's Novellen. To the east of the town lay the vast heathland and rising sandy terrain of the uplands, the Geest; to the north and south lay the rich polderlands, the Marsch, the land reclaimed from the sea, intersected by drainage ditches and divided by old dykes; and to the west, the immense North Sea tidal flats, the Wattenmeer, with its low-lying islands and Halligen (undyked islands), one of the largest continuous areas of mudflats in the world (see map on pages 68–9). Much of Storm's work in prose and poetry is infused with the atmosphere of this remarkable region.

The 'Protestant ascetic' atmosphere of the home in which Theodor Storm grew up, coupled with his mother's inability to show affection to her children, left a lasting mark on his life. He could not remember having ever been kissed or embraced by her.[11] For the affection he needed during his early years he turned primarily to his maternal great-grandmother, Elsabe Feddersen (1741–1829), whose patrician house faced the harbour, and to the local baker's step-daughter, Lena Wies (1797–1869), with her inexhaustible stock of folk-tales and stories. Both are to be found in *Der Schimmelreiter,* and the latter is also described in the prose sketch *Lena Wies* (1873), a literary monument to this Sheherazade of his youth who awakened in him a life-long interest in the superstitions, tales and legends of the region of his birth on which he drew so extensively in his fiction, and who exercised such a considerable early influence on him.

At the age of nine Storm showed a keen interest in music and languages. His literary education began at a celebrated Gymnasium, the Katharineum, in the Baltic city of Lübeck, where he read Goethe's *Faust*, Eichendorff, and Heine's *Buch der Lieder* (*Book of Songs,* 1827), the last making a permanent impression on him. Heine became the 'poet of his youth'. Much later in life he wrote that after reading these 'magical works' of Goethe and Heine it was as if through them 'the gates to German poetry had sprung open for the very first time'.[12]

In 1837 Storm left Lübeck to study law at the University of Kiel. Here, as a close friend of the influential future historian Theodor Mommsen (1817–1903 – the first German to win the Nobel Prize in literature), he enjoyed an intellectual stimulus his law studies did not provide, and discovered the lyric poetry and prose of Eduard Mörike (1804–75), whose novel *Maler Nolten* (*Nolten the Painter*, 1832) he was to recall in his first prose work *Marthe und ihre Uhr* (*Marthe and her Clock*, 1847). The university years also saw Storm's involvement with Theodor Mommsen in a collection of legends, fairy-tales and folk-songs of Schleswig-Holstein, and the production, together with Mommsen's brother Tycho, of a book of poetry, *Das Liederbuch dreier Freunde* (*The Songbook of Three Friends*, 1843). The latter, published in Kiel, contained one hundred and twenty poems, more than forty of which were Storm's.

Among Storm's earliest experiences of love was his infatuation, at the age of nineteen, with an eleven-year-old girl, Bertha von Buchan whom he met at an uncle's house in Hamburg at Christmas 1836. This strange love affair began with the writing of fairy-tales and poems for her, but faded when Bertha, aged sixteen, refused Storm's proposal of marriage, which caused him great misery. Bertha provided the model for the young Elisabeth in *Immensee*. But Storm's demonstrably passionate nature seldom spilled over into his work. He once wrote to a friend: 'I am of a strongly sensual, passionate nature; the reserve in my writings (in the poems it is not so evident) might be based in part on my impulse to keep it to myself; you will hardly ever find the words "love" or "kiss" in my writings.'[13] The drawing-room sensitivities of his largely female readership would also have been a constraining factor.

Storm returned to Husum in 1842 after finishing his studies at Kiel, and set up on his own there in 1843. The eldest among his three brothers and two sisters, he was an attractive young man and much liked in Husum society. He had a fine tenor voice and was intensely musical, and soon founded and trained a small choral society in the town. His musical interests were to feature in Novellen such as *Immensee* and *Journey to a Hallig*, and he was to pass them on to his children – his youngest son Karl became a music teacher and his daughter Elsabe studied music in Weimar.

Storm remained in Husum for the following ten years, building up both his law practice and his social position in the town.[14] At the same time he established himself as a prose writer and poet, publishing a collection of his work, *Sommergeschichten und Lieder* (*Summer Stories and Songs*) in Kiel in 1851, the year his second son, Ernst, was born. The first separate edition of his poems also appeared in Kiel in 1852, containing the evocative and descriptive poem 'Die Stadt' ('The Town'), about Husum, the 'grey town by the sea' – 'one of the first great realistic landscape poems in German literature'.[15]

Am grauen Strand, am grauen Meer
Und seitab liegt die Stadt;
Der Nebel drückt die Dächer schwer,
Und durch die Stille braust das Meer
Eintönig um die Stadt.

Es rauscht kein Wald, es schlägt im Mai
Kein Vogel ohn' Unterlaß;
Die Wandergans mit hartem Schrei
Nur fliegt in Herbstesnacht vorbei,
Am Strande weht das Gras.

Doch hängt mein ganzes Herz an dir,
Du graue Stadt am Meer;
Der Jugend Zauber für und für
Ruht lächelnd doch auf dir, auf dir,
Du graue Stadt am Meer.

By the grey shore, by the grey sea,
And set apart, lies the town;
The fog lies heavy on the roofs,
And through the stillness roars the sea
Dully around the town.

No forest murmurs, nor do birds
Sing constantly in May;
Only the goose on autumn nights,
With its harsh cry, flies by,
On the shore the grasses sway.

Yet all my heart belongs to you,
You grey town by the sea;
The magic of my youth, evermore
Will rest and smile on you, on you,
You grey town by the sea.

In a draft speech for his seventieth birthday in 1887, Storm was to write of his development as a poet:

My lyric poetry was not ripe until my life had acquired an independent meaning of its own and as a young lawyer I had had to take full responsibility for my actions. But when I had written the key songs for *Immensee*, 'Song of the Harp Girl' and 'My Mother Wished it So' . . . and when the poem 'October Song' was also written, then I knew for sure, and was never to be diverted from it, although the world today still hardly knows it, that I belong in the company of those few lyric poets the new German literature possesses: our old Asmus Claudius and Goethe, Uhland and Eichendorff, Heinrich Heine and Eduard Mörike.[16]

In September 1846 Storm married his first cousin, Constanze Esmarch, the daughter of the mayor of Segeberg. Contrary to convention, they were married by a pastor in the Segeberg town hall, Storm rejecting the claim that a church marriage legalised and hallowed a relationship that he considered already sacred. None of his family attended. His rejection of Christianity, its 'external accessories' fabricated by men and what he regarded as the Church's 'interference' in marriage and personal affairs, was to surface throughout his life and work.[17] Storm considered the church, as he did the nobility, to be a 'poison in the veins of the nation'.[18] Yet no direct challenge could ever be given full literary expression for fear of criminal charges for undermining religion and morality. Although initially expressing serious concern at the intermarriage, Storm's father finally consented, but Storm himself later came to share the concern regarding the mental health of some of his children.

Constanze was pretty, intelligent, domesticated and musical, all that could be wished for; but difficulties soon arose within the marriage. Within a year Storm became attracted to Dorothea (Doris) Jensen (1828–1903), the younger sister of his brother's fiancée, who had been in love with him at the age of thirteen. He confessed many years later that Dorothea aroused the passionate side of his nature, while, in the early years of their marriage, his very real love for Constanze was more 'a quiet feeling of sympathy'.[19] The marriage improved with the birth of their first son Hans, Dorothea's honourable conduct in keeping out of Theodor's way, and Constanze's forbearing silence and understanding. Dorothea eventually broke off the relationship and left Husum that year, 1848, the year of revolution in Europe.

The Schleswig-Holstein question – the wars and conflicts over the political and territorial status of the North German territories – dominated Storm's life. The conflagration of 1848 affected him more

adversely than it did any other German writer. From its troubled
aftermath Storm received his baptism by fire as a poet.[20] After severing
its ties with Norway in 1814, the Danish monarchy consisted of three
main parts, the kingdom of Denmark and the duchies of Schleswig
and Holstein, the latter also being a member of the German
Confederation. So whereas Holstein was German, Storm's Schleswig
was linguistically and culturally divided between a Danish population,
primarily in the north, and a German population in the south. When
the German-speaking population in Schleswig opposed Danish rule
and demanded a new and separate constitution and affiliation to
Holstein, and thus the German Confederation, the Danish liberal
movement retaliated by demanding that Schleswig be incorporated
into Denmark. When this incorporation took place in 1848, the
German patriots in Schleswig-Holstein resorted to arms. The war
lasted three years and saw brigades of Danish royalist troops enter
Husum, provoking further rebellion and bloodshed. After the Danish
bombardment of Friedrichstadt in 1850, Storm was witness to the
horrible sights of its wounded as they poured through the streets of his
home town.[21] By the agreements of 1851 and 1852 Denmark pledged to
tie Schleswig no closer to itself than Holstein, but repression followed
the agreements; public meetings were banned, Danish was to be taught
in schools, and officials at all levels who were disloyal or suspected of
disloyalty were removed.[22]

Storm had not himself borne arms, but his patriotic writings of the
time – poems such as 'Ostern' ('Easter', 1848: 'The land is ours, and
should remain so!'), 'Abseits' ('Apart', 1848) and 'Gräber an der Küste'
('Graves on the Coast', 1850: 'Unwillingly must the wild Danish flag be
the guard of honour at your tomb.')[23] – left no room for doubt as to his
real sympathies, and he was forced into exile. Although his was a stance
of local patriotism rather than nationalism, his secretaryship of the
Patriotic Volunteers Society and his signature on a petition for the
termination of Schleswig's personal union with Denmark sealed his
fate. In May 1852 his post of *Rechtsanwalt* (lawyer) was abolished by the
new Danish authorities and he was forced to leave Husum. After
unsuccessfully applying for posts in Gotha and Buxtehude, he had
finally to turn to the less congenial Prussia. In 1853, the year in which

his third son, Karl, was born, he took a post as *Gerichtsassessor* (Assessor), a low rank in the legal section of the Prussian Civil Service, at Potsdam.

The writing and first publication of *Immensee* belong to these years of conflict and reaction. The principal characters fail to grasp happiness from a kind of lethargy, a passive endurance of things, whereas they might have altered the course of events to their advantage by assertive action.[24] In this they reflect the mood of the period, the lethargy into which the greater part of the German middle class, tired of insurrection, cowed by repression and politically apathetic, had sunk after the failed revolution of 1848. During the last years of its existence the German Confederation, rigid and unyielding, remained blind to the need for reform that the revolution had demonstrated. In *Immensee* Storm artistically creates the mood of a whole social class in the aftermath of 1848 and shows himself to be a master of indirect social commentary, an art he was later to develop and refine.[25]

The poetic qualities of this elegiac love story in an idyllic setting are rooted in Storm's early admiration for Goethe, Eichendorff and Mörike. Masterfully employing all the lyrical riches of the age of Goethe, Storm also strikes the balance his public, a largely female readership at this time, looked for between poetry and everyday life.[26] *Immensee* is a lyrical Novelle, 'but not in the sense,' one commentator has pointed out, 'that it is a spontaneous effusion of poetic atmosphere. It is, on the contrary, a remarkable demonstration of the extreme sophistication of Storm's exploitation of themes and motifs and of his high compositional art'.[27]

In a sequence of eight episodes within an opening and closing framework, the narrator, in old age, remembers earlier scenes from his life: an almost fairy-tale childhood, his companion Elisabeth, their mutual love which grew when he left home for university, Elisabeth's eventual marriage to a wealthy suitor at her mother's behest, and his nostalgic meeting with her many years later at her husband's estate at Immensee (Bees' Lake). Moments of climax are heightened by songs in the style of folk-poetry.

In *Immensee* late Romanticism and Realism are fused in Storm's 'poeticised reality', which lifts social experience out of the banal framework of everyday life to ennoble it. Symbols, images and motifs are subtly woven into the fabric of the story, its landscape and everyday setting. A water-lily in the lake at Immensee, to which the narrator tries unsuccessfully to swim at night, symbolises unattainable love.[28] Storm sees the realities of everyday life under the aspect of mutability, subject to the laws of decay and dissolution. His characters are not beings of strong will, rarely combating misfortune, instead watching the storm-clouds gathering which are later to engulf them; 'they yield themselves up to the fate that overtakes them'.[29] The language of *Immensee* is 'concise, almost laconic, very close to the language of everyday speech, and composed of simple sentences, letters and conversations'; it is free from archaisms, dialect words and literary idiom; in its simplicity and directness it is akin to the language of the Volkslied.[30]

After *Immensee* was first published in 1850,[31] Storm gave a copy to Tycho Mommsen who severely criticised it, often unfairly. Storm, however, thoroughly revised it, striking out many passages and rewriting others. The revised version was included in a volume of prose tales and lyrics published in 1851,[32] dedicated to Constanze for her birthday. Commenting in a newspaper in 1853, the year after publication of the first single edition of the work, the great novelist Theodor Fontane (1819–98) placed it 'among the most powerful works we have ever read' and stated that it carried 'the stamp of perfection'.[33] It decisively established Storm's reputation as a writer of fiction, and no less than thirty-five editions, excluding reprints in collected works, appeared in Germany up to 1895.

The years of exile in Berlin and Potsdam proved useful to Storm. He participated in the city's cultural and intellectual life in the literary salons and societies, including the Berlin club 'The Tunnel', frequented by Theodor Fontane and the poet Emanuel Geibel, and the more exclusive circle of the 'Rütli', where he made the acquaintance of the elderly poet Joseph Freiherr von Eichendorff. His appointment to the District Court in Potsdam in 1854 was first without pay, and his father's frequent financial assistance and Constanze's skilled housekeeping were much needed. A daughter, Lisbeth, was born in 1855, who later in her life would be instrumental in the creation of *Hans and Heinz Kirch*.

Also in that year Storm spent a day with Eduard Mörike in Stuttgart, hearing him read his just completed Novelle *Mozart auf der Reise nach Prag* (*Mozart's Journey to Prague*). The two became friends.

The following year, 1856, the family moved to Heiligenstadt, a small town to the south among the wooded Thüringian hills, where Storm was at last given a permanent post as *Kreisrichter* (District Judge). The second edition of his collected verse was also published that year in Berlin, which included the beautiful short poem 'Meeresstrand' ('The Sea-shore', 1854). First written in 1853 with the title 'Am Deich' ('On the Dyke'), it reveals an intense homesickness, evoking images and sounds of his lost homeland, and acute sensitivity to his natural surroundings: 'Grey birds are darting, skimming / Across the darkening sea; / Like dreams the lonely islands / Lie in fog upon the sea.' After a visit to Storm in September 1864, Theodor Fontane noted: 'The setting: the town, the marsh, the uplands, the dykes . . . the sea, the tidal flats . . . – I simply mention them, who wants to describe them, for there is no other locality in Germany that has been described by the same hand so often and so masterfully as by Theodor Storm's.'[34] A year after Storm's death, Fontane described Storm's lyrics as 'equal in quality to the very best ever written' in the German language.[35]

Heiligenstadt was predominantly Catholic, but this did not prevent the free-thinking Storms from establishing themselves in the town. They soon had a congenial circle of friends and Storm again founded and trained a choral society. These years were largely happy ones, although his material circumstances were never easy, since his salary was not large, and the family was increased by two more girls, Lucie and Elsabe. But Storm's official work left him enough time to write more than had hitherto been possible. During his years in exile (1852–64) he wrote seventeen Novellen, fairy- and ghost-stories.

In the year 1864, however, the Schleswig-Holstein problem flared up once again. In response to the German population's renewed demands for the separation of the duchies from Denmark, following the death the year earlier of the Danish king, Friedrich VII, the Danish government annexed Schleswig to Denmark in contravention of the previous agreements of 1851 and 1852. Bismarck reacted promptly: Prussian and Austrian troops invaded both Schleswig and Holstein.

In the same month as the invasion, February 1864, Storm was elected *Landvogt* (District Judge and Chief Constable) in his home town of Husum, and returned there with his now large family to take up his new duties. The year was one of great happiness for both him and Constanze, despite the duchies of Schleswig and Holstein coming under joint Prussian and Austrian administration following the defeat of Denmark. But in May 1865 Constanze died from puerperal fever shortly after the birth of her seventh child, Gertrud. A few days later, together with just his brother Aemil, his three sons and some members of the choral society, a grief-stricken Storm had her body taken in the early hours of the morning to the family vault in the St-Jürgen cemetery in Husum, where she was quietly buried, fulfilling a mutual promise made years before. 'When the inquisitive townsfolk awoke, I had already buried my every happiness,' Storm wrote to Eduard Mörike the following month. His moving poem-cycle *Tiefe Schatten* ('Deep Shadows') describes the vault and the flowers laid on the coffin.

The loss of his 'pearl among women' was devastating for Storm. With her went his confidence in himself and his writing. He felt that his muse had left him. He thought of himself as a 'pensioned off poet' who needed to make a will.[36] Shortage of money and fear of not being able to meet the expenses of his sons' education brought panic. But in spite of his worries, and in accordance with Constanze's own wish, he married Dorothea Jensen in June 1866 in the parsonage of Hattstedt, a village north of Husum (see map on pages 68–9). She had never ceased to love him and was quite ready to care for his many children. They moved into an imposing former merchant's house near the harbour, 31 Wasserreihe, which today houses the Storm Museum and Theodor Storm Society.

Political circumstances caused further worries. The Gastein Agreement of August 1865 provided that Prussia was to administer Schleswig and Austria Holstein, but friction between Austria and Prussia resulted in Prussian troops occupying Holstein in June 1866. After Austria's defeat in the ensuing war with Prussia, both duchies came under Prussian administration. As far as Storm was concerned, one oppressive state had simply been replaced by another. The Prussians had not occupied Schleswig-Holstein 'out of good will', as he brusquely told Fontane, who had invited him to write a 'Victory Hymn' in 1864.[37] And to a friend in 1868 he wrote: 'In Prussia generally, the one in the right is the one with the power!'[38] In 1867 Schleswig-Holstein became part of the North German Confederation, and of the German Empire after Prussia's victory over France in 1871.

After the annexation, Schleswig-Holstein was brought into line with Prussian legislation through extensive administrative reform. Storm's long-held post of *Landvogt* disappeared, and he had to choose in 1868 between an administrative or a legal career. He chose the purely legal post of *Amtsrichter* (District Court Judge) at a much reduced salary, losing almost a third of his income. He and Dorothea had to let out the ground floor of his new home in the Wasserreihe, which was a terrible blow to his much-prized social status and self-esteem. His hostility and anger towards the new Prussian administration is revealed in a letter to Ivan Turgenev whom he had met at Baden-Baden shortly after Constanze's death: 'Prussia sometimes seems to me to be like a child that gets hold of a new toy, and knows of no other way of playing with it than to break it to pieces. The administration has also made it clear to us that it respects no other right of a nation than that forced on it at the barricades.'[39]

The year 1868 saw the publication by Westermann in Braunschweig of the first edition of Storm's collected works in six volumes, and the birth of a further daughter, Friederike. The former event followed his conviction that his life's literary work was at an end. Since Constanze's death three years before, he had written only two Novellen. In the years leading up to the outbreak of the Franco-Prussian War in 1870, he researched in Husum's chronicles and drafted the *Kulturhistorischen Skizzen* ('Cultural-Historical Sketches') which appeared in 1872 under the title *Zerstreute Kapitel* (*Loose Chapters*),[40] but over these years Novellen were conspicuously absent.

The outbreak of the Franco-Prussian War in 1870 reinforced Storm's intense distrust of Prussia's motives and his dislike of war. He had more enthusiasm for Schleswig's struggle within the state than for Prussia's struggle for its borders. When others celebrated Prussia's victory over France, Storm longed for victory over the foreign power in his homeland.[41]

Eine Halligfahrt (*Journey to a Hallig*) was published a few months after Schleswig-Holstein's absorption into Bismarck's German Empire in 1871.[42] This tale of two young people, their boat journey and visit to an old man in voluntary exile on a small hallig in the North Sea tidal flats expresses many of Storm's own reactions to the social and political changes in his homeland since his return in 1864. Through the thoughts and utterances of the old exile, Storm expresses veiled criticism of the increasing Prussianisation of his country, and through local legends of past natural disaster in the region, presents all things, as in *Immensee*, as transient and subject to the laws of decay and dissolution – a message again directed at the Prussian administration. Symbols and folklore motifs are again woven carefully into the story, in depiction of landscape, wildlife and the objects on the hallig,[43] and stranded goods from shipwrecks are tellingly used to suggest the character of the old man and his past. Each in turn, like the statuette of the foam-born goddess in her carriage waiting to be carried away across the blue Aegean Sea, poetically enriches the story and creates an idyllic setting for an island whose environment is, in reality, a hostile and isolated one, the harsh laws of which the old exile is happy to accept in place of the world of his 'power-hungry fellow-creatures' on the mainland. Here we have Poetic Realism at its finest. The hallig's sunken reservoir and surrounding trees and gardens are skilfully presented as a garden wonderland towards which the young couple are drawn as if by magic, and the gulls are portrayed as winged guardians of the island as they circle above it, their flashing, threatening eyes adding a demonic element to the tale.

Storm termed *Journey to a Hallig* 'a description with Novelle-form ingredients'.[44] Dispensing with a tight, unified plot, a climax and dénouement, and a hero/heroine with elaborate social identities, 'it follows a Heinean recipe: in the course of a journey a traveller indulges in a wide range of reflections, historical reminiscences and moods'.[45] It has been suggested that this tale is Storm's personal reassessment of his life at a time of crisis following the death of his wife and the occupation of his country and that it was an exploration of new forms of literary expression.[46]

During the 1860s and 1870s Storm had been rereading Heine,

especially *Reisebilder* (*Travel Sketches*, 1826–31). This work's whimsical amalgam of fact and fiction, autobiography, social criticism, flights of poetic imagination and literary polemic stimulated Storm to strike alternately humorous, ironic, soberly descriptive and elegiac notes, and to interweave them with legends, ghost stories and political references. The narrative style is relaxed and not as taut as it was to become in his later works 'in oils'. As in *Immensee*, hidden references or allusions, rich symbolism and contrasting tones bind the narrative sections together.[47]

Journey to a Hallig strives for and achieves a greater emotional breadth and freedom than Storm's earlier work,[48] at the same time magically evoking his homeland, everything that he held most dear about its stark natural beauty. As in *Immensee*, Storm adopts a narrative frame by means of which the past is brought into the time-domain of the story, a device he was to develop in later Novellen, but here the overall effect is more densely 'layered' than in the earlier work.

The stimulus for writing the Novelle was provided by a sea journey Storm made from Husum to Hallig Süderoog, a remote small undyked island in the North Sea tidal flats, in summer 1869 (see map on pages 68–9). Storm visited the single large hallig-house on its earthwork and noted details of its rooms and their aspects and the hallig's history. Characteristically he missed no detail of the island's flora and fauna, the structure of the earthwork's reservoir and the various items salvaged from stranded ships. The Novelle was completed in the first half of 1871, but although the text was the result of 'long, careful work', Storm came to the conclusion that 'it is not as it should be', and asked the editor to whom he had sent the manuscript to return it.[49] In the second version he achieved a quieter, more relaxed tone, and he removed the original ending after the word 'Requiescat', an outburst against the Franco-Prussian War.

Storm had longed to work among his fellow countrymen again, but the complete absorption of Schleswig-Holstein by Prussia was hard for him to accept. During the years leading up to his early retirement, however, he was to gain two promotions within the Prussian judicial system, finally attaining the post of *Amtsgerichtsrat* (Regional Court

Judge). Glad to feel that most of his children were launched in life by 1880, Storm now felt that he could retire and devote himself completely to writing. He was at the height of his mental powers. Between 1872 and 1880 he had produced some of his finest work 'in oils': *Viola tricolor* (1873), *Pole Poppenspäler* (*Paul the Puppeteer*, 1874), *Aquis submersus* (1876), *Carsten Curator* (1877), *Renate* (1878), *Eekenhof* (1879) and *Die Söhne des Senators* (*The Senator's Sons*, 1880).

Physically, though, Storm was a tired man and had for years been caused gnawing sorrow by his eldest son Hans, who had become an incurable alcoholic and for many years been a constant drain on his financial resources. Not only had his eleven-year medical studies been marked by constant failure in exams, but the posts he eventually obtained – as a doctor on a ship or in a town – had to be given up one after the other, invariably because of alcohol excess. The years between 1877 and 1882 were particularly difficult ones for father and son, Storm's spirits swinging between hope and despair. But the thought of living in the house he was having built in the remote Holstein village of Hademarschen put new life into him. He and his family moved into it in April 1881. Outwardly it was exceedingly plain and unattractive, but had a delightful garden and Storm's study looked out over the countryside he loved. According to his daughter Friederike, his garden was his greatest joy and at this time 'father was always happy'.[50] Hans, it appeared, had a settled job in Frammersbach, Bavaria, and was writing home regularly; he had even sent flowers and written: 'Thank God that everything has changed. I can now look life better in the face.'[51] For the present, Storm had the peace of mind he needed.

It was in the autumn of that year, 1881, that Storm took twelve-year-old Friederike to visit his eldest daughter Lisbeth then living with her husband, a pastor, in the small trading town of Heiligenhafen on the Baltic (see map on page 96). Lisbeth had first met her husband there some years earlier while keeping house for Hans when he had been a local doctor. Along with historical details of the town,[52] Storm learned from his son-in-law the story of a local ship-owner named Johann Brandt and his son Christian: their bitter conflict over Christian's failure to take an interest in his father's expanding shipping business, his long absence at sea, his failure to write home and a final decisive conflict over an unstamped letter, a story which Storm immediately liked, wrote down in detail in his diary, and adopted for his next Novelle. According to Friederike, her father's eyes lit up as he listened to the story;[53] he had writer's block at the time. As soon as he returned to Hademarschen he began work on a new Novelle drawing on the story he had just heard. The first manuscript of *Hans and Heinz Kirch*, one of his most substantial works, was dedicated to 'Gustav and Lisbeth in memory of the autumn days spent in your Heiligenhafen vicarage in 1881'.[54] Its first journal publication was in October 1882.[55] *Carsten Curator* (1877) and *Der Herr Etatsrat* (*The Councellor*, 1881) had both echoed elements of Storm's troubled relationship with his eldest son Hans, and now he again drew on painful personal memories as well as the story of the Brandt father-son conflict.

Outside the nobility, education rather than wealth was the main factor in social stratification in nineteenth-century Germany.[56] There was a strong parental driving force within the *Bildungsbürgertum*, the cultivated and educated class, the élite who enjoyed high social regard and political privileges, to preserve these benefits for their children, particularly their sons. The daughters' social position was won through marriage, not education, as shown in *Immensee*. Storm, therefore, could not contemplate his sons failing to climb the educational ladder to middle-class respectability. But they reacted to his unremitting pressure for academic success with resentment and psychosomatic illnesses, in Hans's case most probably leading to his alcoholism. Hans, whom Storm dearly loved all his life, was demonstrably unacademic and not cut out for the career his father demanded, and his constant ill-health frustrated whatever efforts he did make to please his father.

In this respect, Hans Adam Kirch, the central character in *Hans and Heinz Kirch*, is almost its author's self-portrait: to Hans Adam his self-made shipping business is everything, the one and only ladder to respectability and prestige in his *Kleinbürger* community; for Storm its equivalent was education.[57] Neither father listens clearly to what his son wants from life, and both pay the ultimate price for not doing so. Hans Storm died of tuberculosis alone in a hospital in Aschaffenburg, Bavaria, in December 1886, his father being too ill at the time to be with him. A year later, at what was to be his own last Christmas, after listening to the carol 'Silent Night', Storm broke down and cried: 'Sing no more! Down in Bavaria is a lonely grave, over it blows the wind, and snow is falling in large flakes upon it.'[58] The terrible fate of Hans Adam Kirch had become his own.

But *Hans and Heinz Kirch* is more than a story of father-son conflict. It is a tragedy of the emerging middle classes in a developing industrial society where status is dependent on property, economic power and position in the production process. It is a critique of middle-class values: the idolatry of social status, the obsession with the dignity of work, thrift and industry, and the ascetic attitude towards all joy in life. On a broad social and economic canvas, spanning the years before and after the founding of the German Empire in 1871, Storm shows the effects of these factors on a small, geographically isolated coastal community (see map on page 96). Everything is minutely observed, from the working of the new Prussian administration to the local post office's change of name to the *Kaiserliche Reichspost* and reference to *Reichsgulden* in everyday conversation. Wider context is given by allusions to the corn and coal trade with England, the Harmony Society – the agent of middle-class respectability – the status of the pocket watch, the Social Democrats – an explicit mention unique in Storm's work – the coming of the railway, the telegraph and the steamship, and even the evils of the slave trade. Within a realistic setting, Storm implies not only his contempt for the new Prussian administration but also a marked distaste within his own class, the educated bourgeoisie, for the ethos of the emergent German commercial middle class, a distaste common among his kind at the time.[59] In its critique of the values of the period, *Hans and Heinz Kirch* stands as a refutation of many later criticisms made of Storm's 'provincialism'.

The story is one of Theodor Storm's most powerful Novellen. The economic, compressed narrative reinforces the harsh reality of the tale, yet memorably expresses the intense human relationships within it. In keeping with Storm's own earlier definition of the Novelle, all that is inessential is excluded. The characters are swiftly drawn in the light of others' perceptions, and contrasted one with the other to emphasise the opposing strands of the story. The stooped, gaunt, forever-hurried figure of Hans Adam, with the leitmotif of his strong white teeth, is juxtaposed with the child-like figure of Wieb with her small Madonna face 'on which suffering should not be seen'. Scenes of conflict are skilfully interwoven with scenes of love in which, characteristically in Storm, dialogue is subordinated to atmosphere.

During the eight years Storm enjoyed at Hademarschen with his sons and daughters round him and frequent larger family gatherings, his creative powers showed no diminution. They reached their zenith in his last and most celebrated work, *Der Schimmelreiter,* in 1888, written when he was seventy years old and already weakened by the first symptoms of the cancer of the stomach from which he died on 4 July of the same year. Like his first wife, he was buried at Husum in the St-Jürgen cemetery without religious ceremony, quietly, with no friend speaking at the graveside, as he had stated the wish to be in his poem of 1864, 'Ein Sterbender' ('A Dying Man'): 'And may the priest remain far from my grave, / . . ./ It will not be fitting that a sermon / Be preached about what I have been / . . .'

Storm gave German literature unequalled evocations of his homeland and some of its finest short fiction and lyric verse. His intense visual and aural imagination, his gift for conferring symbolic significance on a wide range of flora and fauna, subtle use of folk legends and mastery of complex narrative structures, make his one of the most distinctive and compelling voices in nineteenth-century German literature. His fiction deserves to be far better known to the English-speaking reader. It seems astonishing that the present selection of Novellen, designed to reflect the variety and development shown by his best work, should include in *Journey to a Hallig* and *Hans and Heinz Kirch* two stories that appear in English translation for the first time.

Notes

1 See E. K. Bennett and H. M. Waidson, *A History of the German Novelle* (London, 1970), pp. 20ff. The term *Novelle* first made its appearance in Germany in the second half of the eighteenth century. According to Bennett and Waidson, the earliest works that can be described as Novellen are the tales contributed by Goethe to Schiller's journal *Die Horen* (*The Seasons*), under the title *Unterhaltungen deutscher Ausgewanderten* (*Conversations of German Refugees*, 1795), which he modelled on the cyclic frame of Boccaccio's *Decameron*. For further studies of the German Novelle see Martin Swales, *The German Novelle* (Princeton, 1977), Clifford A. Bernd, *German Poetic Realism* (Boston, 1981) and Roger Paulin, *The Brief Compass. The Nineteenth-Century German Novelle* (Oxford, 1985).

2 Storm to Gottfried Keller, 14 August 1881, in *Briefwechsel zwischen Keller und Storm*, ed. Albert Köster (Berlin, 1904). Quoted in Bennett and Waidson, p. 163.

3 Bernd, p. 62.

4 Storm to Erich Schmidt, 1 March 1882, in *Theodor Storm. Briefe*, ed. Peter Goldammer, vol. 2 (Berlin, 1984), p. 240.

5 Walter Silz, *Realism and Reality. Studies in the German Novelle of Poetic Realism* (North Carolina, 1954), p. 12.

6 Ibid., pp. 15–16. See also Martin Swales, op. cit. Poetic Realism's tendency towards 'provincialism' could equally be said to reflect simply a Germany at the time that was not organised around capitals, even in the age of nationalism. It remained a land of regions, of *Heimaten*, which were naturally reflected in German literature. See Thomas Nipperdey, *Germany from Napoleon to Bismarck 1800–1866* (Princeton, 1983), pp. 505 ff. In this discussion the term 'regionalism' is preferable to 'provincialism', with all its associations of narrowness and parochialism. See Paulin, p. 111.

7 J. M. Ritchie, *Theodor Storm. Immensee* (London, 1969), p. 35.

8 See Bennett and Waidson, p. 171.

9 See J. G. Robertson, *A History of German Literature*. 4th ed. (London, 1962), p. 486.

10 See David A. Jackson, *Theodor Storm. The Life and Works of a Democratic Humanitarian* (Oxford, 1992), pp. 17–21.

11 See Storm to the Austrian literary critic Emil Kuh, 13 August 1873, in Goldammer (1984), vol. 2, p. 68.

12 'Meine Erinnerungen an Eduard Mörike' in *Theodor Storm-Eduard Mörike, Theodor Storm–Margarethe Mörike. Briefwechsel mit Storms 'Meine Erinnerungen an Eduard Mörike'* (Berlin, 1978), p. 142.

13 Storm to Kuh, 13 August 1873, in Goldammer (1984), vol. 2, p. 71.

14 Margaret Mare, *Theodor Storm and his World* (Cambridge, 1976) provides a detailed account of Storm's life including his early years in Husum.

15 W. Freund, *Theodor Storm* (Stuttgart, 1994), p. 107.

16 Peter Goldammer (ed.), *Theodor Storm. Sämtliche Werke in vier Bänden* (Berlin, 1956), 8th ed. 1995, vol. 4, pp. 552–3. Asmus was the pseudonym of Matthias Claudius (1740–1815), poet and father of German popular journalism. Some of his poems

became folk-songs. Here Storm combines the two names.

17 For a fuller account of Storm's attitude towards Christianity and the Christian church see David A. Jackson, 'Storms Stellung zum Christentum und zur christlichen Kirche' in *Theodor Storm und das 19. Jahrhundert* [International Symposium to mark the centenary of Storm's death], ed. Brian Coghlan and Karl Ernst Laage, (1989), pp. 41–99.

18 Storm to H. Brinkmann, 18 January 1864, in Goldammer (1984), vol. 1, p. 442.

19 Storm to H. and L. Brinkmann, 21 April 1866, in Goldammer (1984), vol. 1, pp. 483–4.

20 See Bernd, p. 29.

21 See Storm to Laura Setza, 14 October 1850, in Goldammer (1984), vol. 1, p. 130. Storm vividly describes the columns of wounded men, women and children streaming through his town after the bombardment.

22 The Schleswig-Holstein question is dealt with in detail in J. A. S. Grenville, *Europe Reshaped 1848–1878* (London, 1976) and in William Carr, *The Origins of the Wars of German Unification* (London, 1991).

23 A poem written in the bloody aftermath of the Danish bombardment of Friedrichstadt. Storm despaired as much over the catastrophic loss of human life as over the lost cause he had supported. Composing the poem in this moment of despondent political passion, at a time of personally felt crisis, he later removed much of its political invective. See Bernd, pp. 63–4.

24 See Bennett and Waidson, p. 168.

25 F. R. Sammern-Frankenegg, *Perspektivische Strukturen einer Erinnerungsdichtung. Studien zur Deutung von Storms 'Immensee'* (Stuttgart, 1976), p. 182.

26 See Ritchie, pp. 36–7. For studies of the nineteenth-century reading public, see C. P. Magill, 'The German Author and his Public in the Mid-Nineteenth Century', *Modern Language Review*, 43 (n.d.), and 'The Reading Revolution and the Rise of the Press', in Thomas Nipperdey, pp. 520–6.

27 Ritchie, p. 21.

28 For a detailed treatment of symbolism in *Immensee* and in Storm's work as a whole see David Artiss, *Theodor Storm: Studies in Ambivalence. Symbol and Myth in his Narrative Fiction* (Amsterdam, 1978).

29 See Bennett and Waidson, p. 168.

30 See Ritchie, pp. 9, 36.

31 In K. L. Biernatzki's *Volksbuch auf das Jahr 1850 für die Herzogtümer Schleswig, Holstein and Lauenberg.*

32 *Sommergeschichten und Lieder (Summer Stories and Songs,* Berlin, 1851).

33 *Preußische [Adler-]Zeitung,* 17 June 1853. Quoted in Goldammer (1995), vol. 1, p. 775.

34 Theodor Fontane, *Unterwegs und wieder daheim.* Quoted in Karl Ernst Laage, *Theodor Storms Welt in Bildern* (Heide, 1987), p. 119.

35 Theodor Fontane, *Sämtliche Werke,* ed. K. Schreinert et al. (Munich, 1963), vol. 1, p. 498.

36 Peter Goldammer, *Theodor Storm. Eine Einführung in Leben und Werk* (Leipzig, 1990), pp. 142–5.

37 Storm to Fontane, 19 December 1864, in Laage (1987), p. 123.

38 Storm to Brinkmann, 21 January 1868, in Goldammer (1984), vol. 1, p. 519.

39 Storm to Ivan Turgenev, 30 May 1868, ibid., p. 526.

40 In Westermann's *Illustrierte Deutsche Monatshefte* for February 1872. *Zerstreute Kapitel* was a general heading given to a series of prose works and sketches which included the 'Cultural-Historical Sketches'. The series appeared in journal form between 1871 and 1873, including *Journey to a Hallig* (1871), and in book form, excluding the 'Sketches', in 1873. These first appeared in book form in 1913 in an edition of Storm's collected works edited by Fritz Böhme (Braunschweig and Berlin).

41 In a letter dated 8 August 1870 to his son Ernst, Storm wrote the following verse: 'Once there's victory over the foreign power, / The power in the homeland destroyed, / Then will I cry: the land is free! / Until then I'll save the cry of joy.' See Laage (1987), p. 135.

42 With other prose pieces under the general title *Zerstreute Kapitel* (*Loose Chapters*) in *Westermanns Illustrierte Deutsche Monatshefte* for October 1871. See note 40.

43 See Artiss, pp. 127–34.

44 Storm to his son Ernst, 16 May 1871. Quoted in Ingrid Schuster, *Theodor Storm. Die zeitkritische Dimension seiner Novellen* (Bonn, 1985), p. 139.

45 See Jackson (1992), p. 185.

46 Karl Ernst Laage and Dieter Lohmeier (eds), *Theodor Storm: Sämtliche Werke*, vol. 2: *Novellen 1867–1880* (Frankfurt am Main, 1987-8), pp. 790–1.

47 Ibid., p. 791.

48 Ibid., p. 790.

49 Ibid., p. 786.

50 Peter Goldammer, '"Ist es nicht langweilig?" fragte Vater. Aufzeichnungen von Theodor Storms jüngster Tochter Friederike', in *Schriften der Theodor-Storm-Gesellschaft*, vol. 44/1995 (Heide, 1995), pp. 51–5.

51 Storm to Paul Heyse, quoted in Heike A. Doane, *Theodor Storm. Hans und Heinz Kirch. Erläuterungen und Dokumente* (Stuttgart, 1985), p. 44. A detailed account of Hans's relationship with his father at this time is given in Ernst Erichsen, *Theodor Storm und sein ältester Sohn Hans* (Hamburg, 1955).

52 Storm's source of historical information, as noted in his diary for 7 October 1881, was Heinrich Scholtz's *Chronik der Stadt Heiligenhafen* (1743) which he had found in the house of his son-in-law, Pastor Gustav Haase, in Heiligenhafen.

53 See Goldammer (Heide, 1995), p. 54.

54 Laage and Lohmeier (eds), vol. 3, p. 794.

55 In *Westermanns Illustrierte Deutsche Monatshefte* (1882). It was revised and first published in book form together with *Schweigen* in Berlin in 1883 under the book title *Zwei Novellen* and dedicated to Dorothea.

56 Eda Saggara, *A Social History of Germany 1648–1914* (London, 1977), p. 253. See also David Blackbourn and Richard Evans, *The German Bourgeoisie* (London, 1991), pp. 185–90.

57 See Doane, p. 76 and Jackson (1992), pp. 125, 213.

58 Erichsen, p. 144.
59 See Jackson (1992), pp. 210–11. For the attitudes of the German propertied and educated bourgeoisie (*Besitz- und Bildungsbürgertum*) at the time, see Blackbourn and Evans, pp. 7ff.

Denis Jackson
Cowes, Isle of Wight
March 1999

Immensee

The scent of a violet rises from these pages,
It grew on the heath outside my town,
Year in, year out; from which kind no one knows,
It was later nowhere to be found.

The old man

O N A LATE AUTUMN afternoon a well-dressed old man walked slowly down the street. He appeared to be returning home from a walk; for his buckle-shoes, of outdated fashion, were dusty. He carried a long gold-headed cane under his arm; his dark eyes, in which his whole lost youth appeared to have taken refuge and which contrasted strangely with the snow-white hair, gazed quietly about him or down into the town which lay before him in the soft evening sunlight. – He appeared almost a stranger; for few passers-by acknowledged him, although many were instinctively drawn to look into those serious eyes. At length he stopped and stood before a tall gabled house, looked once more towards the town, then went into the entrance hall. At the sound of the doorbell, the green curtain at the small living-room window which looked out onto the hall was drawn aside, revealing behind it the face of an old woman. The man beckoned to her with his cane. 'Still no light!' he said with a somewhat southern accent; and the housekeeper let the curtain fall back again. The old man now crossed the spacious hall, then went through a parlour where large oak cupboards filled with china vases stood against the walls, and through a far door entered a small corridor from which a narrow staircase led to upper rooms at the rear of the house. He slowly climbed the stairs, unlocked a door and entered a moderately large room. Here it was peaceful and quiet; one of the walls was almost covered with bookcases and repositories; on the other hung pictures of people and places; before a green-covered table, upon which several opened books lay strewn, stood a heavy armchair with a red velvet cushion. – After the old man had put away his hat and cane in the corner he settled himself in the armchair, and with folded hands appeared to be resting after his walk. – As he sat there, it gradually grew darker; eventually a moonbeam streamed through the window-panes and fell on the oil paintings on the wall, and as the bright band crept slowly onward the old man's eyes instinctively followed it. Now it passed over a small painting in a plain dark frame. 'Elisabeth!' said the old man softly; and as soon as he uttered the name the time changed; *he was back in his youth.*

The children

Soon the charming figure of a small girl approached him. Her name was Elisabeth and she might have been five years old; he himself was twice that age. Around her neck she wore a little red silk kerchief which beautifully set off her brown eyes.

'Reinhardt,' she called, 'we've got a holiday, a holiday! No school for the whole day, and none tomorrow either.'

Reinhardt swiftly put the slate that was already under his arm behind the front door, then both children ran through the house into the garden and through the garden gate into the meadow beyond. The unexpected holiday came at a most opportune time for them. Reinhardt, with Elisabeth's help, had constructed a house from turfs here; they meant to live in it in the summer evenings; but it was still without a seat. He set to work at once; nails, hammer and the necessary planks were already to hand. Elisabeth, meanwhile, walked along the bank and collected the ring-shaped seeds of wild mallow in her apron; she wanted to make chains and necklaces from them for herself; and when Reinhardt had at last finished his seat, in spite of many a crookedly-driven nail, and now emerged into the sunlight again, she had wandered far away to the other side of the meadow.

'Elisabeth!' he called. 'Elisabeth!' And she came, her tresses streaming behind her. 'Come on,' he said, 'our house is ready now. You're all hot; come in, we'll sit on the new seat. I'll tell you a story.'

Then they both went inside and sat down on the new seat. Elisabeth took the tiny rings from her apron and strung them on long threads; Reinhardt began his story: 'Once upon a time there lived three spinners –'

'Oh!' said Elisabeth, 'I know that one off by heart; you shouldn't keep repeating the same old story.'

So Reinhardt had to abandon the tale of the three spinners; instead he told her the story of the poor man who was thrown into the lions' den. 'It was night,' he said; 'you know, really dark, and the lions were asleep. Now and then, though, they yawned in their sleep and stretched their red tongues out, then the man shuddered and thought it was nearly morning. Then suddenly a bright light shone all around, and when he looked up an angel was standing in front of him. It beckoned to him and then walked away into the rocks.'

Elisabeth had been listening attentively. 'An angel?' she said. 'Had it got wings, then?'

'It's just a story,' answered Reinhardt; 'there're no such things as angels.'

'Ugh, Reinhardt!' she said, looking him straight in the face. When he gave her a black look, however, she asked him doubtfully: 'Why do they always say there are, then? Mother and aunt, and at school too?'

'I don't know,' he answered.

'But don't lions exist, either?' asked Elisabeth.

'Lions? Do lions exist? In India they do; there the heathen priests harness them to carriages and drive across the desert with them. When I'm grown up, I'll go there myself one day. It's thousands of times more beautiful than here in our country; there's no winter there at all. You must come too. Do you want to?'

'Yes,' said Elisabeth, 'but then mother must come as well, and your mother too.'

'No,' said Reinhardt, 'they'll be too old by then, they can't come with us.'

'But I'm not allowed to go alone.'

'You will be; you will then really be my wife, and the others won't be able to order you about.'

'But my mother will cry.'

'We'll come back again,' said Reinhardt vehemently. 'Just tell me honestly: do you want to go with me? Otherwise I'll go on my own and then I'll never come back.'

The little girl came close to tears. 'Don't look so cross,' she said; 'I will go with you to India.'

Reinhardt clasped both her hands in boundless joy and pulled her out into the meadow. 'To India! To India!' he sang, and swung her round and round so that the little red kerchief flew from her neck. Then suddenly he released her and said seriously: 'But nothing will ever come of it; you don't have the courage.'

– 'Elisabeth! Reinhardt!' now came the call from the garden gate. 'Here we are! Here we are!' answered the children and scampered off home hand in hand.

In the forest

So the children lived together; she was often too timid for him, he was often too impetuous for her, but for all that they would not be separated; they shared almost every free hour; winters in their mothers' confined rooms, summers in field and woodland. – Once, when Elisabeth was scolded in Reinhardt's presence by the schoolteacher, he banged his slate angrily down on the desk to direct the man's wrath upon himself. It went unnoticed. But Reinhardt had lost all interest in the geography lesson; instead he composed a long poem; in it he compared himself to a young eagle, the schoolmaster to a hooded crow, Elisabeth was the white dove; the eagle swore to take revenge on the hooded crow as soon as his wings were grown. Tears filled the young poet's eyes; he imagined himself as most noble. When he had come home he managed to procure a small vellum-bound book with many white pages; on the first few he wrote, in a careful hand, his first poem. – Soon afterwards he changed school, and here he made a number of new friends among boys of his own age; but his relationship with Elisabeth remained unaffected. Of the fairy-tales which he had told her again and again, he now began to write down the ones she had liked the most; in the process he often felt a desire to insert something of his own, but, he didn't know why, he could never manage it. So he wrote the stories down precisely as he had heard them himself. Then he gave the pages to Elisabeth and she kept them carefully in a drawer; it gave him immense satisfaction to hear her from time to time in the evenings reading those tales from the book he had written, in his presence, to her mother.

Seven years passed. Then Reinhardt had to leave the town to continue his studies elsewhere. Elisabeth could not reconcile herself to the thought that there would now be a time completely without Reinhardt. She was delighted when he said to her one day that he would continue to write down fairy-tales for her as before; he would send them to her with the letters to his mother; she was then to reply to him saying how she had enjoyed them. The day of departure drew nearer, but before that many more poems went into the vellum-bound book. This he kept a secret from Elisabeth, although she was the inspiration for the whole book and for most of the poems, which by and by had filled nearly half its white pages.

It was now June; Reinhardt was to leave the next day. Everyone wanted to celebrate one more festive occasion together. A picnic was therefore arranged in one of the near-by forests for a large party of friends. The hour-long drive to the edge of the forest was made by carriage; the baskets of provisions were then lifted down from the carriage and everyone walked on further. The party had first to walk through a grove of fir trees; it was chilly and gloomy and the ground everywhere was covered with fine needles. After half-an-hour's walk they emerged from the darkness of the fir trees into a bright beech-wood; here everything was light and green, a ray of sunlight occasionally broke through the leafy branches, and above their heads a squirrel sprang from bough to bough. – The party stopped at a spot above which the crowns of ancient beeches grew together to form a broad transparent canopy. Elisabeth's mother opened one of the baskets, and an old gentleman took charge of provisions. 'Gather round me, all you young ones!' he cried. 'And listen carefully to what I say. Each one of you will get two dry rolls for breakfast; the butter has been left at home; you must find something to go with them for yourselves. There are plenty of strawberries in the forest, that is, for those who know where to find them. Those who lack the skill will have to eat the bread dry; but so it is throughout life. Have you understood what I have said?'

'Of course!' the youngsters shouted.

'But listen,' said the old man, 'I've not finished yet. We old folks have roamed about enough in our lives, so we're staying at home for the moment, that is to say under these broad trees, and we'll peel the potatoes and make the fire and lay the table, and at twelve we'll boil the eggs. In return you'll owe us half of your strawberries so that we too can have a dessert. Be off with you now, to east and west, and don't cheat!'

The youngsters pulled all kinds of mischievous faces. 'Stop!' cried the old man again. 'I don't really need to say this to you: anyone who finds nothing need hand nothing over; but pay attention to this carefully, they'll get nothing from us old folks either. And now you've had enough good advice for one day; if you get strawberries too, then you'll manage well enough for today.'

The youngsters were of the same opinion and set off in pairs.

'Come on, Elisabeth,' said Reinhardt, 'I know a glade where there are strawberries; you won't need to eat dry bread.'

Elisabeth tied the green ribbon strings of her straw hat together and hung it over her arm. 'Come on then,' she said, 'the basket's ready.'

Then they went into the forest, deeper and deeper; through damp impenetrable shadows, where everything was silent but for the cries of unseen falcons high above them in the eddies of air; then on through thick undergrowth, so thick that Reinhardt had to go ahead to clear a path, here to break a branch, there to force aside a tendril. But soon he heard Elisabeth calling his name behind him. He turned round. 'Reinhardt!' she called. 'Wait please, Reinhardt!' He could not make out where she was; at last he saw her some distance away struggling with the undergrowth, her fine small head hardly bobbing above the tops of the ferns. So he turned back and led her through the confusion of plants and bushes to an open space, where blue butterflies fluttered among the solitary woodland flowers. Reinhardt brushed the damp hair away from her small flushed face, and would have put her straw hat on her head, but she refused; after he had pleaded with her, however, she consented.

'But where are your strawberries?' she asked at last, as she stood still and drew a deep breath.

'There were some here,' he said, 'but the toads have been here before us, or the martens, or the elves perhaps.'

'Yes,' said Elisabeth, 'the leaves are still there; but don't mention elves here. Come on, I'm not at all tired; we'll go on looking.'

In front of them was a small stream, and beyond it the forest again. Reinhardt lifted Elisabeth in his arms and carried her across. After a while they left the leafy shade again and entered a wide clearing. 'There must be strawberries here,' said the girl, 'it smells so sweet.'

They went searching around the sunny glade, but found none. 'No,' said Reinhardt, 'it's just the smell of the heather.'

Raspberry bushes and holly grew everywhere in confusion; a strong smell of heather, which together with the short grass carpeted the open areas of ground, filled the air. 'It's lonely here,' said Elisabeth. 'I wonder where the others are?'

Reinhardt had given no thought to the way back. 'Wait a minute; which way is the wind?' he said and lifted his hand. But there was no wind.

'Quiet,' said Elisabeth, 'I thought I heard them talking. Call to them, in that direction.'

Reinhardt called, cupping his hands round his mouth: 'Come over here!' – 'Over here!' came the reply.

'They're answering!' said Elisabeth and clapped her hands.

'No, it was nothing, it was just an echo.'

Elisabeth clasped Reinhardt's hand. 'I'm afraid!' she said.

'You mustn't be,' said Reinhardt. It's magnificent here. Sit over there in the shade, in the heather. Let's rest for a while; we'll be sure to find the others.'

Elisabeth sat down under an overhanging beech tree and listened carefully in every direction; Reinhardt sat a few paces away on a tree stump and gazed silently across at her. The sun was directly overhead; it was a scorching midday heat; tiny, brilliant steel-blue flies with quivering wings hovered glittering in the air; all round them a faint buzzing and humming, and sometimes the hammering of a wood-pecker and screeching of the other woodland birds could be heard deep in the forest.

'Listen!' said Elisabeth. 'Bells ringing.'

'Where?' asked Reinhardt.

'Behind us. Can't you hear? It's midday.'

'Then the town is behind us, and if we go straight on in that direction we'll meet the others.'

So they started their journey back; they had given up looking for strawberries, for Elisabeth had grown tired. At last the sound of the others laughing filtered through the trees; then they saw a white cloth gleaming on the ground, the picnic table, on which strawberries were heaped in abundance. The old man had a napkin in his buttonhole and was continuing his moral lecture to the youngsters while he energetically carved away at a joint.

'Here come the stragglers,' cried the youngsters when they saw Reinhardt and Elisabeth coming through the trees.

'Over here!' called the old man. 'Empty out your hankies, tip up your hats! Show us what you've found.'

'Hunger and thirst!' said Reinhardt.

'If that's all,' replied the old man, holding up the full bowl towards them, 'then you can keep them. You know the rules; lazy people don't get fed here.'

He was prevailed upon at last, however, and now the picnic began; and a thrush sang from the juniper bushes.

And so the day passed. – But Reinhardt had found something after all; although it was not strawberries, it had grown nonetheless in the forest. When he returned home he wrote in his old vellum-bound book:

> Silent falls the wind,
> Here on the side of a hill;
> Beneath the spreading branches
> The child sits alone and still.

> She sits among wild thyme,
> She sits in scent so rare,
> The blue flies buzz about her,
> And glitter in the air.

The forest stands so silent,
She knows its soul, it seems;
Upon her brown, brown tresses
The golden sunlight streams.

Far off laughs the cuckoo;
And now I understand:
She has the golden eyes
Of the queen of the forest land.

She was not merely his protégée, she was also the expression of all that was most lovely and wonderful in his unfolding life.

The child stood at the wayside

Christmas Eve drew near. – It was still afternoon when Reinhardt and his fellow-students sat together at the old oak table in the Ratskeller. The lamps on the walls were lit, for here below it had already grown dark; but the guests were thinly gathered and the waiters lent idly against the pillars. In a corner of the vaulted room sat a fiddler and a zither-player, a girl with fine gypsy-like features; their instruments rested on their laps and they seemed to be preoccupied with their thoughts.

A champagne cork popped at the students' table. 'Drink up, my Bohemian beauty!' cried a young man of Junker-like appearance, holding a full glass towards the girl.

'I don't want to,' she said, without moving.

'Sing then!' cried the Junker and tossed a silver coin into her lap. The girl ran her fingers slowly through her dark hair while the fiddler whispered in her ear; but she shoved his head away and rested her chin on her zither. 'I'm not playing for him,' she said.

Reinhardt jumped to his feet, glass in hand, and stood in front of her.

'What do you want?' she asked defiantly.

'To look into your eyes.'

'What have my eyes got to do with you?'

Reinhardt, his eyes gleaming, looked down at her. 'I know very well they're deceiving me!' – The girl leaned her cheek in her open hand and gave him a sly look. Reinhardt raised his glass to his mouth. 'To your beautiful, wicked eyes!' he said and drank.

She laughed and tossed her head. 'Give it here!' she said, and fastening her dark eyes on his, slowly drank the rest. Then she struck a chord and sang in a deep impassioned voice:

> 'Today, just today
> Is my beauty displayed;
> Tomorrow, tomorrow
> Away it must fade!
> Only this hour
> Are you my own;
> For I shall perish,
> And perish alone.'

While the fiddler played a postlude in fast tempo, a new arrival joined the group.

'I called for you, Reinhardt,' he said. 'You'd already left, but the Christ-child had paid you a visit.'

'The Christ-child?' said Reinhardt. 'He doesn't visit me anymore.'

'What do you mean! Your whole room smelt of Christmas tree and brown biscuits.'

Reinhardt set down his glass and reached for his cap.

'Where are you going?' asked the girl.

'I'll be back soon.'

She frowned. 'Stay!' she said softly, with a seductive look in her eyes.

Reinhardt hesitated. 'I can't,' he said.

She laughingly prodded him with the tip of her shoe. 'Go!' she said. 'You're not worth it; you're all worthless.' And as she turned away from him, Reinhardt slowly climbed the cellar stairs.

Outside in the street it was deep twilight; he felt the fresh winter air on his hot forehead. Here and there the brilliant glow from a lighted Christmas tree shone from the windows, now and then from within could be heard the noise from tiny whistles and tin trumpets and the jubilant voices of children. Bands of beggar-children went from house to house or climbed up onto the railings by the side of the steps and tried to catch a glimpse through the windows of the pleasures denied to them. Occasionally a door would be flung open and scolding voices would drive a swarm of such small guests from the well-lit house into the dark lane; at one house an old carol was being sung in the hall, girls' voices clearly audible. But Reinhardt did not hear them, he walked quickly past everything, from one street to the next. When he reached his lodging it had grown almost dark; he stumbled up the stairs and entered his room. A sweet smell met him; it reminded him of home, it smelt like the Christmas room in his mother's house. His hand trembled as he lit his lamp; a large packet lay there on the table and as he opened it the familiar brown festive biscuits fell out; on some of them the initial letters of his name were sprinkled in sugar; no one else could have done that but Elisabeth. Then a small packet emerged containing fine-embroidered linen, handkerchiefs and cuffs, and lastly letters from his mother and Elisabeth. Reinhardt opened the latter first. Elisabeth wrote:

The beautiful sugar letters will no doubt tell you who helped with the biscuits; the same person has embroidered the cuffs for you. Christmas Eve will be very quiet here at home; my mother always puts her spinning wheel away in the corner at half-past nine; it is extremely lonely this winter now that you are not here. Last Sunday the linnet you gave me died; I cried bitterly, I always took great care of him. He always used to sing in the afternoons when the sun shone on his cage; as you know, mother often hung a cloth over it to make him quiet when he sang his heart out. So it is much quieter now in the small room except that your old friend Erich visits us from time to time. You once said he looked like his own brown frock-coat. I always think about that when he comes to the door, and it is really so funny; but don't tell mother, she gets so easily annoyed. – Guess what I am giving your mother for Christmas! You can't guess? Myself! Erich is drawing me in black chalk; I have had to sit for him three times already, each time for a whole hour. I quite loathed the idea of a stranger getting to know my face so well. Nor did I wish it, but mother persuaded me; she said it would give dear Frau Werner such enormous pleasure.

But you are not keeping your word, Reinhardt. You have not sent any fairy-tales. I've often complained about you to your mother; but she always says you have so much more to do now than childish things like that. But I don't believe it; it is something else.

Reinhardt next read his mother's letter, and when he had read both letters and slowly refolded them and put them away, an overwhelming homesickness came over him. For a time he walked up and down his room; he spoke quietly, then almost inaudibly, to himself:

> He had almost lost his way,
> And knew not where to roam;
> The child stood at the wayside,
> And beckoned him towards home!

Then he went to his desk, took some money from it and went down into the street again. – Here, meanwhile, it had grown quieter; the Christmas trees were no longer lit, the processions of children had ceased. The wind swept through the lonely streets; old and young sat together as a family in their houses; the second part of Christmas Eve had begun. –

When Reinhardt neared the Ratskeller he heard violin-playing and the zither-girl's song coming up from its depths; the cellar door bell now rang below, and a dark figure reeled up the broad dimly-lit stairs. Reinhardt stepped into the shadow of the houses and then quickly walked by. After a while he reached a jeweller's well-lit shop, and after buying a small cross of red coral returned the same way he had come.

Not far from his lodgings he noticed a little girl clad in wretched rags standing in front of a tall front door, struggling in vain to open it. 'Shall I help you?' he said. The child did not answer, but let go the heavy door handle. Reinhardt had already opened the door. 'No,' he said, 'they might drive you away; come with me! I'll give you some Christmas biscuits.' Then he closed the door again and clasped the little girl by the hand, and she went in silence with him to his lodgings.

He had left the lamp burning. 'Here are the biscuits,' he said, and put half of all he possessed into her apron, but none with the sugar lettering. 'Now run home and give your mother some too.' The child looked shyly up at him; she appeared to be unaccustomed to such kindness and unable to give an answer. Reinhardt opened the door and lit her way, and now the little thing with her biscuits flew like a bird down the stairs and out of the house.

Reinhardt poked the fire in his stove and put the dusty inkstand on his table; then he sat down and wrote, and wrote letters the whole night long to his mother and to Elisabeth. The rest of the Christmas biscuits lay untouched beside him; but he had buttoned on the cuffs from Elisabeth, which looked distinctly odd with his white fluffy woollen house-coat. He was still sitting there when the winter sun fell on the frozen window panes and revealed to him a pale, serious face in the mirror opposite.

At home

When Easter came, Reinhardt journeyed home. On the morning after his arrival he went to see Elisabeth. 'How you've grown!' he said, as the pretty, slender girl came smiling towards him. She blushed, but made no reply; the hand he had taken in his during her welcome she sought gently to withdraw. He looked questioningly at her; she had not done that in the past; it now seemed as if something foreign had come between them. – And so it remained even after he had been home for some time and returned day after day to see her. When they sat alone together, pauses arose, which he found awkward and then sought anxiously to avoid. So as to have a definite occupation during the holidays, he began to instruct Elisabeth in botany, to which he had intensively devoted himself in the first months of his life at university. Elisabeth, who was accustomed to following him in everything, and was quick to learn, entered willingly into this. Excursions were now made several times a week out into the fields or the heathland; and when they brought home the green botanist's vasculum full of plants and flowers at midday, Reinhardt would return again a few hours later to sort and share out the joint findings with Elisabeth.

It was for this purpose that he entered the room one afternoon as

Elisabeth stood by the window fastening fresh chickweed to a gilded birdcage that he had not seen before. In the cage sat a finch which fluttered its wings and pecked screeching at Elisabeth's finger. Reinhardt's cage-bird had once hung in that spot. 'Did my poor linnet turn himself into a goldfinch after his death?' he asked jovially.

'Linnets don't usually,' said her mother, who sat in her armchair spinning. 'Your friend Erich had him sent over for Elisabeth at lunch-time today from his estate.'

'From what estate?'

'Don't you know?'

'Know what?'

'That a month ago Erich inherited his father's second estate at Immensee?'

'You haven't said a word to me about it.'

'Well,' said her mother, 'you've not asked a single word about your friend, either. He is a very nice, sensible young man.'

Her mother left the room to see to the coffee; Elisabeth had her back turned towards Reinhardt, still busy creating her small bower. 'One more minute,' she said, 'then I'll be ready.' – As Reinhardt uncharacteristically did not answer, she turned round. A sudden expression of sorrow lay in his eyes which she had never seen in them before. 'What's wrong, Reinhardt?' she asked, stepping closer to him.

'Wrong?' he asked, his thoughts elsewhere, and letting his eyes musingly rest in hers.

'You look so sad.'

'Elisabeth,' he said, 'I can't bear that yellow bird.'

She looked at him in astonishment; she did not understand him. 'How strange you are,' she said.

He took both her hands, which she let quietly rest in his. Her mother soon returned to the room.

After coffee she sat down at her spinning wheel; Reinhardt and Elisabeth went into an adjoining room to put their plants in order. Stamens were now counted, leaves and blossoms carefully opened out, and two specimens of each kind laid between the pages of a large folio volume to dry. It was a still, sunny afternoon; only the spinning wheel whirred in the next room, and the sound of Reinhardt's low voice was heard from time to time as he named the orders and families of the plants or corrected Elisabeth's awkward pronunciation of Latin names.

'I am still missing the lily of the valley from the other day,' she said, when all the plants had been identified and arranged.

Reinhardt pulled a small white vellum-bound volume from his pocket. 'Here is a spray of lily of the valley for you,' he said, taking out the half-dried plant.

When Elisabeth saw the hand-written pages, she asked: 'Have you written any more fairy-tales?'

'They're not fairy-tales,' he replied, handing her the book.

There were many poems, most filling no more than one page. Elisabeth turned one page after another, appearing to read only the headings: 'When she was scolded by the schoolteacher'; 'When they were lost in the forest'; 'With the Easter fairy-tale'; 'When she wrote to me for the first time'; they were nearly all in the same vein. Reinhardt looked searchingly at her, and while she kept on turning the pages, he saw a delicate blush rising over her clear features and gradually covering them. He wanted to see her eyes; but Elisabeth did not look up, and when she got to the end, she silently laid the book down in front of him.

'Don't give it back to me in that way!' he said.

She took a brown sprig from the tin case. 'I will put your favourite plant in it,' she said and placed the book in his hands.

Eventually the last day of the holiday arrived, and the morning of departure. In response to her request Elisabeth was granted permission by her mother to accompany Reinhardt to the mail-coach stage a few streets away from their house. When they stepped out of the front door Reinhardt gave her his arm, and made his way in silence beside the slim girl. The nearer they came to their destination, the more he felt he had something urgent to say to her before he departed for such a long time, something on which everything of worth and pleasure in his future life depended, yet he could not think of the key word. Troubled, he walked more and more slowly .

'You'll be late,' she said. 'St Mary's clock has already struck ten.'

But he did not quicken his pace. Finally he said, stammering: 'Elisabeth, you will not be seeing me again for two years – when I come back will you still be as fond of me as you are now?'

She nodded and looked warmly into his eyes. – 'I have defended you,' she said after a pause.

'Me? Who did you need to defend me against?'

'My mother. We spoke for a long time about you last night when you had gone. She thought you weren't as sincere as you once were.'

Reinhardt fell silent for a moment; but then he took her hand in his, and, looking seriously into her childlike eyes, said: 'I'm just as sincere as I ever was; you must believe that! Do you, Elisabeth?'

'Yes,' she said. He let go her hand and walked quickly with her along the last street. The nearer he came to the parting, the happier his face grew; he walked almost too quickly for her.

'What's the matter, Reinhardt?' she asked.

'I have a secret, a grand secret!' he said and looked at her with glowing eyes. 'When I come back in two years, you'll find out.'

Meanwhile they had reached the mail-coach; they were just in time. Reinhardt took her hand once more. 'Goodbye!' he said. 'Goodbye, Elisabeth. Don't forget.'

She shook her head. 'Goodbye!' she said. Reinhardt got in, and the horses moved off.

When the coach rounded the first corner, he saw the figure dear to him once more as she slowly retraced her steps.

A letter

Almost two years later Reinhardt was sitting in front of his lamp among books and papers expecting a friend with whom he was in the habit of joint study. Someone came up the stairs. 'Come in!' – It was the housekeeper. 'A letter for you, Herr Werner!' Then she went away.

Since his visit home Reinhardt had not written to Elisabeth and had not received any letters from her. This one was not from her either; it was his mother's writing. Reinhardt opened it and read the following:

At your time of life, my dear child, almost every year has a character of its own, for youth is always making progress. And here too there has been change, which will probably hurt you at first, if I have rightly understood you. Yesterday Erich at last obtained Elisabeth's consent to marry him, after he had twice asked her unsuccessfully over the last three months. She had always been unable to make up her mind; now she has really done so at last; she is still so very young. The wedding will take place soon, and her mother will go away with them.

Immensee

Again years had passed. – On a warm spring afternoon, a young man with strong, sun-burnt features made his way down a shady forest road. His serious grey eyes peered intently into the distance, as though at last he expected a change in the monotonous road, of which, however, there was still no sign. Finally a horse-drawn cart came slowly up the road. 'Excuse me, my friend!' called the traveller to the farmer beside it. 'Is this the right way to Immensee?'

'Keep straight on,' replied the man and touched his broad-brimmed hat.

'Is it far from here?'

'The gentleman's almost there. Not half a pipe of tobacco, then you're at the lake; the manor house is close by.'

The farmer drove past; the other quickened his pace as he walked beneath the trees. After a quarter of an hour the shade on his left suddenly came to an end; the way led by a precipice, the crowns of ancient oaks scarcely reaching to the top of it. Beyond them a broad, sunny landscape opened out. The lake lay far below, peaceful, dark blue, and almost entirely surrounded by green sun-lit forest; only in one place was there a gap which provided a distant view until this too was closed off by blue mountains. Directly opposite, in the middle of the green foliage of the forest, was a snow-like layer – fruit trees in blossom, out of which, on the high shore, rose the manor house, white with red tiles. A stork flew up from the chimney and circled slowly over the water. – 'Immensee!' cried the traveller. It was as though he had now reached his journey's end; he stood motionless and looked out over the tops of the trees at his feet to the other shore where the reflection of the manor house gently swayed on the water. Then he resumed his way.

The way down the mountainside was now quite steep so that the trees below again provided shade, at the same time hiding the lake from view, which glittered only occasionally through gaps between branches. Soon the road rose gently upwards again, and now the trees on either side disappeared; instead, vine-slopes stretched along the way; on both sides of the road stood fruit trees in blossom, full of humming, rummaging bees. An imposing man in a brown frock-coat approached the traveller. When he had almost reached him, he waved his cap and cried in a ringing voice: 'Welcome, welcome, brother Reinhardt! Welcome to the Immensee estate!'

'God greet you, Erich, and thank you for your welcome!' cried the other in return.

Then they had come together and shaken hands. 'Is it really you?' said Erich, looking closely into his old schoolfriend's serious face.

'Of course it's me, Erich, and you are your old self; only you look rather more cheerful than you always used to look.'

At these words a pleasant smile made Erich's simple features even more cheerful. 'Yes, brother Reinhardt,' he said, shaking his hand once again, 'but since then I have won the great prize, as you well know.' Then he rubbed his hands and cried cheerfully: 'This will be a surprise! She doesn't expect him, never in all eternity!'

'A surprise?' asked Reinhardt. 'For whom?'

'For Elisabeth.'

'Elisabeth! You've said nothing to her about my visit?'

'Not a word, brother Reinhardt; she's no idea, nor has her mother. I've written to you in secret, so that the joy will be the greater. I always used to have my quiet little plans, as you know.'

Reinhardt grew pensive; he appeared to find it more difficult to breathe the nearer they drew to the estate. On the left of the road the vineyards now came to an end and gave way to an extensive kitchen garden which stretched down almost to the shore of the lake. The stork had meanwhile settled on the ground and was sedately strolling about between the vegetable beds. 'Hey!' shouted Erich, clapping his hands.

'That long-legged Egyptian is stealing my short pea-sticks again!' The bird rose slowly and flew onto the roof of a new building that lay at the end of the kitchen garden, the walls of which were covered with espaliered peach and apricot trees. 'That's the distillery,' said Erich. 'I built it two years ago. My late father rebuilt the farm-buildings; the house was built by my grandfather. And so, step by step, we make progress.'

As he spoke these words they entered a spacious forecourt, bounded on its sides by the farm-buildings and at its end by the manor house, both wings of which adjoined a high garden wall; behind this could be seen the lines of dark yew hedges, and here and there lilac trees hung their blossom-laden branches down into the courtyard. Men with faces heated by sun and toil crossed the courtyard and greeted the two friends while Erich called across an instruction or a question about the day's work to one or other of them. – They had reached the house. They entered a lofty, cool entrance-hall, at the end of which they turned left into a rather darker side-passage. Here Erich opened a door, and they went into a spacious room opening into the garden, the Gartensaal; because of the luxuriant foliage covering the windows, both its halves were filled with green twilight. Between the windows, however, the two tall, wide-open folding doors admitted the full glare of the spring sun and provided a view into a garden with precisely laid out flower-beds and high steep hedgerows, divided by a broad straight path from which could be seen the lake and the forest on the other side of it. When the two friends entered the room, the breeze carried a current of scents towards them.

On the terrace in front of the door to the garden sat a white, girl-like figure. She stood up and walked towards the visitor, but half-way stood as though rooted to the ground, staring motionless at the stranger. With a smile he offered her his hand. 'Reinhardt!' she cried. 'My God, it's you! – We haven't seen each other for so long.'

'So long,' he said, and could say no more; for when he heard her voice he felt a faint physical pain around his heart, and he looked at her standing before him, the same gentle, graceful figure to whom, years ago, he had said goodbye in his home town.

Erich had remained standing by the door, his face beaming. 'Now,

Elisabeth,' he said, 'you didn't expect him, did you? Never him, in all eternity!'

Elisabeth looked at him with sisterly eyes. 'You're so good, Erich!' she said.

He took her slender hand affectionately in his. 'And now that we have him,' he said, 'we shan't let him go again so easily. He has been roaming the world for so long, we want him to feel at home again. Just look how foreign and distinguished-looking he has become.'

Elisabeth cast a shy glance at Reinhardt's face. 'Throughout the time we haven't been together,' he said.

At this moment Elisabeth's mother came through the door with a small key-basket on her arm. 'Herr Werner!' she said, as she caught sight of Reinhardt. 'Well, a welcome guest as much as an unexpected one.' – The conversation now took its steady course of questions and answers. The ladies settled to their work, and while Reinhardt enjoyed the refreshments prepared for him, Erich lit his meerschaum pipe and sat smoking and talking next to him.

The next day Reinhardt accompanied him outdoors; across the fields, to the vineyards, the hop-garden, the distillery. Everything was in excellent order; those who worked in the fields or tended the vats in the distillery all had a healthy and satisfied appearance. At midday the family would come together in the Gartensaal, and the day would be spent, depending on the hosts' available time, more or less together. Only in the hours before dinner, as during the first of the day, would Reinhardt remain in his room working. For many years he had collected verse and songs current among the people wherever he could find them, and he now settled down to organise his treasured collection, and where possible to enlarge it with new transcriptions from the locality. – Elisabeth was gentle and friendly at all times, accepting Erich's constant unvarying attention with almost humble gratitude, and Reinhardt wondered occasionally if the spirited child of former times had promised to be a rather quieter wife.

Since the second day after his arrival he had been in the habit of taking a walk along the shore of the lake. The path led close by the bottom of the garden. At the end of it, on a projecting mound, stood a seat under tall birch trees; Elisabeth's mother had christened it 'the evening seat' because it faced directly west and, because of the sunset, was occupied mostly at this time. – One evening Reinhardt was returning from a walk along this path when he was surprised by rain. He sought shelter under a lime tree at the water's edge, but the heavy drops soon penetrated through the leaves. Resigning himself to being wet through, he slowly made his way back. It was almost dark; the rain fell more and more heavily. As he approached the 'evening seat' he thought he could make out the white figure of a woman between the shimmering birch trunks. She stood motionless and, so he believed as he approached her, turned round towards him as if expecting someone. He thought it was Elisabeth. When he hastened his steps, however, to meet up with her and walk with her through the garden back to the house, she slowly turned away and disappeared into the dark side-paths. He could make no sense of it, but he was almost angry with Elisabeth, although he doubted whether it had been her. He shrank, however, from asking her about it; indeed, on his way back he did not go into the Gartensaal, so as to avoid the possibility of seeing Elisabeth entering through the garden door.

My mother wished it so

Some days later, it was already towards evening, the family sat together as usual at this time of day in the Gartensaal. The doors stood open; the sun had already set behind the forest on the other side of the lake.

Reinhardt was asked to tell the company about some folk-songs he had received by post that afternoon from a friend living in the country. He went up to his room and came down immediately with a rolled-up package of papers which appeared to consist of neatly hand-written sheets.

Everyone sat down at the table, Elisabeth at Reinhardt's side. 'We'll read them at random,' he said. 'I haven't looked through them myself yet.'

Elisabeth unrolled the manuscript. 'It's music,' she said. 'You must sing this one, Reinhardt.'

And he began reading through some Tyrolean Alpine songs, occasionally briefly humming the lively tunes. A general cheerfulness

pervaded the small gathering. 'But who wrote these lovely songs?'
Elisabeth asked.

'Oh,' said Erich, 'you can tell by just listening to them; journeyman-
tailors and hairdressers and such happy-go-lucky people.'

Reinhardt said: 'They're not written; they grow, they drop out of the
air, they drift over the land like gossamer, this way and that; they're sung
in a thousand places at the same time. We find our own deeds and
sufferings in these songs, as if we had all had a common share in them.'

He took another sheet: 'I stood high up in the mountains . . .'

'I know that one!' cried Elisabeth. 'You start, Reinhardt; I'll help
you.' And then they sang the tune which is so mysterious that it is
impossible to believe it was conceived by man; Elisabeth's alto voice
could just be made out accompanying Reinhardt's tenor.

Her mother, meanwhile, sat occupied with her sewing. Erich, with
folded hands, listened attentively. When the song had ended, Reinhardt
quietly put the page to one side. – Up from the lake shore through the
stillness of the evening came the jingle of cow-bells; they listened
instinctively; then they heard a boy's clear voice singing:

> 'I stood high up in the mountains,
> And looked down to the valley below . . .'

Reinhardt smiled. 'Can you hear it? So it goes from mouth to
mouth.'

'It's often sung in this region,' said Elisabeth.

'Yes,' said Erich, 'it's Casper the cowherd; he's driving the heifers
home.'

They listened for a while longer until the jingling faded away behind
the farm buildings. 'These are the voices of nature,' said Reinhardt,
'from the depths of the forest; only God knows who first found them.'

He drew out a fresh sheet.

It had quickly grown darker; the red glow of evening lay like foam
over the forest on the other side of the lake. Reinhardt unrolled the
sheet; Elisabeth laid her hand on one side of it and looked at it with
him. Then Reinhardt read:

My mother wished it so,
She chose, so long ago;
The one my heart possessed
My heart must now forget;
It did not wish it so!

My mother is to blame,
She brought me only pain;
What once was pure and strong
Now is sin and wrong.
Where am I to turn!

For the pride and joy of my life,
All I have reaped is grief.
Would it had never been so,
Would I could a-begging go
Across the brown, brown heath!

During the reading Reinhardt felt an imperceptible trembling of the paper; when he had finished, Elisabeth quietly pushed her chair away and went silently out into the garden. Her mother's gaze followed her. Erich wanted to join her, but her mother said: 'Elisabeth's got something to do outside.' And so things rested.

Outside, the evening spread more and more over the garden and the lake, the moths whirred past the open door through which the ever-intensifying scent of the flowers and bushes wafted indoors; from down by the water came the croaking of the frogs, beneath the windows a nightingale sang, and another deeper in the garden; the moon looked over the trees. Reinhardt looked for a further moment at the place where Elisabeth's slender figure had disappeared between the arboured walks; then he rolled up his manuscript, took his leave of the others and walked through the house down towards the water.

The forest stood silent and cast dark shadows far out over the lake, while the centre of it lay in the sultry half-light of the moon. An occasional gentle rustling rippled through the trees; but there was no wind, it was just the breath of the summer night. Reinhardt walked on along the shore. A stone's throw from it he could make out a white water-lily. He was suddenly struck with a desire to see it more closely; he threw off his clothes and stepped into the water. It was shallow. Sharp plants and stones cut into his feet, and yet he still did not reach a depth enough to swim. Suddenly everything beneath him was gone, the water swirled completely over him and it was some time before he came to the surface again. He struck out with hands and feet and swam round in a circle until he was sure of the place where he had entered the water. Soon he saw the lily again; it lay alone among the broad glossy leaves. – He swam slowly out, sometimes lifting his arms out of the water so that the falling droplets of water sparkled in the moonlight; but it was as though the distance between himself and the flower remained the same; only the shore, when he looked round, lay increasingly uncertain in the haze behind him. He would not abandon his venture, however, but swam on vigorously in the same direction. At last he came so close to the flower that he could clearly distinguish the silvery leaves in the moonlight; but at the same time he felt himself entangled as though in a net; the smooth stalks reached up from the bed of the lake and entwined themselves around his naked limbs. The unfamiliar water lay dark all around him, and behind him he heard the leaping of a fish; a sudden eerie feeling overcame him in the strange element, making him tear violently at the tangle of plants and swim in breathless haste to the shore. When he looked back at the lake, the lily lay as before, distant and alone upon the dark depths. – He dressed and walked slowly back to the house. When he entered the Gartensaal from the garden he found Erich and Elisabeth's mother preparing for a short business journey they had to make the following day.

'Where have you been at this late hour?' Elisabeth's mother called out to him.

'Oh,' he replied, 'I wanted to go out to the water-lily; but I couldn't reach it.'

'Would you believe it!' said Erich. 'What did you want with the water-lily?'

'I knew it well once in the past,' said Reinhardt. 'But that was long ago.'

Elisabeth

On the following afternoon Reinhardt and Elisabeth wandered along the other side of the lake, now through the woods, now along the prominent high-rising shoreline. Erich had given Elisabeth the task, while he and his mother were away, of acquainting Reinhardt with the beautiful views of the immediate surroundings, particularly of the estate itself from the shore on the other side of the lake. They now went from one place to the next. Eventually Elisabeth grew tired and sat down in the shadows of some overhanging branches. Reinhardt stood facing her, leaning against a tree trunk; then he heard the call of a cuckoo deeper in the forest, and it suddenly occurred to him that all this had happened before. He gave her a strange smile. 'Shall we look for strawberries?' he asked.

'It's not the time for strawberries,' she said.

'But it soon will be.'

Elisabeth quietly shook her head; then she stood up and they both continued on their way; and as she walked by his side his gaze constantly turned towards her; for she walked gracefully, as if she were carried along by her clothes. Often without thinking he would drop a step or two behind so as to keep her completely fixed in his view. So they came to an open space overgrown with heather with a far-reaching view of the country around. Reinhardt stooped and picked something from the heather. When he looked up his face wore an expression of deep anguish. 'Do you know what this flower is?' he said.

She gave him an inquiring look. 'It's Erica. I've often picked it in the forest.'

'I have an old book at home,' he said. 'I once used to write all kinds of songs and verses in it; but I stopped a long time ago. There's still a wilted spray of Erica in it. Do you know who gave it to me?'

She nodded in silence, but lowered her eyes and looked only at the heather that he held in his hand. So they stood for a long time. When she looked up at him again, he saw that her eyes were full of tears.

'Elisabeth,' he said, 'beyond those blue mountains lies our youth. What happened to it?'

They spoke no more, but walked together in silence down to the lake.

The air was close, in the west dark clouds were gathering. 'There'll be a thunderstorm,' said Elisabeth as she quickened her pace. Reinhardt nodded quietly, and they both hurried along the shore until they reached their rowing boat.

During the crossing Elisabeth let her hand rest on the gunwale. Reinhardt glanced over at her while he rowed; but she looked past him into the distance. So his eye fell on her hand where it remained, and this pale hand revealed what her face had concealed from him. He saw on it that faint trace of secret grief that so readily takes possession of a woman's beautiful hands which rest at night on a broken heart. – When Elisabeth felt his eyes resting on her hand, she let it slip slowly over the side into the water.

On reaching the courtyard they found a knife-grinder's barrow at the front of the manor house; a man with flowing, curly black hair busily trod the wheel and hummed a gypsy melody between his teeth while a tethered dog lay panting nearby. In the hall, clad in rags, stood a forlorn-looking girl with beautiful features; she held out her hand, begging, towards Elisabeth. Reinhardt felt in his pocket; but Elisabeth anticipated him and hastily emptied the whole contents of her purse into the beggar's open hand. Then she quickly turned away, and Reinhardt heard her sobbing as she went up the stairs.

He wanted to detain her, but he changed his mind and remained at the foot of the stairs. The girl was still standing in the hall, motionless, the alms she had received in her hand. 'What else do you want?' asked Reinhardt.

She started. 'I don't want anything else,' she said, then turning her head towards him and staring at him with her lost-looking eyes, she walked slowly towards the door. He called out a name, but she heard nothing more; with head bowed, her arms crossed on her breast, she walked away across the courtyard.

> For I shall perish,
> And perish alone!

An old song rang in his ears, he caught his breath; after a brief moment he turned and went to his room.

He sat down to work but could not focus his thoughts. After an hour of vain effort he went down into the family living room. No one was there in the cool green twilight; on Elisabeth's sewing table lay a red ribbon that she had worn round her neck in the afternoon. He took it up in his hand, but it caused him pain, and he laid it down again. He felt tense and restless; he went down to the lake and untied the boat, rowed across the water, and walked once again along all the paths he had just walked together with Elisabeth. When he again returned to the house it was dark; in the courtyard he met the coachman who was taking the coach-horses out to graze; the travellers had just returned. Entering the hall, he heard Erich striding up and down in the Gartensaal. He did not go in to him; he stood still for a moment, then quietly climbed the stairs to his room. Here he sat down in the armchair by the window; he pretended to himself that he wanted to hear the nightingale that sang below in the yew hedges; but he heard only the beating of his own heart. Everything had become quiet downstairs, the night was seeping away, he did not feel it. – So he sat for a number of hours. At last he stood up and leaned out of the open window. The morning dew was dropping gently between the leaves, the nightingale had stopped singing. Gradually the dense blue of the night sky was displaced by a pale yellow glow from the east; a fresh wind arose and stroked Reinhardt's hot brow; the first lark climbed into the air rejoicing. – Reinhardt turned swiftly round and went to the table, groped for a pencil, and when he had found one sat down and wrote a few lines with it on a blank sheet of paper. When he had finished, he took his hat and cane and, leaving the sheet behind, carefully opened the door and went down to the hall. – The dawn still lingered in every corner; the large house cat stretched itself on the straw mat and rubbed its back against his hand which he instinctively held out towards it. Outside in the garden, however, the sparrows were already holding forth from the branches and proclaiming to everyone that night was over. Just then he heard the opening of a door from above; someone came down the stairs, and as he looked up, Elisabeth stood before him. She laid her hand on his arm, her lips moved, but he heard no words. 'You won't come back,' she said at last. 'I know it, don't try to deceive me; you will never come back.'

'Never,' he said. She let her hand drop and said nothing more. He went across the hall towards the door; then turned round once more. She stood motionless on the same spot and looked at him with lifeless eyes. He took a step forward and stretched out his arms towards her. Then he forced himself to turn away and went out through the doorway. – The world outside lay in the fresh morning light, the dew-drops hanging in the spiders' webs sparkled in the first rays of the sun. He did not look back, but walked quickly away; and the silent farmstead receded further and further behind him, and before him rose the great wide world.

The old man

The moon no longer shone through the window-panes, it had grown dark; but the old man still sat with folded hands in his armchair, gazing into the interior of the room. Gradually, before his eyes, the dark twilight around him changed into a broad dark lake; black stretches of water lay one behind the other, each deeper and more distant, and on the last, so distant that the old man's eyes hardly reached it, a water-lily floated alone among broad leaves.

The door opened and bright light flooded the room. 'It's good that you've come, Brigitte,' said the old man. 'Just put the lamp on the table.'

Then he moved the armchair to the table, took one of the opened books and became engrossed in studies to which he had once devoted the energy of his youth.

Journey to a Hallig

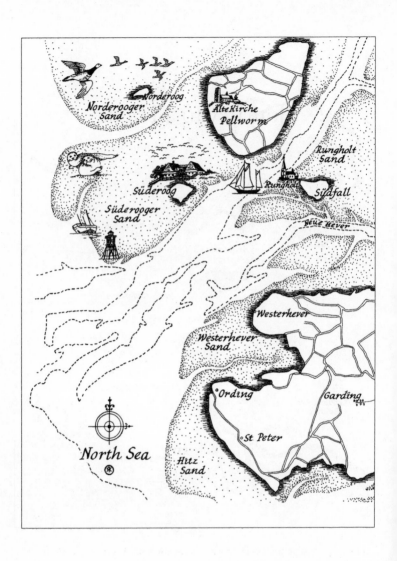

Norderoog

Norderooger
Sand

Alte Kirche
Pellworm

Rungholt
Sand

Süderoog

Rungholt

Südfall

Süderooger
Sand

Neue Hever

Westerhever

Westerhever
Sand

Ording

Garding

North Sea

St Peter

Hitz
Sand

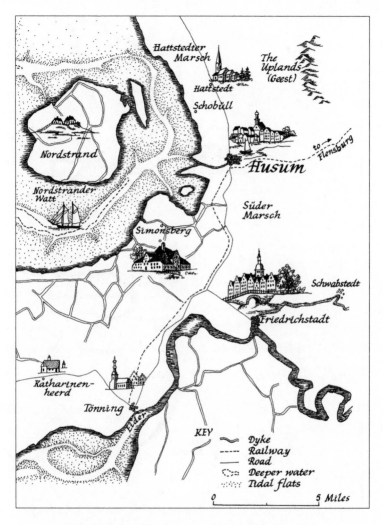

The west coast of Schleswig, Storm's home town of Husum in North
Friesland, the offshore islands, Hallig Süderoog and the North Sea tidal flats
(the Wattenmeer), the setting for *Journey to a Hallig*. Rungholt church indicates
the location of the town of Rungholt before its destruction by the sea in the
fourteenth century

(Based on a local map showing the area c. 1860; drawn by Ruth Knight)

THERE WERE ONCE vast forests of oak along our coast, and so dense were the trees that for miles a squirrel could spring from branch to branch without touching the forest floor. At weddings, when the processions led through the forest it is said that the bride needed to remove the coronet from her head, the branches hung so low. During the days of high summer constant cool shade could be found beneath the leafy domes where the boar and the lynx still roamed, while above, seen only by the eyes of hunting falcons, a sea of sunshine flooded the tops of the trees.

But these forests have long since disappeared; only occasionally is a petrified root still dug out of the dark earth of the moors or out of the mud of the tidal flats, which gives us descendants a sense of just how violently those crowns of leaves must have once swayed in their struggle with the north-west storms. So when we stand on our dykes today, we look into a vast treeless landscape as if into an eternity, and it was rightly said by that female inhabitant of a hallig coming here to the mainland from her small island for the first time: 'My God, how enormous the world is; and there's Holland too!'

* *

And how pleasantly the wind blows on these dykes! I have just come home; where better could I have enjoyed a Sunday morning!

The first warm spring rain on the polders had already made the endless pastures green; the innumerable cattle grazed again on the covering of grass in which the ditches between the fens sparkled like ribbons of silver in the morning sun. On this side and that, the bellowing of cattle, alternating and responding in infinite gradations and tones, rose up and sounded far out over the vast empty landscape. And how active the starlings were, those winged friends of cattle! A noisy flock of them rose up from the polder, swirled round and round in front of me, then settled in a dense swarm on the ridge of the dyke, immediately walking seawards down its slope, briskly pecking around them as they went.

From below, along the side of the river which ran into the sea from the town, the newly-laid straw covering that protected the toe of the dyke from the gnawing tide gleamed invitingly. – How delightful it was to stroll on this fine carpet! – It was still early morning; a dreamlike feeling of youth came over me, as if this day was going to bring me something inexpressibly lovely. A time comes to everyone when even the ghosts of happiness are still welcome. – And behold! – while the water softly, almost silently, washed up to my feet, suddenly, with light inaudible steps, memory walked beside me. It came from the distant past; but the hair, in short loose curls, was still as blonde as it once was. – It was the figure of you, Susanne, that appeared to me; I saw your sharply defined young face again, the small hand that pointed excitedly into the distance – how clearly I saw it all!

On this very shore, on a carpet just like this one, we walked together then too. Your parted lips drank in the moist refreshing air; sometimes, when the gentle south-east breeze gusted, your hand reached for the blue veil and put it back over your tiny summer bonnet. Then you stood still and looked up, listening; your young, inquisitive eyes searched the clear sky. 'I can only see one!' you cried. 'There it is, climbing into the sky over there!' And now I heard it too, far away and as high as it was possible to hear; the whole sky above seemed to be one ceaseless sound of larks singing. The tiny singers themselves, however, disappeared from our eyes in the dazzling intensity of the light that streamed through it. – And in silence we walked on; the world so still and clear and the larks constantly singing; what should we have talked about!

But we were not alone. The Frau Geheimrätin, Susanne's mother, is no less unforgettable to me; she had filled her handkerchief with mushrooms picked on the slope of the dyke and now walked, like the odour of the earth itself, at our side. She was a most imposing lady, and even the little monsters of the deep, the crabs, appeared not to deny her due respect. They had crawled up onto the shore, and sat at the water's edge on the straw covering sunning themselves and rolling their button-like eyes; but when the reflection of the Geheimrätin with the enormous purple cockade fell upon them, they snapped furiously with their claws and darted sidewards back into the abyss. – After a while we had climbed aboard a small boat; it was called the *Good Fortune*; the name stood embossed on the transom in gold letters. We had all happily embarked, except that the old lady had let out a delicate cry when her mushrooms, which she had offered to the 'dear captain' for safe-keeping, flew unceremoniously down into the vessel's open hold.

And the sails billowed gently and the boat drifted quietly on; the water could be heard at the bow rippling against the keel. After an hour we had left the large neighbouring island behind us and now drifted on the broad tide. Close by us a gull glided over the water; I saw its yellow eyes peering down into the depths. 'Rungholt!' cried the boatman, who had just shifted the sails to tack.

The Geheimrätin, who – I don't know by what art – again carried her bag of mushrooms in her hand, looked all about her. 'All I see is the boundless ocean!' she said, packing away her pince-nez and placing it in her belt. The boatman, resting on his arms and leaning overboard, turned his weather-tanned face towards the lady, but after he had scrutinised her with an expression of pitying contempt for a few seconds continued to stare silently out to sea.

'You should look,' I said, 'where according to Seneca all earthly things are kept most safely!'

'And where might that be, my dear?'

'In the past – in the secure land where Rungholt lies. In King Abel's time, and also much later, it stood above the sea in the sunshine with its splendid gabled houses, its steeples and mills. The ships from Rungholt sailed over all the seas of the world and carried home treasures from every part of it. When the bells rang for mass, the market and the streets filled with fair-haired women and girls hurrying to church in silk garments, and at the time of the equinoctial storms the men, especially when they had come home from their feasts, would clamber up onto their high dykes again, stick their hands in their pockets, and shout mockingly down at the roaring sea: "You can't touch us now, Wild Hans!" But that red-blooded paganism that stills lurks inside us all –'

'I'd kindly ask you to leave me out of that!' the Geheimrätin broke in with a somewhat taut smile.

I nodded in agreement. 'It rose up again against the pale Christian

God that had been imposed. The men of Rungholt – at least, according to the religious chroniclers – summoned a priest one day and ordered him to give Communion to a sick pig. This angered God and he made his waters rise as in Noah's time; and they rose over the dykes, mills and steeples. And Rungholt with its fair-haired women and its defiant men' – and I pointed behind us where the water swirled in the sun from the keel of our boat – 'lies down there, lost and invisible on the floor of the sea. Only occasionally in fine weather when the pennant hangs limply from the mast in the stillness of midday and the sailors are snoring in the cabin, then – as people say – "it rises up." – Then anyone with keen eyes who looks overboard into the water can see the steeples with golden weathercocks rising up out of the green gloom; he or she might perhaps even recognise the roofs of the old houses and see strange slow-moving creatures crawling in the seaweed that has grown over them, or might look down between the jagged gables into the narrow lanes where shellfish and amber have obscured the gateways to the houses and the never-resting ebb and flow of the tide plays with the treasures of sunken ships. – Even the sailors below decks wake and sit up, for they hear the sound of ringing beneath them from the deep – it is the bells of Rungholt.'

Meanwhile, Susanne had approached and was listening wide-eyed; but confronted with this tale of the sea, she felt in need of a more knowledgeable authority.

'Do they really ring?' she asked the boatman. 'Have you heard them yourself?'

This sounded so delightful that even the old salt's cheeks dissolved into a smile; and he spat far out into the sea before answering: 'Not heard 'em in my lifetime.'

And we sailed on over Rungholt. But in spite of the boatman's cool response, Susanne stole a glance overboard a few times into the water. The midday stillness had begun to hang oppressively over the sea. And when she saw that I had noticed her glances, she blushed slightly and smiled; for my eyes might have revealed to hers how ready I was myself to believe in wonders.

In front of us a grey dot now appeared on the horizon, gradually broadening and finally rising up as a small green island before us. A winged guard appeared to surround it; as far as the eye could see along the shore, the air was swarming with great white birds rising and falling through each other in ceaseless silent turmoil. Continually occupying the same space in the air, they were like a huge drifting wreath which appeared to encircle the whole island; their powerful outstretched wings showed like translucent marble against the midday sky. – It was almost like a fairy tale; and it occurred to me that my friend Aemil, a man with a passion for regattas, claimed to have heard enchanting music coming from that spot when he had passed it one mild summer's evening in his boat. The moon, he said, had stood over the quiet island, and as he rowed for home after a long rest, he had heard no other sound in the night and over the sea than those ghostly sounds gradually dying away behind him.

* *

But even so, this was no magic island but a hallig of old North Friesland which had been rent into these smaller islands by the great flood of five hundred years ago; the white birds were herring gulls which glided along the shore above their nesting grounds, *Larus argentatus*, long ago recorded and classified by natural scientists. Soon afterwards, as we rode in the wagon beneath the circling birds, I clearly saw, above our heads, their flashing eyes and strong, front-tipped bills. At the same time a hoarse 'Gack! Gack!' rang out at short intervals, similar to that of our geese, only more hurried and more wild. Susanne pressed her head anxiously against her mother; but our driver, laughing, cracked the whip and the aerial rabble flew off cackling in all directions.

And there on the high earthwork, in the middle of the bare treeless island, lay the large hallig-house with the steeply pitched straw-thatched roof in which the 'Cousin' whom we were visiting, a fine old bachelor, had lodged with its taciturn occupants for many years. 'The cogs of state machinery' – so he had announced his move from the mainland to me at the time – 'are becoming far too much for me; I know there are people who are delighted about it; but for myself, I can't stand being prodded in the coat-tails all the time.' – And so, with his library and collections of all kinds of objects, he had been drawn to the isolation of the sea, where he felt himself outside the range of the odious machinery.

The nocturnal music was without doubt to be attributed to him; for not many years before he had been considered a talented violinist in the town in which he then lived; although, for as long as I can remember, he had declined every request to play with the comment that all that was over. I heard him play only once myself, when I was still living in my parents' house; this one occasion, however, later proved the cause of repeated disappointments for me: when I attended concerts given by world-famous virtuosi, I seldom took anything away from them but a dreamlike longing for our Cousin's playing. Nevertheless, it was said that during my later absence from the homeland he took up his violin again, for a short time, and as in times past inspired everyone with his playing. I never learned any further details. Our Cousin was in general a cheerful old gentleman whose congenial eyes did not reveal the often deep emotion for which they stood sentry guard.

But our wagon had already arrived at the foot of the earthwork, and there above, in the doorway beneath the stone gable, he himself stood, the short, slightly-built man with deep-set eyes and thick white hair. 'Welcome to our small land of freedom!' he called out, as he hurried down and helped the servant-boy put the ladder against the wagon. And indeed, it was free enough here; apart from the earthwork crowned with the wide house nothing showed above the green surface of the island but a scattered herd of grazing sheep; even the grass was so short that it hardly created an obstacle for the long-legged crane-flies that clambered about amongst it.

Our Cousin had furnished the largest room of the house as his living room, the so-called *Pesel*. Cupboards with books, collections of conchylia and other objects, cards and copperplate engravings of works by Claude Lorrain and Ruysdael covered the white-washed walls. From the top of the writing desk, beside a statuette of Venus with a dolphin, overshadowed as it were by a tree of coral from a South Sea island, the powerful face of Beethoven on the familiar massive bust looked down on us.

When we entered the room a small bird flew towards us, fluttered hesitatingly to and fro for a moment, then settled itself on its master's hand, its active tiny head looking up at him. 'Just a sparrow!' said our Cousin with a smile, responding to the old lady's astonished look. 'The sparrow, you know, is like a human being, it's without value, but carries the possibility of great things within itself. This fellow here and I, we get on splendidly together.' – At his nod the bird flew away again and settled on a bough of the coral tree above the head of the foam-born goddess, as if waiting, as in legend, to be harnessed together with merry companions in front of her carriage to carry her across the blue Aegean Sea to the shade of her divine groves. But we were soon sipping, out of dainty cups, the drink of the modern world; I don't mean coffee but tea, at which we coastal folk, even on a hot midsummer's morning, do not turn up our noses.

Through the windows, which at the front of the house faced south, the green expanse of the hallig could be seen, and on the distant shore the surf shimmering silver in the sun. Our boat could not be seen from here; but to the west, the mast of another small vessel stood in the air; it had recently gone aground here and was now the property of the inhabitants of the hallig. – What indeed were not stranded goods here! The big black dog that now ran about the house no less than the noble Alicante we later drank at table. And what about our Cousin's library? –

Following my natural impulses, I rummaged among the bookcases and was just leafing through a battered copy of *Hesperus* when a small hand gently laid itself on the first blank page of the book. The name 'Emma' was written on it with a cross underneath.

I can still hear the sigh of innocent sympathy that Susanne uttered at the sight of it. 'Who was that, uncle?' she called. 'Did you know her?'

'Know her, my child?' repeated the old man, brushing his finger along a row of books. 'All these are stranded goods; nearly everything here is an antique! The original owners foundered or perished; their books were scattered all over the world, fished up by tradespeople and sold; and now they will remain here for a while until their present owner meets the same fate. – But nevertheless, I do know this Emma, even if she doesn't know that I have made her posthumous acquaintance.'

Susanne looked eagerly into our Cousin's increasingly expressive eyes.

'Look!' he continued, taking the book from my hand and opening a few pages, 'here it is clear: she loved, suffered and died. The pencil marks here beneath her favourite passages tell me this short tale, the dried forget-me-not, the cross as well. She was an old maid and ugly enough for her beautiful eyes to have pleased no one, not even the one who never thought how happy he made her on that spring day when without a thought he gave her the faded flower that he had just as thoughtlessly picked a while before. A pretty face like yours will never understand that; but' – and he looked half in sadness and half in tender admiration into the face of the young girl – 'it's true, isn't it? No one will suffer because of you!'

Susanne opened her lips as though she wanted to ask a question; but our Cousin passed his hand gently over her blonde hair; then turned and with almost tender care returned the book to its place. He might well have felt that I had noticed; for he said with a smile: 'Well, well! That's not just *Hesperus*, there's a poor true human heart in it as well.'

Under the bookcase at that moment I caught sight of the black violin case I used to know so well, and what could be more natural, after such a conversation, than to remind the old gentleman of that melody I had heard him play in my boyhood and to beg him to let me hear it again now. – But he appeared almost alarmed. 'No, no, my boy!' he said, pushing the case hastily away into the farthest corner. 'Can't you see it's a small coffin? The dead should be left in peace.'

And so nothing more was said about violin-playing.

To most people, our Cousin's extremely sensitive attitude, which conflicted with the external conditions of his life, undeniably made him an odd sort of fellow. Nor did he fail, on more than one occasion during the course of the day, to astonish the Geheimrätin, who had a rare knack of touching on a sensitive nerve.

The fine old lady could not get over the fact that he, 'a highly-educated gentleman', had exchanged the refined society of his earlier domicile for this featureless waste populated only by hallig people and a tame sparrow, and raised the subject time and time again. – The small scene that this caused between the old lady and gentleman is one I shall never forget.

'Frau Cousine!' said the old gentleman with great emphasis, letting an orange he had already grasped in his hand fall back into the crystal bowl – for we were just having dessert after finishing lunch – 'Here on November nights, when our house is in the grip of a storm, and we spring shaken from our beds – when for a brief moment, just as the clouds have raced away from the moon, we glimpse the sea through the window, a sea whipped up by the storm just down there at the foot of our earthwork, which at this moment is the only thing rising above the foaming, raging mountains of water – you cannot imagine, Frau Cousine, how pleasant it is to feel oneself being ruled by a force other than our small power-hungry fellow-creatures!'

I may have nodded silently in response, for I should not have known, as even now I do not, of anything of consequence to be said against this. 'Frau Cousine', however, certainly did not want to believe it, but continued to argue vehemently for the mainland and its respectable society. The old man listened patiently for a while; but then a quiver began to develop roguishly around his still fine mouth.

'I will tell you frankly,' he said, 'the way Their Excellencies and Privy-High-God-Knows-What-Councillors began to multiply in our good town, not so long ago, was extremely disturbing to me.'

I saw the most condescending smile spread across the face of the old lady.

'But, good heavens, what did it matter to you – ?'

'To me, Frau Cousine? It certainly did matter; they walked about in the sunshine everywhere; where I liked to walk. But while they still hang by their strings they are often quite despicable figures, and you have to get out of their way to avoid being hit by their wooden arms.'

The Geheimrätin grew agitated.

'But, my dear Cousin, my late husband – '

'Of course, of course, Frau Cousine!' And he laid his hand on her arm to calm her. 'I know a whole bunch of them who all go about with extraordinary airs; but if you removed their rankings from the court register – I'll wager! – those fellows would sit there like empty shells; I can already see their eyes glazing over while their bit of rank consciousness evaporates.'

'But, Cousin!' The Geheimrätin took advantage of a momentary pause. 'My wonderful late husband – '

And the old man again laid his hand on her arm to calm her.

'Of course, of course, Cousin! I'll do no one an injustice, there are also some excellent people among them!'

And suddenly turning towards me, he began to talk more and more quickly and vehemently; at last, sincerely but in vain, he evidently tried to suppress some plain speaking.

The Geheimrätin had folded her hands in resignation and said nothing more; our Cousin, however, had jumped up, and with a flushed face he flung open the door and cried: 'Mantje, a glass of water!'

But before Mantje had the time to appear, he ran to fetch it himself.

The old lady appeared to let out a gradual sigh of relief.

'A pleasant man, our Cousin,' she said, giving a slight cough, 'but just the same, I much prefer to see him here on his island.'

But he soon re-entered the room.

'I have cut our meal short in an unseemly manner,' he said apologetically. 'Well, you know: the heart grows older but still no wiser! – Let us drink Martje Flor's health according to the custom of the country!' He filled the glasses and lifted his own. 'Frau Cousine! Susanne! My dear boy! To good health in our old age!'

And we drank in a manner that appears peculiar to this most serious of all toasts, in silence, then shook one another's hands.

The story behind it, however, deserves wider telling. Once when Tönningen, the largest town in the district of Eiderstedt, was being besieged by the Swedes, a group of enemy officers had taken up quarters in the neighbouring parish of Kathrinenheerd and behaved badly there; they ordered wine and caroused as though they were the rulers here. Martje Flor, the ten-year-old daughter of the house, indignantly looked on at the orgy of drinking, thinking of her parents who had to suffer it under their roof. One of the drinkers then held out a full glass towards her and loudly asked why she stood there so gloomily; she should propose a toast instead! And Martje walked with her glass up to the table where the enemy soldiers were sitting and said: 'To good health in our old age!' – And at the child's words the whole room became quiet.

Since that day everyone at home has understood very well when at the close of a meal the landlord proposes to his guests the toast: 'And now – to Martje Flor's health!'

* *

When the meal was finished and we had gathered outside the front door, our Cousin led us in weighty silence along the side of the house to its south-west corner. Here he pushed open a small, almost hidden gate beneath an overhanging elder; and we looked down, as though seeing a miracle, into a large tree-filled garden, which in this place, surrounded by bleakness, no one would ever have expected. From the island, it was completely concealed from the eye, and lay below in a basin-shaped hollow in the earthwork, along the steeply inclined sides of which, between different kinds of fruit trees, stretched a row of flourishing vegetable beds.

From the bottom of the hollow sparkled a small pond enclosed within a high privet hedge. Just then, a white cat on its way down from the house appeared on the steep path that ran along beside it; but a moment later it disappeared into the shadows of the fruit trees in the garden, which spread their thick branches out over the path. The shiny leaves shone the deepest green as though they had never been touched by a voracious insect; but just where the crowns of the trees reached the upper perimeter of the garden they were completely cropped as if by hedging-shears, which, as our Cousin explained, was a result not of any cultivation but of the north-west winds.

Our 'Mamma's' attention was caught by a pump which stood in the small pond not far from the entrance; and while the old man, vigorously pumping its handle, began to explain the reservoir's fresh-water supply to her and its significance to the hallig, Susanne and I went down into the sheltered garden retreat where the sunshine, as if captive, slept on the green foliage. We slowly followed the white cat and disappeared as it did beneath the thick foliage of the apple trees which almost touched Susanne's bright golden hair; all around us hung the fragrance of plumed pinks and roses which bloomed high between the vegetable plots. If my memory serves me rightly, we had been drawn imperceptibly into that dreamlike state into which, in the summer stillness amid the weavings of nature, a young couple will so easily drift: they say nothing, and they almost begin to talk, but it is just the sound of the invisible life in the foliage and the air, just the breath of the summer winds which carry the pollen from one flower to another. I believe we were sitting on a small wooden bench and looking – who knows how long we had been there! – through the gaps in the fence at the glistening water below, when suddenly the accentuated tones of the Geheimrätin called me back up to the surface of life; and soon afterwards the old man also appeared and with cheering words induced us into the house for coffee.

But I soon stole away to look in my own way, alone and undisturbed, at the various rooms of the large quadrangular house.

I stood for a while in a kind of carpenter's shop and chatted with the son of the house, who combined, like Crusoe, every trade from seal hunter to carpenter, and who was working at that moment in the latter capacity on the blocks for a sailing boat for which he had received an order from a neighbouring island.

Next I came to a row of somewhat gloomy stalls. They were empty as the livestock were out on the hallig grazing; only the white cat now sat here on the manger, and some hens ran cackling in and out of the hole in the wall; on the walls here and there I saw a seal's skin nailed up to dry.

At the end of the stalls, set at right angles to them, even quieter and in deeper gloom, was the barn; and there in the middle of it stood the new boat, still smelling of forest resin, as yet untouched by any wave. It goes without saying, I climbed aboard; I sat on the oarsman's bench and thought of our Cousin and why he had just disowned his violin-playing to us.

It was completely isolated here. The tiny, cobweb-covered windows were so high that they afforded no view. I heard not a sound from the house; but although the wind had almost totally subsided by midday, from the walls outside came a kind of wind music that gave me a sense of what would be the storm's vast registers of sound when it performed its sea-concert around All Saints' Day. After a while light footsteps mingled with these aerial sounds; they came from the stalls, and when I looked up Susanne stood in the doorway, her tiny bonnet swinging to and fro on its ribbons.

'Why did you run away, then?' she called, defiantly throwing back her head. 'Mamma is sitting indoors over a sea chart and Uncle has set up a large telescope at the open window. But I don't want to look through a telescope.'

'So come on board my boat!' I replied, moving to one side on the thwart. 'It's a safe new vessel.'

'You want me to get into that boat? What for? It's so gloomy here.'

'Just listen to how the gentle spirits play music!'

She listened for a moment, then she came nearer; already she had placed her tiny foot on the gunnel.

'What's stopping you, Susanne? Have you no confidence in my seamanship?'

She looked at me; there was something of the blue radiance of a precious stone in this look, and I wondered if any harm might one day come to me from these eyes. I might have stared at her most strangely at this moment; for, as though becoming afraid, she slowly withdrew her foot.

'It would be better if we went down to the shore!' she said quietly. 'I should like to see the herring-gulls' nests!'

So I left my fine vessel and we walked out of the house, the bright daylight streaming almost blindingly into our eyes. – Paying no heed to the old lady and gentleman, we went down the earthwork and across the hallig towards the shore. We picked a stem of fragrant sea-wormwood and a violet bloom of sea-lavender on the way, there was nothing else that could have attracted our attention. At many of the often deep watercourses, which covered the whole hallig like a web, we had to wander up and down before we found a spot to jump over. But Susanne had had sessions at a girls' gymnasium, and on her shoulders were the invisible wings of youth; I clearly heard their rhythmic swish when she put her small foot down to jump and then quickly flew over.

A light wind had sprung up when we reached the shore. The sea, which with the incoming tide was just a stone's throw from the grassy foreshore, now lay like smooth silver under the slanting rays of the afternoon sun; the roar of the surf could be heard far out round the shore of the island. In the air, as in the morning, the great herring-gulls still rose and fell, only now, as no light from above shone through them, the snowy-whiteness of their wings was emphasised even more against the blue sky. We also saw smaller dark birds with stork-like bills which, as though with shrill war-cries, shot here and there through the teeming mass of large gulls.

And now Susanne let out a cry of delight; in a cluster of seaweed, surrounded by a reddish wreath of crushed shellfish, lay two large grey-green eggs, six steps further on another two, and there, somewhat to one side, gleamed three smaller oystercatcher's eggs. Most of these eggs lay on the bare sand, for, as our Cousin said: 'These creatures are not too fussy about their home life.' The birds squawked and screeched, but Susanne, unconcerned and with eyes bright with curiosity, walked further and further on from nest to nest.

I had sat down on the shore facing the sea. For a while I watched Susanne. Where my thoughts then wandered I should hardly have been able to explain to myself, but my eyes spelled out again and again the long familiar name 'Good Fortune' on the transom of our boat rocking on the water not far off, the gold lettering sparkling in the sun. The lapping of the water, the gentle movement of the wind – it is strange how it makes us dream.

When I stood up, there was nothing to be seen of Susanne. I walked on a short distance along the shore, while above me the gulls danced like enormous snowflakes in the air. I shouted, sang – no answer. Finally, far away in a depression in the ground, I saw her kneeling in the sand. In the clear light of the early evening sun I made out one of the large eggs in her hand; motionless she held her ear inclined towards it as though she wanted to eavesdrop on the awakening life that was enclosed within it. Just above her, however, hovered two of the powerful birds which had detached themselves from the long chain; they emitted their hoarse calls and beat their white wings as if in anger. Instinctively I stopped; so wild and yet so charming was this scene. The kneeling figure of the girl remained motionless. Then one of the incensed birds darted down so steeply at her that it seemed as if it would seize hold of her curls with its bill.

Susanne let out a loud scream, so that even the birds flew off to one side, startled; then she hurled the egg far away from her and, just as she had earlier leaped over the narrow watercourses, flew upon me and flung both arms round my neck.

> Breath need only quiver,
> A spark light up the eyes;
> And angels start to weave
> A fateful paradise.

So says the poet. – But this breath seldom quivers. – I was a young lawyer and had long been advised by well-meaning people that if I wanted to 'prosper' in my work, I should not only lay my grey Hecker hat aside but also shave off my moustache. I had failed to do both, I was too reckless and carefree; but now a heavy weight seemed to lie on my heart, and, curiously, while the breakers sounded monotonously in my ears, and the girl's blonde head still rested on my shoulder, I could not turn my thoughts to anything better than taking up a position once more in battle order against this tyranny of public opinion; indeed, even the Hecker hat and the moustache began to rise up against me like two enemy ghosts.

'Susanne,' I said at last, resignedly, 'we must be off home, it will be late soon.'

This was decidedly awkward; I still recall how Susanne pushed me away from herself in alarm and then, blushing to the curls on her forehead, stood helplessly in front of me. And it was little less awkward when, to make amends, I clasped both her hands and said to comfort her: 'It was just the angry birds, I know.'

But however it was – as we now returned home it was somehow different from before; she had put herself under my protection. Still from time to time, when a bird's cry sounded above us, she would quickly turn her head as though the winged enemies were coming after her to avenge their destroyed brood; and when we came to a watercourse she would offer me her hand as a matter of course, and it was unmistakable that we now flew over it together.

When we arrived on the earthwork our Cousin was standing at the door.

'Susanne, my dear child,' he said in an oddly mysterious way, 'your mother's inside; I'd like a word with our young friend here.'

And he gripped me under the arm and led me round to the back of the house. Here he stopped and looked long and affectionately into my eyes.

'My dear boy!' he then said, 'now I know why you wanted that old love song from me, for I will confess to you that it was a love song, a real one. And as it's been with you all these long years and has accompanied you to this goal' – our Cousin paused for a moment – 'when the two of you visit me in the near future, I do believe I'll find the melody again.'

How was I to answer such an embarrassing speech!

'I don't understand you, Cousin!' I said.

'You don't understand me?'

I had to repeat myself; but then it became clear.

From his room our Cousin had directed his telescope at each of the islands and halligen in turn, the Geheimrätin looking eagerly through it too, 'until finally,' he continued, 'our own shore, and you and Susanne, like figures in a landscape painting, appeared in our lens. Frau Cousine looked with motherly pride at you both, but suddenly she sprang back into the room with an "Oh, good heavens! I don't understand the situation at all!" and urgently pushed me in front of the telescope. Now I looked through it – "Extraordinary!" I cried too. "But not totally incomprehensible!" and "My heartiest congratulations, Frau Cousine!" For don't deny it, Cousin! You held her properly in your arms, and all I say is: Hold her tightly, my boy, hold her tightly! For this child is a blessing to God and to all men!'

The old man's face beamed for joy, and my own heart began to pound heavily within me. But what use was that!

'I am sorry,' I said, 'but take the good wishes back, because there is nothing at all in it, Cousin!'

'Nothing?'

'No, nothing!'

And I now explained to him that it had simply been the big birds.

'Extraordinary!' He looked at me in some doubt for a while; then, as though suddenly decided, he clasped my hand firmly and said: 'My dear boy, I now believe that *you* don't understand the situation at all.'

Whether in the meantime Susanne had also enlightened her mother in this matter, I don't know; I noticed only a somewhat more solemn manner about the old lady as we entered the room than was customary with her.

Not long afterwards it was time to leave. The ladies drove; I walked down to the shore accompanied by our Cousin. When the wagon had almost reached us, the old man held my arm yet again and led me a short way along the water's edge.

'So, there's really nothing in it, my boy?'

'Really nothing, Cousin!'

He looked at me sadly.

'Well, come and stay with me on my hallig; we'll find some additional space for you at Easter; consider it!'

And he clasped both my hands firmly.

Then we joined the boat. When we were some way out from the land in deep water, we could still see our Cousin waving his cap in farewell and the evening sun shining on his white hair.

The wind veered after sunset; a gentle breeze blew from the south-west; in front of us the moon rose out of the dark water and lit up the sea with its soft light. The Geheimrätin had wrapped her silver-fox-lined silk satin coat round herself and because of the cold settled below in the boat's open hold. Beside me Susanne, wrapped in a soft shawl, leaned against the bulwark; her face appeared almost colourless in the evening light.

Once, from afar, the whimpering of an animal was carried across the water towards us, and the boatman said it was a young seal searching for its mother. Then it was quiet again, with only the sound of the waves against our boat. But we remained standing looking out over the sea. Where our gazes wandered in this vast empty world, who could possibly say! Or whether Susanne still gave a thought to the angry birds? She gave no hint of it to me, and nor did I find out later. I am equally uncertain if the boat's goblin was on board. Once, as I turned my head, I seemed to see something shrouded in fog huddled up on the bowsprit beneath the jib-sail, but I paid no attention to it. Two young eyes, as calm as the evening, which turned towards me from time to time, were a sweeter mystery. But I certainly felt that spirits were sailing with us, which even the proximity of the Geheimrätin could not counter.

When we finally returned home along our dyke towards the town, a lark was still singing unseen in the fading light above the polder. On the other side the moon was up and shed a golden sparkling light on the mud exposed by the ebbing tide.

* *

There are days that are like the rose, fragrant and radiant, then everything is over; no fruit follows them, but also no disappointment, no continuing cares from day to day. – I kept my hat and my moustache until finally both became the general fashion and were absorbed in it. On the other hand, it has not been vouchesafed to me to know whether in the course of life the look of those blue eyes, besides the radiance of a precious stone, might not also have taken on something of the same hardness. The day on our Cousin's hallig, and in the middle of it Susanne's sweet youthful figure, remain for me, like Rungholt, safely locked away in the secure land of the past.

* *

Some years later I again visited our Cousin on his hallig; but not with another person, as he so sincerely had in mind for me at that time. His mind still seemed active, but he mostly preferred to rest his body in the comfortable armchair by the window and let his eyes rather than his feet wander across the hallig to the shore. As I sat there opposite him, I saw two of those white gulls fly out of the blue sky towards the house. They settled half-way up the earthwork, and our Cousin opened the window and threw pieces of bread and meat out to them which he had had in readiness beside him on the window-ledge. 'I used to go to them,' he said, 'now they have to come to me.'

Now they look in vain for their friend. It is true he remained on his hallig, but they carried him out of the house; the green turf lies protectively over him. He was bold enough to retire here in peace, well knowing that the storm could one day drive the tide to his very grave, that the tide could churn it up and carry him in his narrow resting-place out to the open sea. But how could he have feared those great forces under whose protection he believed himself so happily secure!

The excellent old man, apart from his library and his handwritten papers, had also bequeathed to me his Cremona violin, which by the terms of his will I, completely ignorant of the art of violin-playing, may neither give away nor sell, only bequeath. So now it lies undisturbed among other memorabilia. Among his papers, however, some brief notes were found in the hand of the deceased which suggested that there had been a particular motive at the time for his flight from the world. The date given on them accorded with this, belonging to the last years before his move to the hallig. He was then still living in his own house which was situated close to the town in a tree-filled garden. From his living room on the upper floor, through some lime trees standing outside, the heathland could be seen beyond green fields; in those days it still extended far to the west. I still recall – for I used to sit there with him – how much he loved this view. The heathland was a familiar place to him; not only because he was constantly searching it in his entomological and botanical studies, but also because he found there, as he expressed it, 'the necessary rest from life'.

Sitting by this window I am urged to think of him as he wrote down the lines that now lie before me in his small but clear handwriting. They read:

How wonderful it looks from here in the October afternoon! The sun still shines so golden; but beneath its rays the leaves are already loosening and sinking silently onto the wet grass; the naked branches are showing more and more. From below, out of the elderberry bushes, a thrush called; after a while it called again, away in the distance – everything is saying farewell.

The pale grey twilight of the autumn evening has spread, the house and garden are already lying in shadow, beyond the heath the sun has set. Only far away in the sky, at the point to where the birds are now flying like shadows, is there still a brightly lit stretch of clouds. They are hanging over a spot beyond the horizon, which my eyes can still reach. But even there the golden day will soon fade.

When I looked back into the room, a soft glow of that evening light still lay on my black violin case, which has stood unopened there beneath the bookcase for years now. I once bought the violin it contains from the personal estate of a Florentine musician who died young, and only since then have I known that I can play. I found a verse inscribed in Italian on the inner rim of the case, and strangely, when I translated it into our language it felt as if I had previously written these now German lines myself, and I searched for them for a long time among my old papers, in vain. But as soon as I touched the violin with my bow it sang and the sound swelled to such power as to make even me tremble. It was not I alone who created these tones; this violin contained a spiritual inheritance, and I was the rightful heir, who increased it by his own efforts. For a long while now it has rested soundless in its black case; for I recognised years ago that only up to a certain stage in life does that electric current flow through our nerves, the current that carries us beyond ourselves and irresistibly sweeps others with it too.

And now? This evening?

I must look in the mirror so that I don't forget my grey hair.

No, no! I will take my violin, my sounding soul, out of its coffin, and my hands shall not tremble.

* *

Eveline led me into the hall. It was still empty, but the candles were already lit; beneath the crystal chandelier stood an opened grand piano.

'You'll be playing here!' she said. 'Your violin's there on the small table.'

'Will I, Eveline?'

She put her hand to her cheek, as she did at times, and looked at me seriously.

'But you promised me!'

'And before such distinguished company?'

For looking down from the walls, depicted in large, though fairly mediocre, lithographs in thick gilt frames, were almost all the first rank in our court register.

She laughed.

'Sh! Don't mock! They are papa's penates. Why don't you look at my pictures, hanging modestly but consolingly among them?'

And to be sure, Goethe and Mozart, although in smaller format, were represented too.

The invited company thronged into the hall from the other rooms.

'Au revoir!' Eveline said.

She hurriedly offered me her hand, her dark eyes glanced at me; then she went towards the people entering. I sought out a place for myself in the farthest corner. The soft, somewhat weary sound of her voice still hung in my ear; her simplest words often seem to convey, I'm not sure, something like the painful anticipation or the secret promise of happiness. But soon my worthy Cousin, the Geheimrat, joined me and said something about art, while I examined the invited company who, chatting and passing compliments, were still taking their places, and compared them with those whose portraits hung on the walls.

And now a chord was struck. Adolf, our music director, began the Largo from Beethoven's D major Sonata. It became completely quiet and remained so; for he knew, when the time was right, how to bring his Beethoven so impressively to everyone's ears that only a great intellectual or an ill-mannered lout would have preferred to hear his own voice at that moment. It seemed to me, in fact, at the beginning of the minuet, as if a rapturous sigh went through the whole hall. Is not music the art that makes all people believe they are children of the same star!

Then the music director presented his young group of singers. There were clear, pleasant voices among them, and they sang the tea-and-coffee ditties they could perform so well, which come and go like butterflies. They also sang the songs of the great new composer in which Eichendorff's wonderful lyrics have been expressed in music for the first time. Innocently, the young voices floated above the depths of these songs. – I do not know whether or not

Kapellmeister Johannes Kreisler would have fled; I sat quite still listening to the sweet, fresh, lark-like voices of youth. And between the songs always the contented clapping and kind words of the older ladies and gentlemen and the loud compliments of the young cavaliers. Why ever not?

And now – I almost believe my chest was pounding – I myself stood by the grand piano. Eveline had set the violin quietly in front of me and then just as quietly retreated. Spohr's ninth concerto lay opened. Adolf looked at me. 'Shall we begin, then?'

We knew each other well. Years ago, many an evening, many a night had seen us thus together. My bow already lay on the strings; some piano chords, and the first note flew firm and crystal-clear through the hall.

And my violin, or rather my soul, sang. It sang as Nöck by the waterfall did, who the children said had no soul. – You know this, my muse, for you stood opposite me beside the picture of your favourite, the young Goethe, your beautiful hands folded in your lap. Your eyes were full of devotion and I drank the exhilarating godly strength of youth from them. And the walls of the hall faded and the rushing waterfall ceased, and all the young birds that had just sung so loudly fell silent, listening. You and I were one, beautiful youthful goddess; I stood on high, supreme; I felt the sparks fly beneath my bow; and I held them all in a breath-taking spell for a long, long time.

We had come to the end. Adolf lifted his hands from the piano, looked up at me, and nodded slightly.

And as I put down my bow, the young men looked up at me, half shyly, with large amazed eyes, as though they had suddenly discovered that I was still one of their number, whom they had not recognised, who had now suddenly cast aside the mask of age.

Not until Adolf had moved his stool and stood up was the stillness broken, and the audience pushed its way towards us. Only I knew that Eveline's hand suddenly lay in mine. Or was it the hand of my muse which once again fleetingly touched me?

* *

They criticised you for your behaviour, Eveline.

And if you had all spoken the truth – let us be! Even Mother Nature, of which she is simply a part like the rose, can give us nothing other than what we ourselves give to her. Perhaps human beings can advance no further, and we die lonely as we were born lonely. And yet, what would life be if there were no roses!

* *

Do you know that there is such a thing as second sight? – Now and then, as though it cannot wait until its time has come, the future casts its phantom into the present. – You suspected nothing of it, but I saw it; it was in the middle of the candle-lit hall. You had been dancing and sat breathless in the corner of the sofa; then I saw your face change, your features became sharp, your cheeks limp and pallid. I stretched out my hand to take the rose quietly from your hair, the rose that sat there, a mockery of your poor face. But it disappeared as I looked hard at you; you smiled, you were eighteen years old once more. The ghost faded powerlessly away; but I still saw it like a veiled threat standing in the distance.

Oh, Eveline! The river of beauty pours forever through the world, but even you are just a sparkle on a wave that lights up and fades; and all the future will one day become the present.

> Born in one's own heart,
> Never possessed, yet lost.

How strange, those words on my violin case!
Even that is now over. –

* *

There appear to be one or two pages missing here from our Cousin's notes; for the following, which starts on a new page, is apparently the end of a lengthy memoir.

– 'But the trace of eternal youth in me has touched your heart, however much your young lips might tremble with pride. One day, when you too belong to the departed souls, whose mouths thirst in vain after the goblet from which youth drinks its fill before their eyes, the memory of me will suddenly come over you; perhaps one quiet evening when you see the sun setting behind a harvested field, perhaps – even this is possible – in the look of death, in that last moment when all spirits of this world leave you. And now go, Eveline; for they are all in your service!'

Her hand trembled; I had only just realised, it lay in mine. But she quietly withdrew it and left.

'Good night, Eveline!'

But you, muse of song, don't leave me yet! Let me lean my head on your shoulder, for I am tired, tired as a hunted animal; and if I should quietly bleed, lay your hand on my wound! –

* *

Here these notes end. No ribbon, no lock of hair, no flower lay with the yellowed pages.

Who was this Eveline who was able to stir this aging heart again so deeply? – I know of no one by that name. Requiescat! Requiescat!

Hans and Heinz Kirch

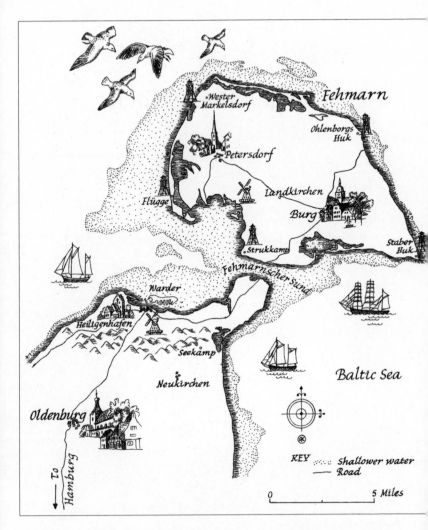

North-east Holstein, with the Baltic trading town of Heiligenhafen and the
surrounding coastal region, the setting for *Hans and Heinz Kirch*. The railway
first came to Oldenburg in 1881, but did not reach Heiligenhafen until 1898

(Based on a local map showing the area c. 1860; drawn by Ruth Knight)

CLOSE BY THE WATER on a rising Baltic shore lies a small town whose squat church tower has looked out over the sea for well over five hundred years. A few cable-lengths from the shore, parallel to it, lies a narrow island known here as the Warder, from which, in spring, the ceaseless cries of shore birds and waterfowl are carried across to the town. In clear weather reddish-brown roofs and the spire of a steeple also appear on the island opposite, which forms the shore of the strait, and when the twilight has dimmed the scene, the beacons of two lighthouses are lit there and cast a shimmer of light over the dark sea towards the near shore. However, any stranger who wanders through the town's rising and falling streets, where here and there roughly-paved steps lead across the pavement to the small houses, will not escape the feeling of complete remoteness, especially if he has descended to the town on the landward side, from across the long chain of hills. Until recently, the so-called town bell hung in a wooden belfry in the market-place, as it had for centuries. At ten o'clock every evening, as soon as the church bell had rung, it too used to peal the hour, and woe betide any servants or even son of the house who ignored its call, for shortly afterwards all the keys would be heard turning in the doors up and down the streets.

Hard-working people live in this small town, however, well-established townsfolk, independent of the money and influence of the wealthy landowners of the neighbourhood; and a small patriciate has formed from these, whose more imposing properties with their wide stone-walled steps behind the shelter of mighty lime-trees from time to time interrupt the low rows of houses. But up to the last decade, even the sons from these families had to follow the same path that their parents and forefathers had trodden to achieve prosperity and social standing; only a few of them studied the sciences, and among the well-educated Bürgermeister of the town there would seldom be a local man. If the provost were to ask the boys at the annual examination in the rector class what they wanted to be when they grew up, the one to rise proudly from his school bench was the one who ventured to answer 'Shipmaster!' Ship's boy; captain of a family vessel, then of one's own vessel; then at around forty, a ship-owner; and soon a senator in one's home town – so went the progression to civic honours.

In the church built by a duke in the thirteenth century the spacious Shipmasters' Gallery is to be found, immediately recognisable from the model of a barque in full rigging suspended from its ceiling and the bold metal sconces prominently mounted on its walls for the evening service. Every citizen passing the helmsman's examination and owning his own vessel always had a right to sit up here; and those established as merchants, the town's first ship-owners, also used to worship here among the other captains while their wives sat below, for they were above all still seafaring folk and the small suspended barque was their distinctive symbol.

It is understandable that even many a young sailor or helmsman from the lower middle class, instead of being filled with devotion on entering the church, would be seized with the ambition of gaining a place for himself up there one day, and despite the compelling sermon, would return to his quarters or his vessel with aroused worldly desires rather than godly thoughts.

To these striving and industrious people belonged Hans Adam Kirch. Through ceaseless effort and saving he had risen from the status of leaseholding shipmaster to that of ship-owner. Admittedly he could only afford a cutter, but when all the other shipmasters were already at home sitting comfortably by their stoves he was out tirelessly, even well into the winter, sailing the Baltic, carrying freight not only for others but also on his own account, transporting the produce of the region, corn and flour, to coastal towns large and small; and not until the water off the bays threatened to freeze over did he too secure his boat to a pile and sit up in the Shipmasters' Gallery for the Sunday service among the dignitaries of his home town. But long before the beginning of spring he was out again in his cutter; in every Baltic coastal town people knew the dark-haired, stooped figure of the small, lean man in the blue loose-fitting sailing jacket; everywhere he was stopped and spoken to, but he answered only abruptly, he had no time; he was seen striding resolutely through the lanes as though he were mounting a jack-ladder. And this driving determination bore fruit; a plot of meadow land was soon added to the house inherited from his father, sufficient for both summer and winter fodder for two cows; while the cutter was at sea, these were meant to further his business ashore. A few years earlier Hans Kirch had quietly taken a wife, and now dairy farming was added to the small business they had run till then; there were a few pigs, too, to be fattened as provision for the cutter during commercial voyages; and since his wife, whom he had chosen uncharacteristically from a penurious schoolmaster's family, knew only his strong will, and furthermore had pinched and scraped for fear of her husband's well-known sudden anger, he was also accustomed, on each trip home, to finding a fine pile of small change in the house.

After a few years the marriage produced a boy who was brought up with the same thrift. 'Good money down the drain!', ran the saying around the town; Hans Adam had cast it at his wife when one week-day she had bought her young boy a treacle tart. But despite this thrift, which closely resembled meanness, the captain was and remained a trustworthy businessman who rejected every improper advantage; not only because of his innate honesty, but also because of his ambition. He had achieved his place in the Shipmasters' Gallery, but now higher honours were sweeping through his mind which he did not cast aside; the seats on the town council, although they generally belonged to the influential families, had been occupied from time to time by the petty bourgeoisie. In any case, his Heinz should have the way prepared for him; people even said he was the image of his father; the sharp inquisitive eyes, the head full of dark-brown curls were inherited from his father, but instead of the bent back he had the slim build of his mother.

What affectionate feelings Hans Kirch did possess, he expressed towards his son. On every trip home, even before reaching the Warder, he squinted through his glass to see if he could make him out on the quayside; and should mother and child come on board after he had moored, he would lift little Heinz onto his arm before offering a welcoming hand to his wife.

When Heinz reached the age of six, his father took him to sea with him for the first time, as a 'play-bird' as he put it. His mother gazed anxiously after them; but the boy was delighted with his shining little hat and ran joyfully up the narrow gangway onto the ship; he was thrilled to become a shipmaster now just like his father, and quietly decided to help as best he could. They had put out to sea early in the morning; now the midday sun shone down upon them on the blue Baltic waters across which a mild summer's wind drove the cutter only slowly onwards. After lunch, before the captain went to his cabin for his midday rest, Heinz was entrusted to the ship's boy, who was busy splicing some severed boat's rigging on the deck; the small boy, too, received a few ends of rope which he eagerly tried to weave together.

After an hour or so Hans Kirch climbed up from his cabin and called out, still half asleep: 'Heinz! Come here, Heinz. It's time for coffee!' But neither the small boy nor any answer came in response to the call; instead the sound of a child singing came from the bowsprit. Hans Kirch turned deathly white; for there, almost at the furthest point of the jib, he had caught sight of his Heinz. On the windward side, leaning comfortably against the slightly billowing sail, the small boy sat as if he were resting from his work. When he became aware of his father he gave him a friendly nod; then continued to sing unconcerned while the sea broke against the bows; his large childish eyes shone, his dark-brown hair blew in the gentle breeze.

Hans Kirch, however, stood motionless, paralysed with fear; only he knew how easy it was for the sail to flap in the light airs and knock the child into the deep in front of his eyes. He wanted to call out, but the words stopped in his mouth – children, like sleepwalkers, should be left alone; he wanted to lower the rowing boat and steer for the vessel's bow; but even that idea he discarded. Then the boy himself made a decision; he had had enough of singing, he wanted to go to his father now and show him his ropes. Cautiously, beneath the foot of the jibsail which still billowed out to the side of him, he made his way back; overhead a gull screeched high in the sky; he looked up, then quietly clambered on. With bated breath, Hans Kirch remained standing by the cabin, his eyes following the child's every movement, as though it were vital to hold him in his gaze. Suddenly, in response to a hardly perceptible movement of the boat, he turned his head sharply: 'Port!' he shouted to the helmsman, 'Port!', as though he would burst his lungs. And the man at the helm followed with a slight pressure of the hand, and the slackening sail filled again.

At that same instant the boy had sprung down onto the foredeck and now he ran excitedly with outstretched arms towards his father. The danger-hardened man's teeth still chattered. 'Heinz, Heinz, don't ever do that to me again!' In relief he pressed the small boy to him; but already the abating fear had given way to rage against the culprit. 'Don't ever do that to me again!' he repeated, but a suppressed rage now sounded in his voice; his hand lifted as if about to fall upon the boy, who was looking up at him in astonishment and fear.

But this time it was not to be; the captain's anger turned on the ship's boy who was about to push by in his casual manner, and with fear in his eyes little Heinz had to watch his friend Jürgen being most cruelly beaten by his father, and he did not know why.

When Hans Kirch wanted to take Heinz on board the vessel again the following spring, the boy had hidden himself away, and when finally found had to be dragged to the boat by force; nor this time did he sit singing under the jibsail; he feared his father, yet at the same time was defiant towards him. The father's affection diminished correspondingly the more self-willed the boy became; he even believed himself that he loved in the son only the heir to his ambitious plans.

* *

When Heinz reached the age of twelve his sister was born; an event the father accepted as something which simply could not be helped. Heinz had grown up to be a wild boy; but in the rector class few were ahead of him. 'He's very gifted!' observed the young teacher. 'One day he could well grace the pulpit here.' But Hans Kirch laughed. 'Nonsense, Herr Rektor! It's not a question of money, but it's obvious you're not from these parts.'

Nonetheless, the very same day he went to see his neighbour, the pastor, whose garden extended from the front of the house to the street. The pastor received the visitor somewhat brusquely. 'Herr Kirch,' he said, before allowing him to speak, 'your boy Heinz has broken the end-windows of my stable again!'

'If that's what he's done,' replied Hans Kirch, 'then I'll replace them and Heinz will get the stick; this game's too expensive.'

Then, while the other nodded in agreement, he broached what had brought him here: he asked the pastor to take Heinz on for private lessons, such as he used to give to some day-boarders and sons of respected members of the community to further his somewhat small stipend. When after a few questions the pastor agreed to do this, Hans Kirch tried to reduce the fee; but as the pastor appeared not to be listening, he did not pursue it further; for Heinz should learn more than the rector class was now able to offer him.

That same evening Heinz received his promised punishment, and on the following afternoon when he sat with the other students upstairs in the pastor's study he received an additional sharp telling off from the good Reverend to go with it. But hardly had the boisterous group of boys, after a thankfully completed lesson, stormed down the stairs and out into the garden when the pastor, a much-relieved man, heard a loud cry of pain from below his window. 'I'll teach you to tell tales!' yelled an angry boy's voice, and again the pitiful cry rang out. But when the pastor opened his window he saw below only his pale-blond day-boarder, who had disclosed Heinz's misdemeanour to him that morning, busily engaged with his handkerchief wiping blood from his mouth and nose. That he had actually been up to such a trick the boy was not of course inclined to disclose; but neither did he reveal at this moment who had given him the bloody warning as he left the class.

The pastor had not been blessed with a son; he had only two daughters, some years younger than Heinz and not at all bad to look at. But Heinz did not concern himself with them, and one might have believed he kept to the rule that an able youth should not concern himself with girls, had not little Wieb been living in the house opposite the pastor's garden. Her mother was a seaman's wife, a laundress who unfortunately kept her child cleaner than her reputation. 'Your mother's an amphibian too!' a burly lad had once shouted into the girl's face just after a lesson about these creatures. – 'No she's not, why?' the incensed Wieb had retorted. – 'Why? Because she's got one man afloat and one ashore!' The comparison was inappropriate, but the boy had satisfied his malicious intention.

The pastor's daughters nevertheless kept up a playing companionship with the seaman's child; mostly of course during workdays and when the Bürgermeister's daughters were not with them; when they wore their white dresses with blue sashes they preferred not to play with little Wieb. If they met the young girl standing quietly and shyly in front of the garden gate, or if the younger, good-natured Bürgermeister's daughter actually asked her in, then they would indeed speak to her in a most friendly, though very hurried way. 'You'll still come and see us tomorrow in the garden, won't you, Wieb?' In late summer they would pop an apple into her pocket, adding: 'Wait a moment, we'll find another one for you!' And little Wieb would steal away in bewilderment with her apples out of the garden and into the lane. But if Heinz came by he would snatch them away from her and throw them angrily back into the garden, right among the smartly-dressed children, so that they flew screaming into the house; and then when Wieb cried over her lost apples, he would wipe away her tears with his handkerchief: 'Hush, Wieb; for every apple I'll get you a whole pocketful out of their garden tomorrow!' – And she knew he always kept his word.

Wieb had a small 'Madonna face', as the art-loving school rector had once said, a gentle face on which suffering should not be seen; but the little Madonna nevertheless liked to eat the pastor's red apples, and Heinz climbed the trees at every opportunity and stole them for her. Then Wieb would tremble; not because she thought stealing apples was a sin, but because on these occasions the pastor's older day-boarders would sometimes attack and beat her friend about the head until the blood flowed. But when after a successful expedition Heinz beckoned her into the avenue behind the house, kneeled on the ground before her and crammed his booty into her small pockets, she would smile at him in sheer delight, and the strong youth would swing his protégée into the air with both arms, joyfully exclaiming: 'Wieb, Wieb, dear little Wieb,' and whirling her round with him in a circle until the red apples flew out of her pockets.

Sometimes too, at such moments, he would take the little Madonna by the hand and go with her down to the harbour. Should everyone on the ships be below decks he would unmoor a boat, slip his protégée quietly aboard, and row with her round the Warder and far out into the strait. If, meanwhile, the boat's theft was noticed and loud angry words were carried across the water to them from the ship to which the boat belonged, then he would begin to sing loudly so that little Wieb should not be frightened; but if she heard them, then he would row even more energetically and shout: 'We must get far away from all these awful people!' One afternoon, when Hans Kirch was away on his ship, they even dared to moor over on the island where a relative of Wieb's, whom she called 'Möddersch', lived in the large village. It was the time of the great St Michael's Fair, and after they had had a cup of coffee with Möddersch they hurried between the booths and into the midst of the bustling crowd, Heinz making room for them both with some good shoving with his elbows. They had ridden on the merry-go-round, eaten gingerbreads and stood by many a barrel organ when Wieb's blue eyes caught sight of a small silver ring displayed among chains and spoons in a goldsmith's booth. Dispiritedly she played with the remaining wealth in her hands, just three six-pfennig pieces; but Heinz, who had sold all his rabbits the day before, still had eight shillings left after the day's extravagance, and these plus the three six-pfennig pieces were happily sufficient to secure the ring. Both their pockets were now quite empty, and for a go on the merry-go-round Möddersch had to pay out a further shilling – it cost so much because this time Wieb wanted to ride on a huge lion instead of an ordinary seat; then, just as all the lamps between the pearl and gold embroidered draperies were lit, the fun was over for them, and the old woman too now made to return home. While Heinz pulled hard on the oars, they cast many a look back and their hearts were full of joy as they watched, in the advancing darkness, the gleams of light from the many lamps on the merry-go-round pulsating above the now invisible village; but Wieb had her silver ring, which she never let go from her finger.

* *

Hans Kirch, meanwhile, had sold his cutter. In a stately schooner built at the local yard he shipped corn to England, at first for clients but more and more on his own account, and returned with cargoes of coal. And so to the corn business was added coal, and this too, like the dairy farming, had to be managed by his wife. Regarding Heinz, if on his return, in answer to the direct question: 'Has the boy been behaving himself?', he received an affirmative answer, he did not seem greatly concerned about anything else; only at the end of term was he in the habit of visiting the rector and the pastor to find out how the boy was doing at school. The report was always the same: studying was child's play to him; he always had too much time left over; for he was as wild as the devil, no boy was too big for him nor any peak too high.

According to the rector, a quite unaccustomed and gratified smile would often appear on Hans Adam's face when he received such comments, and he would just say, 'Ah, well', as he shook the rector's hand on parting.

However right Heinz's teachers might have been, the protective relationship with little Wieb continued, a subject many a spiteful young lad contrived to comment on behind their backs. He was also seen out walking on Sundays with his mother to a sparse copse not far from the town, and on the way back to be carrying his small sister on his back in addition to an empty picnic-bag. Sometimes the gradually growing Wieb also joined these Sunday walks. The quiet Frau Kirch had taken to the sensitive girl and would say: 'Let her come along, Heinz; she won't be with that wretched mother of hers then.'

After his confirmation Heinz had to make a couple of voyages aboard his father's schooner, no longer as a 'play-bird' but as a strictly disciplined ship's boy; but he coped with it, and after the first voyage home Hans Kirch patted him on the back while giving his wife her share of his satisfaction with a quick nod of his head. The second voyage was with another master; for the growing trade at home demanded the personal attention of the owner of the business. Then, after two further voyages aboard larger vessels, Heinz returned to the parental home as a sailor. He was now seventeen years old; the blue peakless sailor's cap with its bright coloured brim and fluttering ribbons admirably suited his fresh brown complexion, which even the pastor's daughters noticed when they peeped through the fence on hearing him playing with his sister in their parents' garden next door. And even Hans Kirch himself, during service on Sundays, could not refrain from squinting down from the Shipmasters' Gallery at his handsome boy sitting next to his mother. His eyes would also occasionally wander across to an epitaph where the marble bust of an imposing figure of a man wearing a great extended wig was to be seen among trophies of victory; a man like his Heinz, just an ordinary citizen's son, who as a commander of three of His Majesty's ships had returned nonetheless to his home town. But no, such a lofty plan for his son was not yet in Hans Kirch's mind; for the time being it was only to be a voyage on board the Hamburg-registered ship *Hammonia* to the China Sea, from where it would be a year before Heinz returned; and today was his last in the parental home.

Not without tears, this time, had his mother packed his chest, and after coming home from church she placed her own hymn-book on top of it. The father had also spoken little to his son in these last few days, apart from what was necessary, but on this last evening, when they met in the dark hall, he grabbed for his hand and shook it fiercely. 'I'll not be idle here, Heinz; for you, just for you! And come back safely as well!' He uttered these words hastily, then let go of his son's hand and hurried out into the yard.

Heinz gazed after him in surprise for a while; but his thoughts were elsewhere. He had seen Wieb again the day before; but it had only been an opportunity for a few fleeting words; now he wanted to take his leave of her, to row her round the Warder again as before.

It was a cool May evening; the moon hung over the water as he made his way down to the harbour; but Wieb was not yet there. True, she had told him she had to do a few small jobs for an old lady in the evenings, but all the same, he could hardly contain his impatience while he walked up and down the lonely quay: he scolded himself and did not know why the pounding of his heart almost snatched his breath away. At last he saw her coming down from the higher street above him. In the moonlight, which shone directly on her, she appeared to be so tall and slender that at first he was almost in despair that it really might not be her. However, she had wrapped the upper part of her body in a large shawl; she had not needed covering for her head, for her blonde hair rested like a small bonnet above her delicate features. 'Good evening, Heinz!' she said quietly as she stepped towards him, and shyly, almost like a stranger, he touched her hand which she held out to him. In silence he led her to a boat that lay in the water beside a large Kuff. 'Come on, it's all right!' he said when he had stepped aboard, stretching out his arms to her as she hesitated on the steps of the quay. 'I've got permission. We won't be told off this time.'

When he had caught her in his arms he slipped the mooring, and the boat glided out of the shadow of the large ship and across the shimmering surface of the moonlit water.

She sat opposite him on a thwart in the stern of the boat; but although they had travelled beyond the tip of the Warder, where some startled gulls woken from sleep were shrieking, still no further word was spoken between them. There was so much that Heinz wanted to say to little Wieb in this hour of parting, and now it was as if his lips were sealed. It was the same with the girl too; the further out they went and the more quickly the short evening passed, the quieter and more anxious she became as she sat there; and his eyes almost devoured the childlike figure with whom he now drifted so alone between the sky and the sea; hers, though, were turned away into the night. Then a sudden feeling welled up within him and the boat shuddered from his brisk pull on the oars which made her small head turn abruptly, and the blue radiance of her eyes met his. But that too passed quickly, and something like anger overcame him; he did not know whether against himself or against her, because she sat so strangely opposite him, because all the words that raced through his mind refused to fit her. He forced himself to reflect on the past: had he not on more than one occasion, abroad, whirled the most obdurate of young lasses in his arms, even also whispered a high-spirited word in her ear; but the chaste young figure opposite was quite clearly indifferent to such things.

'Wieb,' he said finally, sounding almost pleading, 'little Wieb, today's the last for a long time.'

'Yes, Heinz,' and she nodded and looked down. 'I know that.' It was as though she had wanted to say something else, but she did not say it. The heavy shawl had slipped from her shoulders, and when she retrieved it and now clasped it to her breast with her hand, he missed the small ring on her finger that he had once helped her to buy at the fair. 'Your ring, Wieb!' he cried instinctively. 'Where have you left your ring?'

For a while she sat motionless; then she got up and stepped over the next thwart towards him. She had to place one hand on his shoulder in the swaying boat while she reached with the other into a slit in her clothes and pulled out a length of cord to which the ring was fastened. With halting breath she removed the cap from her friend's brown locks and slipped the cord round his neck. 'Heinz, oh please, Heinz!' The full radiance of her blue eyes settled in his; her tears fell onto his face and the young couple flung their arms round each other's necks and the tempestuous Heinz almost kissed his little Wieb to death.

It must have been quite late when they returned their boat to the big ship; they had not heard the hours being struck; but every light in the town appeared to be out.

When Heinz returned to his parents' house he found the door locked. His mother answered his knock from the hall; his father had already retired to his room and taken the key with him. But at last Heinz heard his steps too coming slowly down the stairs from the bedroom above. The door was then quietly opened, and after Heinz had been let in, just as quietly closed; not until after he had uttered his 'Good evening' did Hans Kirch look at him. 'Didn't you hear the town bell? Where have you been wandering?'

The son saw the anger flare in his father's eyes; he was pale to the roots of his dark hair, but he said quietly: 'Not wandering, father'; and his hand instinctively touched the small ring which he kept safe beneath his open waistcoat.

But Hans Kirch had waited up too long for his son. 'Just watch out!' he shouted, thrusting the heavy key towards his son's face. 'Don't ever knock on your father's door like that again! It might stay shut.'

Heinz had drawn himself up to his full height; his face reddened; but his mother had put her arms round his neck and the angry response, already formed on his lips, never came. 'Good night, father!' he said, and quietly squeezing his mother's hand, he turned and went upstairs to his bedroom.

＊ ＊

The next day he was gone. His mother went quietly around what had suddenly become an empty house to her; little Wieb's heart had grown heavy; thoughtfully and almost with fondness she examined the red weals on her arm – her mother's reward for disturbing her night's rest: they were almost like a token of Heinz which she would always keep; only Hans Kirch's thoughts and inclinations turned busily to the future.

After six weeks a letter had come from Heinz; it carried good news; because of courageous intervention at the right moment, the captain had voluntarily increased his pay. His mother entered the room just as her husband was tucking the letter into his pocket. 'May I read it too?' she asked timidly. 'You've good news?'

'Yes, yes,' said Hans Kirch, 'but nothing in particular, beyond wishing to be remembered to you and his sister.'

The next day, however, he began to make all sorts of errands into the town; in the shade of the lime-trees he was seen entering in turn each of the large houses with their wide stone-walled steps. Who could know how soon the young man would have his helmsman's examination behind him; there was now a need for him too to move up the ladder. He had been a member of the college of deputies for some years; now a seat on the council was vacant; its occupant was to be appointed by the remaining members of the council.

But Hans Adam's hopes were dashed; within a few days the vacant seat was filled by his former colleague, a fat master baker, for whom he was certainly no match in either wealth or girth. He had just emerged ill-tempered from a meeting of the deputies, at which the baker's place had now become empty, and was standing chewing his resentment away on a small plug of tobacco under the tail of the giant fish, caught here in '70 and still hanging by the door of the town hall in commemoration of the event, when an elderly but buxom woman crossed the market-place and came straight towards him; a boy laden with two large sides of bacon followed her.

'It's not going at all your way, Hans Adam!' she shouted from some way off.

Hans Adam raised his head. 'There's no need to shout across the street, Jule. I know that without you telling me.'

It was his elder sister, who after her husband's death hawked bacon with Kirch zeal around the town. 'And why shouldn't I shout?' she retorted, 'I don't mind if everyone hears! You're an old skinflint, Hans Adam; but you've a good head on your shoulders, which is the last thing any of those on the council want, unless it happens to be sitting on their own; that old loafer suits them much better, particularly when they can't ignore us middle-class folk.'

'Tell me something I don't know!' replied her brother angrily.

'Oh yes, Hans Adam, you're too clever for me, or else you wouldn't live in our parents' house for next to nothing!'

The good woman could never get over the fact that her brother had once been offered a higher price for the family house, by someone keen to buy it, than that at which he had acquired it in the division of their inheritance. But Hans Kirch was well used to this reproach, he gave it no further attention, at this moment it simply appeared to act as a spur to recovery after the blow he had received. Outwardly he stared at the ground as though he saw something in front of him on the pavement, but his thoughts were already restlessly occupied with preparing a new way towards his objective: it was self-evident, further acquisition had to be made, and more saved; the power of money eventually had to open this door when the next opportunity came; and should it not be of any use to himself, then it would certainly help his Heinz, with his better schooling and bolder character, as soon as he had completed his customary years as a captain at sea.

With a swift movement Hans Adam lifted his head. 'Do you know, Jule' – he put the question almost casually – 'whether your neighbour Schmüser still wants to sell that large warehouse of his?'

Frau Jule, who with her last remark had wanted to provoke a completely different answer from him and had been waiting for it for some time, retorted angrily that it would be best if he enquired himself.

'Yes, yes; you're right.' He nodded quickly and had already taken a few steps towards the street in which Fritz Schmüser lived when his sister, paying no attention to the boy groaning beneath the bacon, tried to detain him further; he must not escape so easily. 'Hans Adam!' she called. 'Just wait a minute! Your Heinz . . .'

At the sound of this name Hans Adam suddenly halted. 'What do you want, Jule?' he asked hurriedly. 'What's this about my Heinz?'

'Nothing much, Hans Adam; but you probably don't know what your smart lad got up to on his last evening here!'

'Well?' he exclaimed, as she paused for effect. 'Out with it, Jule; it won't be a song of praise for sure!'

'It all depends, Hans Adam, it all depends! There wasn't much time for good-byes at the old aunt's; but why shouldn't he take the spruced up Wieb, the sailor's lass, out for a row from nine to eleven? It must have been cold comfort out there in the sound; but we older ones know what's what, the young ones have their own fire with them.'

Hans Adam was trembling, his upper lip rose to expose his full set of teeth. 'Stop prattling!' he said. 'Just say where you heard that from!'

'Where from?' Frau Jule let out a merry laugh. 'The whole town knows, most of all Christian Jensen in whose boat the pleasure-trip took place! But you're a hothead, Hans Adam, from whom people can easily get an angry answer; and who's to know whether the spruced up daughter-in-law is in your favour or not? And by the way' – she took hold of her brother's lapel and pulled him close to her – 'in view of the new relationship, it's surely for the best that you didn't get a seat on the council.'

Having happily delivered herself of her message, she turned to go. 'Come Peter, get along!' she called out to the boy, and soon they had both disappeared down one of the lanes off the market-place.

Hans Kirch stood rooted to the spot as though thunderstruck. After a while he stirred himself almost mechanically and set off for the lane where Fritz Schmüser's warehouse was situated; but he suddenly turned back again. Soon he was sitting at home at his desk with his quill pen swiftly writing a letter to his son, pouring out the surge of anger from that last evening which the mother's intervention had prevented from being fully expressed.

* *

Months went by; the places from which Heinz had agreed to write must
have long been passed, but Heinz still did not write; then came news of
the ship, but no letter from him. Hans did not let that trouble him too
much. 'It'll come soon,' he said to himself. 'He's well aware what there
is for him here at home.' And with that, after he had acquired
Schmüser's warehouse at a low price, he worked vigorously at the
expansion of his business and let nothing distract him. However, when
he returned home from the extra voyages, some to home ports, once
even to England with his schooner, the first hurried question to his wife
was always: 'Any letter from Heinz?', and invariably the only answer he
received was a sad shake of the head.

The anxiety that he could not ultimately suppress was dispelled
when the newspapers announced the return of the *Hammonia*. Hans
Kirch walked restlessly around the house and yard, and mother and
daughter frequently heard him talking fiercely to himself; for the boy
would soon be coming in person and he intended to give him a sharp
lecture. But a week passed, and a second, and Heinz had not come.
From inquiries it was finally learned that on the voyage home he had
agreed with the captain to take another job; it was not established
where. 'He wants to defy me!' thought Hans Adam. 'We'll see which
one of us keeps this up the longest!' The mother, who knew nothing of
her husband's letter, went about in sorrow, and unable to understand
her son; and whenever she dared to ask her husband about Heinz, he
either gave no answer at all or insisted that she never mention the boy
to him again. In one way at least his behaviour was different from that
of most men: he did not burden the poor mother with the blame for this
lamentable state of affairs; but nonetheless, Hans Adam was now
difficult to live with.

Summer and autumn passed, and the more time went by, the more
firmly resentment took root in his heart; his son's name was no longer
mentioned in his own house, and people were afraid to ask after Heinz.

It was already spring again when one morning, from his front door,
he saw the pastor with his pipe in his mouth standing by his front
garden fence. Hans Kirch had some business further up the street and
was about to pass by with a quiet touch of the hat; but the neighbourly
pastor called loudly across to him with all the dignity of his pastoral

office. 'Well, Herr Kirch, still no news from Heinz?'

Hans Adam was startled, but he stood still; the question had not been put to him for some time. 'Let's talk about something else, if you don't mind, Herr Pastor!' he said abruptly.

But the pastor did not feel at all prompted to respond to this request. 'My dear Herr Kirch, it's now almost two years; you should really be concerned about your son!'

'I should have thought, Herr Pastor, according to the Fourth Commandment it would be just the opposite!'

The pastor took his pipe from his mouth. 'But not according to the Commandment in which, according to God's Word, all the others are included, and what could be closer to you than your own flesh and blood!'

'Don't know, Reverend,' said Hans Kirch, 'but I'll stick to the Fourth.'

There was something in his voice that warned the pastor not to continue in this vein. 'Well, well,' he said to placate him, 'he's sure to return, and when he does – he's your kind, Herr Kirch – it won't be empty-handed!'

Something of the smile that showed on the pastor's face during these last words also transferred itself to the other's face, and while the pastor, with a polite wave of the hand, returned to his house, Hans Kirch made his way up the street to his large warehouse in a more cheerful mood than he had been for some time.

* *

On the following day, the old postman walked down the same street. He strode hurriedly and held a thick letter in his hand which he appeared to have taken out of his leather postbag in anticipation; just as hurriedly at his side, talking excitedly to him, walked a blonde girl of about sixteen years of age. 'From an old friend, you said? Don't tease me any longer, Marten! Go on, tell me who it's from?'

'You silly young thing,' cried the old man, waving the letter in front of her eyes. 'How can I know that? I only know who it says I have to give it to.'

'Who to, who to, Marten?'

He stood for a moment and held the address side of the letter towards her.

The girl's opened lips expressed a sound that did not conclude in a word.

'From Heinz!' she said at last, shyly, and like a bright flame happiness glowed on her young face.

The old man gave her a kindly look. 'From Heinz?' he repeated mischievously. 'My dear Wieb, you can't tell that just by looking!'

She said nothing; but as he strode off in the direction of Kirch's house she continued to walk by his side.

'So?' he said. 'You really think I should have another one in my bag for you?'

She suddenly halted, and while she was sadly shaking her head the postman walked on with the thick letter.

When he entered Kirch's house the mother was just coming out of the kitchen with a steaming bowl; she was on her way with it up to a small room on the top floor in which little Lina lay with measles. But Marten called out to her: 'Frau Kirch! Frau Kirch! What will you give for this letter?'

She had soon read the address in her husband's name and recognised the writing. 'Heinz!' she cried. 'Oh, from Heinz!' And something like a cheer burst from this quiet breast. Then the child's voice came from upstairs. 'Mother! Mother!'

'I'm coming, I'm coming, my child!' Then after a grateful glance towards the postman she flew up the stairs. 'Oh, Lina, Lina! From Heinz, there's a letter from our Heinz!'

Below in the living room Hans Kirch was sitting at his desk, two opened account ledgers in front of him; he was busy with the accounts of his losses, which had turned out to be unusually large at this time. Irritably he listened to the loud voices outside which disturbed him in his reckonings; when the postman entered he shouted at him: 'What were you making that noise for, outside with my wife?'

By way of answer, Marten handed him the letter.

Almost grudgingly he peered at the address with his keen eyes, which still had no need of glasses. 'From Heinz,' he growled after he had carefully examined all the postmarks. 'And not before its time!'

Old Marten waited in vain to see a spark of joy in the father's eyes; but all he noticed for his trouble was a trembling of the hand, which Hans Adam could not control as he reached for a pair of scissors to open the letter. And just when he was about to use them, Marten touched his arm. 'Herr Kirch, I need to ask for thirty shillings!'

'Why?' – he threw the scissors down – 'I don't owe the post anything!'

'Sir, you can see the letter isn't stamped.'

He hadn't noticed; Hans Adam clenched his teeth; thirty shillings; why not put them down as a loss too! But that was a trifle, it wasn't that at all; no – it was what lay behind it! What had the pastor been babbling about recently? He wouldn't return empty-handed! – not empty-handed! Hans Adam laughed furiously to himself. – He didn't even have the postage! And he – he should be the one to win a seat on the council, a position which had proved to be too lofty for him, the father!

Hans Kirch sat silently and stiffly at his desk; his thoughts raged only in his mind. His ship, his warehouse, everything that he had acquired with difficulty over so many years rose up before him, and, as if of its own accord, merged into the impressive sum of his work. That he should have to give all that to this . . . His thoughts failed to complete the sentence; his head burned, there was a roaring in his ears. 'Wretch!' he suddenly shouted. 'You'll not enter your father's house in this way!'

The letter was thrown down at the alarmed postman's feet. 'Take it,' he said. 'I'm not paying for it; it's too expensive for me!' And Hans Kirch grabbed his quill pen and leafed through his account ledgers.

The good-natured old man picked up the letter and tried some modest persuasion; but the master of the house drove him away, and he was relieved to reach the street without meeting the mother a second time.

As he continued on his way towards the southern end of the town, Wieb was just returning from the same direction; she had taken an order to the distillery which was the last house there. Her mother, after the sudden death of 'her man at sea', had formally become the legitimate wife of 'her man ashore' and had opened a sailors' tavern with him down by the quayside. Little good was said about the new enterprise; but when the burning red lamp above the door cast its light

towards the ships on autumn evenings, the taproom inside was soon full
to bursting, and outside, the distillery at the end of the town enjoyed
good custom.

As Wieb approached the old postman she noticed straight away that
he now looked quite grumpy – and then she saw that he still had Heinz's
letter in his hand. 'Marten!' she cried out – she could not help herself –
'The letter; you've still got it? Wasn't his father at home then?'

Marten's face was grave. 'No, child, his father was certainly not at
home; the old man Hans Kirch was there; but the letter was too
expensive for him.'

The girl's blue eyes gave him a startled look. 'Too expensive,
Marten?'

'Yes, yes. Imagine, he was asked to pay thirty shillings for it.'

After these words Marten put the letter in his leather postbag and
went on with another, which he had drawn out at the same time, to the
next house.

Wieb remained standing in the lane. She looked at the door for a
while, which had closed behind the old man; then, as if suddenly struck
by a thought, reached into her pocket and jingled what sounded like
small silver coins. Yes, Wieb really did have money in her pocket; she
even counted it, and it was a whole handful she had taken that very
morning behind the bar. True, it did not belong to her, she knew that
quite well; but what did she care, her mother could beat her as much as
she liked for it! 'Marten,' she said hurriedly when he emerged again
from the house, and held out a handful of small coins towards him,
'here's the money, Marten; give me the letter!'

Marten looked at her in complete astonishment.

'Come on, give it to me!' she insisted. 'Here's your thirty shillings!'
And when the old man shook his head, she grabbed hold of his postbag
with her free hand. 'Oh, please, please, dear Marten, I want to read it
just once, together with his mother.'

'Child,' he said, catching her hand and looking kindly into her
anxious eyes, 'if it were up to me we could come to some arrangement;
but even the postmaster cannot sell you a letter.' He moved away from
her and strode off on his round.

But she ran after him, held onto his arm, from her innocent mouth came the most charming words of entreaty and flattery for old Marten, and in her head were the most stupid of notions; could he at least lend her the letter; he would have it back this very same evening.

Old Martin was caught in an intense conflict with his generous nature; but in the end he had no choice, he had to push the child forcibly away from him.

She did not follow; she pressed her hand to her brow beneath her golden-blonde hair as though she had to think about something; then she let the money fall back into her pocket and walked slowly towards the quayside. Those who passed her on the way looked at her in surprise; for her hands were pressed to her breast and she was sobbing wildly.

* *

Fifteen years had passed. The small town appeared hardly to have changed at all; just a new house had been built in the market-place for a young merchant from one of the established families; telegraph wires had been strung along the lanes and the sign outside the post office now read in gold letters: 'Imperial Post Office'; as always, the sea rolled its waves up the shore and when the north-west wind veered to the east-north-east, the high tide washed the walls of the distillery which even now still had its best custom from the red lamp; but the end of the railway was still some miles away inland behind the chain of hills; even the Bürgermeister's seat on the council, in spite of the new blessings, was still occupied in the good old manner by an educated man, and the town council maintained its former respectability even though Senators had been transformed into 'Aldermen' and Deputies into 'Town Councillors'; one young Councillor had even proposed the abolition of the town bell as an antiquated custom, but two old members of the council had given the bell their support – in their youth, the bell had impelled them home from many a folly: why shouldn't the young folk of today, and the servants, be subject to the same discipline? And so just as before, when it struck ten from the church tower the little bell continued to chime in response and frighten the young couples apart as they chattered by the fountain in the market-place.

The Kirch household was not so unchanged. Heinz had not returned home; he was missing; only a formal declaration was needed to confirm that he was legally dead; most young people did not know that old Kirch had ever had a son. At the time the incident had taken place, however, old Marten had related the story of the letter to others on his rounds, and a good deal had been said about the father and son; and not just about them – also of the mother, of whom people never spoke, it was reported that when details of the incident finally reached her ears, she had protested to her husband for the first time. 'Hans! Hans!' she had addressed him, without paying attention to the maid eavesdropping at the kitchen door, 'you had no right to do that without me! We can now only pray that the letter will not be returned to its sender; but God will not burden you with such heavy guilt.' And Hans Adam, while her eyes looked fully and tearlessly at him, had not responded, not with a single word. She, however, had not only prayed, but had sent off enquiries everywhere after her son, though always in vain; fearlessly she paid the costs incurred from the small cashboxes she kept. And Hans Adam, although he soon noticed this, never intervened. He himself did nothing of the sort; he doggedly told himself that the boy had to communicate differently, whether by letter or in person, or never knock at the door of his parents' house again.

And the son had never knocked on their door again. Hans Adam's hair had greyed somewhat more quickly; silent grief, however, had gnawed the mother's heart away at last, and when her daughter grew to womanhood, she broke down. Only one thing had remained firm within her, the conviction that her Heinz would return one day; but even that she bore in secret. Not until what seemed to be her rapidly approaching end, after a sharp decline in her strength, did it once escape her lips. It was a bright and frosty Christmas morning; supported by her daughter, she was struggling upstairs to the bedroom. Just when she was half-way up, breathing heavily and leaning against the banister, looking about helplessly, the winter sun suddenly streaked through the pane above the front door and filled the dark hall with its pale light. The sick woman turned her head towards her daughter.

'Lina,' she said secretively, and her dull eyes suddenly glowed in eerie transfiguration. 'I know, I shall see him again! He'll come one day when we least expect it!'

'You think so, mother?' the daughter asked, frightened.

'My child, I don't think so; I'm certain of it!'

She had then nodded to her daughter with a smile; and soon she was lying between the white sheets which in a few days time would be enfolding her dead body.

During this last period of her life Hans Kirch had hardly left his wife for a moment; his assistant, who until then had only lent a hand with the business, had become quite bewildered by the sudden responsibility thrust upon him, but even now the son's name was not mentioned between the parents; only when the dying woman's already fading eyes opened wide and looked around the empty room as though searching for something had Hans Kirch, as though in promise, taken her hand and squeezed it; then her eyes had closed for her last rest.

But where was Heinz Kirch, and what was he doing in the hour of his mother's death?

* *

A few years later the pitched roof of Hans Kirch's house was dismantled and a full second storey was built on; and soon a young household was installed on the upper floor, for his daughter had married the son of a wealthy citizen of a neighbouring town who had then entered her father's business. Hans Kirch contented himself with the rooms on the old ground floor; the office next to the front door also served as his living room. Behind it, looking out onto the courtyard, was the bedroom; and there he sat amid his business without the need for climbing stairs, and despite approaching old age was still able to oversee affairs and direct his young partner. But it was not the same with the other side to his life; more than once there had been a change on the council, but Hans Kirch had not lifted a finger; even though he had been appealed to, not a single word for or against the new appointments had escaped his lips.

On the contrary, he now often went for a stroll with his hands behind his back, sometimes by the harbour, sometimes in the park, whereas he usually looked on all walkers with disdain. In the descending twilight he could be seen out in the open, sitting on the high shore across the bay, looking out to sea, apparently oblivious of the few people who passed by. If a ship happened to emerge out of the sunset and come towards him in full sail, he would remove his cap and run his other hand trembling over his grey head. But no, miracles didn't happen any more; why should Heinz be on that ship? And Hans Kirch would give himself a shake and almost angrily set off for home.

The entire ambitions of the household now took another form, represented by his son-in-law. Christian Martens had known no rest until the family had become members of the Harmony Society, which, as was well known, admitted only respectable citizens. The young husband, as his father-in-law had promptly and thoroughly established, was a conscientious worker and in no way a spendthrift, but – to be considered a fine gentleman, to exchange warm handshakes with respected members of the community, perhaps even to wear a solid gold chain on a brown velvet waistcoat – all this he had to have too. Although Hans Kirch had at first resisted joining the Society, when he was offered a regular game of 'Sixty-Six' in a small, quiet room with some old seafaring gentlemen he went along to the Society with his daughter and son-in-law.

So time had passed, when one sunny morning in September Hans Kirch stood at his front door; with his bent back, stooped head, and as usual both hands in his pockets. He had just returned from his warehouse, but curiosity had driven him outside again, for through the window he had noticed on the left of the market-place, where there were usually only hens and children running about, a large crowd of adults, men and women, obviously in lively discussion with one another. He raised his hand to his ear to overhear something; but they were standing too far away from him. Then a stocky though aged-looking woman detached herself from the crowd; she might have been half-blind, for she felt her way with a walking stick; nevertheless, she was soon making her way towards the Kirchs' house quickly enough. 'Jule!' growled Hans Adam. 'What does Jule want?'

Since the time her brother had refused her a larger loan for a purchase, only an occasional word or greeting had passed between them; but now she stood before him; she had first gestured towards him with her stick from some way off. A first impulse made him want to turn and go indoors, but he stayed where he was. 'What do you want, Jule?' he asked. 'What's the meeting about over there in the market?'

'What's the meeting about, Hans? Will you lend me the hundred Thaler if I tell you?'

He turned to go into the house.

'No, stay!' she cried. 'You'll get to know anyway; your Heinz has come back!'

The old man gave a start. 'Where? What?' he exclaimed, and turned his head in every direction. The bacon-hawker saw with pleasure how his hands trembled inside his wide pockets.

'Where?' she repeated, slapping her brother on his bent back. 'Pull yourself together, Hans! He's not here yet, he's in Hamburg in a seamen's hostel on the Johannisstraße!'

Hans Kirch groaned. 'Women's twaddle!' he muttered. 'Gone seventeen years; he's not coming back – he's not coming back.'

But his sister wouldn't let him go. 'It's not women's twaddle, Hans! Fritz Reimers has written home to say he's with him in the hostel!'

'Yes, Jule, and Fritz Reimers has lied more than once!'

His sister crossed her arms angrily under her full bosom. 'Quaking again over your money-bags, are you?' she cried scornfully. 'Oh well, they betrayed our Lord Jesus for thirty pieces of silver, so well may you disown your own flesh and blood for thirty shillings. But now you'll have him every day again! He's certainly not going to be a senator now; you'll just have to accept him as you yourself have made him!'

But her brother's hand gripped her arm; his lips had curled back to reveal the still full set of strong teeth. 'Nero! Nero!' he called hoarsely into the open doorway, while the stirring of the large house dog was heard inside. 'Damn you, woman, need I clear you from the door with dogs!'

Frau Jule's moral indignation, however, was probably not so profound, six months ago had she not herself more or less forced her own daughter to marry a drunkard in order to attract his capital to her business? It had simply provoked her, as she later admitted, to tease her brother occasionally about the hundred Thaler. And so she was close to making it up with him when an older man came towards them from the direction of the market-place. It was the shopkeeper from the corner opposite. 'Come, neighbour,' he said, taking hold of Hans Adam's hand, 'we'll go to your room; the street's no place for this!'

Frau Jule nodded her broad head a few times. 'I think so too, Herr Rickerts,' she said, while she felt for the street with her stick. 'You can tell him better yourself; he won't believe his sister! But Hans, what if you're short of money to get to Hamburg?'

She got no answer; Herr Rickerts had already gone with her brother into his room. 'So you know, neighbour,' he said, 'it's quite right; I've read the letter from Fritz Reimers myself.'

Hans Kirch had sat down in his armchair, and with his hands on his knees stared in front of him. 'From Fritz Reimers?' he asked at last. 'But Fritz Reimers is a windbag, a real fool!'

'Quite so, neighbour, and this time too he wrote home of his own shame. In the evenings, at the seamen's hostel on the Johannisstraße, they all sat together in the tavern bar, German seamen, but from all over the world; Fritz Reimers and two of our youngsters were among them. They discussed all sorts of things, and finally, where each of them had first cried as a baby. When it came to Reimers' turn he sang – you know it well, neighbour – that silly song in which they turn the huge fish at the entrance of our town hall into a miserable little plaice; but hardly had the word been sung when someone from the other end of the table shouted: "That's no plaice, it's the tail of a killer whale, and it's double the length of your arm and leg put together!"

'The man who said this was perhaps ten years older than our youngsters who were sitting there, and called himself John Smidt.

'Fritz Reimers, however, didn't answer, but sang on, as it says in the song: "And they trade, said he, quite a lot; they've two boats, said he, and a yacht!" '

'The cheeky scoundrel!' exclaimed Hans Kirch. 'And his father sailed in my schooner right up to his death!'

'Yes, yes, neighbour; John Smidt banged the table too. "It's an ill bird that fouls its own nest!" '

'Quite so!' said Hans Kirch. 'He should have banged him on his thick skull!'

'He didn't do that; but when Reimers asked him what he knew about it, John Smidt said –'

Hans Kirch had seized the other's arm. 'John Smidt said –?' he repeated.

'Yes, neighbour,' – and the narrator's voice became quieter – 'then John Smidt said that his name was actually Heinz Kirch, and asked him if he could believe it. – You know of course, neighbour, our youngsters sometimes give themselves other names when abroad, Smidt or Mayer, or anything that comes to mind, especially if there's something not quite right when changing ships. Of course, I've only been here sixteen years; but from hearsay, this man must be just like your Heinz!'

Hans Kirch nodded. It was extremely quiet in the room, only the pendulum ticked in the wall clock; the old shipmaster seemed to feel a chilling hand waiting for the grasp of his own.

The shopkeeper broke the silence first. 'When do you want to go, neighbour?' he asked.

'This afternoon,' said Hans Kirch, standing up as straight as he could.

'You'd better go with enough money, they say your son's clothes are not in the best of shape.'

Hans Kirch winced. 'Yes, yes, I'll go this afternoon.'

* *

There had been a listener to the conversation; the young wife who had come to see her father had heard her brother's name through the half-open door and stood listening. Without going in, she now flew back upstairs to her own living room where her husband, sitting by the window, had just lit a Havana cigar from the Sunday box as a special treat. 'Heinz!' she cried out to him in excitement, just as her mother had done long ago. 'News of Heinz! He's alive, he'll soon be with us!' And in a rush of words she explained what she had overheard in the hall below. But suddenly she stopped and looked at her husband who was thoughtfully puffing out clouds of smoke.

'Christian!' she cried and knelt down in front of him. 'My only brother! Aren't you pleased?'

The young man laid his hand on her head. 'I'm sorry, Lina; it was so unexpected. For me your brother has never existed; it will all soon be quite different.' And cautiously and sensibly, which was proper for a right-thinking man, he then began to set out for her how this homecoming, no longer in doubt, would unsettle, even shake, the foundations of their future existence. That the son's long absence had provided on his part, even though he hardly admitted it to himself, a second reason to court Hans Adam's daughter, went unmentioned, however much it now pressed on his mind.

Frau Lina had listened attentively. But as her husband fell silent, she shook her head smiling. 'If only you knew him. Oh, Heinz was never self-interested.'

He looked at her fondly. 'Of course, Lina; we must learn to come to terms with this; all the more if he returns as you once knew him.'

The young wife threw her arms round her husband's neck. 'Oh, you are good, Christian! You'll certainly become friends!'

Then she left the room, went into the bedroom, then the parlour, and to the stove. But her eyes shone no more with happiness, a cloud had just been cast over her joy. Not that her husband's thoughts oppressed her; no, it was only that such a thing could be possible; she hardly knew herself why everything now appeared so bleak to her.

* *

A few days later Frau Lina was upstairs busily preparing the room for her brother; but even today her heart was heavy. The letter in which her father had announced his and his son's homecoming contained no word of a happy reunion between them; instead, it revealed that the new-found son had at first sought to hide himself from his father under his adopted name and might well be accompanying him home unwillingly.

When on the appointed Sunday evening the young married couple had gone outside to the carriage drawn up before the house they saw, in the light which came from the open hall, a man descend whose weather-beaten face with full red beard and short cropped brown hair seemed to indicate an age of almost forty; a scar that ran across his brow and one eye might well have contributed to making him appear older than he actually was. Hans Kirch slowly clambered down after him from the carriage. 'Well, Heinz,' he said, pointing to each of those named in turn, 'this is your sister Lina, and this is her husband Christian Martens. You must try to get on together.'

Heinz now shook hands in exactly the same manner with each of them in turn and with a dry '*Very well!*' He did this with an awkward embarrassment; the manner of his homecoming might well have troubled him, or he felt a reserve in his relatives' welcome; for certainly they had painted a different picture of the homecomer for themselves.

After they had all entered the house, Frau Lina took her brother upstairs to his room. It was not the same any more, where he had once slept as a boy everything up here was new, but he seemed not to notice. The young wife set the luggage, which she had carried up after him, down on the floor. 'This is your bed,' she said, removing the white bedcover and folding it up. 'Heinz, my brother, you should sleep like a top here!'

He had discarded his coat and with rolled-up sleeves gone to the wash-stand. He now quickly turned his head and his shining brown eyes rested in hers. 'Thank you, sister,' he said. Then he dipped his head into the bowl and splashed the water about as is common among those who wash in the open. His sister, leaning in the doorway, looked on in silence; her woman's eyes examined her brother's clothes and clearly recognised that everything had been recently acquired; then her gaze rested on the man's brown sinewy arms which displayed still more scars than his face. 'Poor Heinz,' she said, nodding towards him, 'they must have done a lot of hard work!'

He looked at her again; but this time a wild fire burned in his eyes. '*Demonio!*' he cried, shaking his outstretched arms. 'Every kind of work, sister! But – *basta y basta!*' And he dipped his head into the basin again and threw water over himself as if he wanted to rinse down God only knew what.

At the evening meal, which the family took together, conversation was difficult. 'You've travelled far, brother-in-law,' said the young husband after several futile attempts; 'you must tell us everything about it.'

'Far enough,' replied Heinz; but it did not lead to any account of things; he gave only short general answers.

'Let him be, Christian!' exhorted Frau Lina. 'He needs to sleep here at home for one night at least.' Then, however, so that the first evening was not too quiet, she herself began to bring up the few memories she had of her brother's youth, either from her own experience or from her mother's tales.

Heinz listened quietly. 'And then,' she continued, 'that time you had the big anchor with your name tattooed on your arm! I can still remember how I screamed when you came home so burned, and how we called the doctor. But' – and she hesitated a moment – 'wasn't it on your left forearm?'

Heinz nodded. 'Might well have been; it was just a boys' prank.'

'But Heinz – it isn't there any more. I thought things like that never disappeared!'

'Must've done, sister; there are terrible illnesses in those parts; you've often got to be thankful when they don't strip the skin from your body.'

Hans Kirch had only half an ear for what was being said. More than usually stooped, he ate his meal in silence, only occasionally throwing one of his sharp looks at the homecomer, as though considering what remained to be done with this son.

But in the days that followed, the household remained silent. Heinz neither inquired after earlier acquaintances nor spoke about what he might do next. Hans Adam asked himself whether his son expected the first word to come from him, or whether he ever gave a thought to the morrow. 'Yes, yes,' he muttered, vigorously nodding his grey head, 'he's become used to things over these last seventeen years.'

But Heinz appeared not to feel at home. After smoking his cigar for a short while in his sister's room, he would feel a need to leave the house again, and go down to the harbour where he would shout a few words to one or other of the shipmasters, or call at the big warehouse where he watched the off-loading of hard coal or other work with indifference. Once or twice, as he sat below in the office, Hans Kirch had opened one of the account ledgers in front of him so that he could gain an insight into the current position of the business; but every time, after a quick thumbing to and fro of the pages, he had laid it down again as if it were something strange.

In one respect, however, much to the relief of the young husband, he appeared to conform to the description of her brother that Frau Lina had sketched for him in their first conversation: the homecomer appeared to have no thought of exercising his rights as a son.

There was another thing that had not escaped her woman's eye. Just as her brother had once gone around with her, his much younger sister, had told her things and played with her, with her and – as she knew from her mother – with someone else too, whom he had so far not asked after and whom she had avoided mentioning; now in just the same way, sitting outside on the steps in the afternoon, he would let the shopkeeper's little son scramble about on his lap and pull at his hair and beard, and then he would laugh just as Frau Lina seemed to remember hearing her brother Heinz laugh in the garden, or on those Sunday walks with their mother. It was on the second day after his return, as she was just going out through the front door in hat and scarf to meet him, that she had so found him. The young rascal was standing on his lap and holding him by the nose. 'You're fibbing, you big shipmaster!' he said, shaking him vigorously.

'No, no, Karl, *by Jove*, mermaids do exist. I've seen them with my own eyes.'

The boy let him go. 'Really? Can you marry them then?'

'Oho, my lad! Of course you can! Over there in Texas, there are all kinds of things to see, I knew someone once who had a mermaid; she was always kept in a huge water barrel in his garden.'

The young lad's eyes lit up; he had only once seen a young seal like that, and he had had to pay a shilling for it. 'Listen,' he said secretively, nodding towards his bearded friend, 'I'll marry a mermaid, too, when I grow up!'

Heinz looked thoughtfully at the boy. 'Don't do that, Karl; mermaids are unfaithful; it would be better to stay in your father's shop and play with your neighbour's cat.'

His sister rested her hand on his shoulder. 'You wanted to go to mother's grave with me!'

And Heinz lifted the boy to the ground and went with Frau Lina to
the cemetery. And later he also let her talk him into visiting the old
pastor who now managed the large vicarage with the help of a
maidservant, and he even paid a visit to Aunt Jule to whom he had given
little thought as a boy.

* *

Sunday morning had arrived and the young married couple prepared
themselves for the customary churchgoing; even Heinz had announced
he would go. Hans Kirch had been particularly quiet the evening
before and his daughter, who knew him well, glanced anxiously at his
face several times. But at last she felt relief as she heard him open and
close the large hall cupboard from which he was accustomed to taking
out his Sunday coat for himself.

But shortly afterwards, when the three churchgoers entered the
downstairs room, Hans Kirch was standing by the window, hands
behind his back, in his everyday clothes and looking out onto the empty
lane; hat and Sunday coat lay carelessly slung over the chair at the desk.

'Father, it's time to go!' Frau Lina reminded him shyly.

Hans Adam had turned round. 'Just go!' he said bluntly, and the
daughter saw his lips tremble as they closed over his strong teeth.

'Why, aren't you coming with us, father?'

'Not today, Lina!'

'Not today, when Heinz is back with us again?'

'No, Lina.' He spoke the words quietly, but it was as if they had to be
immediately followed by an outpouring of feeling. 'I've no wish to be
alone in our Shipmasters' Gallery today.'

'But, father, you always are,' said Frau Lina hesitantly, 'Christian
always sits below with me.'

'Yes, yes, your husband, your husband!' – and an angry look shot
from beneath the bushy brows at his son, and his voice grew louder –
'that's where your husband belongs. But old mariners who at thirty-
five still let their father's ships be commanded by other captains, who
should have sat somewhere else long ago, those I have no wish to see
below me in a pew.'

He paused and turned back to the window, and no one had answered him; but then Heinz laid the hymn-book that his sister had given him on the desk. 'If that's all it is, father,' he said, 'then the old mariner can stay at home; many a Sunday he's only listened to the whistling of the wind in the rigging.'

But the sister seized her brother's and then her father's hands. 'Heinz! Father! Let it rest for now! Listen to God's Word together; you'll come back with good thoughts and can then discuss what should be done next!' And now, perhaps because the furious man had been at least temporarily calmed by the venting of his anger with a word or two – what she herself had not expected she had achieved: both of them went to church.

But Hans Kirch, sitting up among the other old captains and shipowners and staring as usual at the marble bust of the old commander, was aware how below all eyes gazed towards the homecomer. The old commander had also been a boy of the town, a schoolmaster's son, a schoolmaster's grandson like Heinz; how differently he had returned home!

No conversation between father and son took place either after church or in the afternoon. That evening Frau Lina drew her brother into her bedroom. 'Well, Heinz, have you talked to father yet?'

He shook his head. 'What should I talk to him about, sister?'

'You know perfectly well, Heinz. He wants to have you up there in the church with him. Tell him you'll take your helmsman's examination – why does it take you so long to say it?'

A contemptuous smile distorted his face. 'What a tremendous question this old Shipmasters' Gallery is!' he cried. '*Todos diabolos.* An old lad like me sitting on a school bench again! I've steered many an old barque without it, you know!'

She looked at him fearfully; the brother whom she was beginning to get used to suddenly seemed a stranger to her, even eerie. 'Steered?' she repeated quietly. 'Where have you steered to, Heinz? You've not got very far.'

For some moments he glanced sideways at the floor; then he stretched out his hand to her. 'Maybe so, sister,' he said calmly, 'but – I can't be like you just yet; I'm always having to remind myself where I am going; you don't know, none of you know, sister! Half a man's life – yes, think of it, even more than half a man's life without an honest roof over his head; only the wild sea or wild men or both together! You know nothing of it, I tell you, the shouting and the swearing, my own included; oh yes, sister, mine too, it still sounds in my ears; I must first be quieter, otherwise – it's impossible!'

His sister put her arms round his neck. 'Of course, Heinz, of course, we'll be patient; oh, it's good that you're with us now!'

* *

Suddenly, God knows from where, a rumour arose and spread wildly from door to door: the homecomer was not Heinz Kirch at all, it was Hasselfritz, a boy from the poorhouse who had gone to sea at the same time as Heinz, and from whom nothing had been heard either. And now, after circulating for a short while, the rumour had found its way into Kirch's house. Frau Lina held her head in her hands; she must have heard through her mother of that other, who had had brown eyes like Heinz and like him had been an intelligent wild lad, in fact, people had once found a similarity between them. Supposing all the joy should now have been for nothing, supposing it was not her brother! Her face went a bright red; she had hung her arms about his neck, she had kissed him. Frau Lina suddenly avoided touching him; surreptitiously, however, and more frequently, her eyes passed over her guest's rough features as she inwardly strove to recognise the boyhood face of her brother among the shadows of the past. When her young husband warned her to be careful, Frau Lina suddenly recalled how casual her brother had recently seemed to her by their mother's grave; he had leaned both arms on the surrounding iron railings and stared at the other graves to either side of him as if he were bored; as if, as in church during the Lord's Prayer following the sermon, he was just waiting for the visit to come to an end.

To both husband and wife the brother's whole behaviour now appeared far coarser than before; his shuffling about on chairs, his lack of regard for Frau Lina's clean floorboards. Heinz Kirch, everyone said it, and the impression also remained in Frau Lina's own memory, had been a fine young fellow. When both of them shared their doubts with Kirch, the same had already occurred to him too; but he had kept silent so far and was silent now; he simply pressed his lips together more firmly still. But when soon afterwards he saw the old pastor with his pipe standing by his front garden fence he could not miss the opportunity to approach him, as though by chance, and make inquiries in a roundabout way.

'Yes, yes,' said the old man, 'it was most decent of Heinz not to begrudge me a visit straightaway on his second day.'

'Duty, Herr Pastor,' retorted Kirch. 'But you must be in the same position as I am; it takes skill to discover the old Heinz in this fellow with the red beard.'

The pastor nodded. His face suddenly wore an expression of oratorical inspiration. 'Yes, a beard!' he repeated emphatically, with a gesture of the hand, as if in the pulpit, 'as you say, Herr Kirch; and indeed, since this unseemly ornamentation became the fashion, it's become impossible to recognise the boys in the young men anymore, unless they mention their names first – I've experienced it myself with my boarders! There was that blond Dithmarscher – your Heinz once gave him a bloody lesson, but he seems to have forgotten about it now – he looked just like a snowy lamb when he left here; and years later when he came into my quiet room so unexpectedly – he was a lion! I assure you, Herr Kirch, a real lion! If his dull old eyes hadn't fortunately still been up to it, this old man might have dropped dead as a result of it!' The pastor drew on his pipe a few times and pulled his velvet cap more firmly over his grey head.

'But of course,' said Hans Kirch, feeling he had evoked a favourite topic, and returning to his own subject again, 'my Heinz shows no such signs as your Dithmarscher.'

But the old man continued in his own way. 'Good Lord, no!' he said contemptuously, with a movement of his hand as though sweeping aside his poor sight. 'A man, a real man!' Then he raised a forefinger and, with a mischievous smile, described a straight line across his brow and one eye: 'He's also won a decoration; in a fight, Herr Kirch, in a fight; just like a student in the old days! In my time, seamen and students, they were the men of liberty, we always stood together!'

Hans Kirch shook his head. 'You're mistaken, Herr Pastor; my Heinz was only in trading ships; in a storm, a fragment of wood, a swinging yard can do the same.'

'Crede experto! Trust the expert!' exclaimed the old man, secretively raising the left earflap of his cap, behind which the faint trace of a scar was visible. 'In a fight, Herr Kirch; oh, we've also fought for our country!'

A smile flitted across the old seaman's face, momentarily revealing his strong teeth. 'Yes, yes, Herr Pastor; of course he was no coward, my Heinz!'

But the glowing pride that brought forth these words soon disappeared; the picture of his brave boy faded before that of the man who now lodged under his roof.

Hans Kirch quickly took his leave, giving up competing any further with the ramblings of old age.

That evening there was a ball at the Harmony Society. Heinz wanted to stay at home, he would be out of place there, and the young couple, who had only casually mentioned it to him, agreed; for they considered Heinz, and they were surely correct, not yet ready to present to the Society. Frau Lina wanted to stay at home too, but she had to give in to pressure from her husband, who had purchased new finery for her. Hans Kirch went too for his game of Sixty-Six; an inner disquiet drove him from the house.

So Heinz remained at home alone. When everyone had gone, he stood with his hands in his pockets by the window of his dark bedroom which faced north-east towards the sea. The weather was unsettled, the clouds raced across the moon, but he could still see the white crests of the waves in the deeper waters beyond the Warder. He stared at them for a long time; gradually, when his eyes had accustomed themselves to the dark, he also noticed a bright haze over the island opposite; it could not be coming from the lighthouse; but the large village was there, where he had heard there was a fair that day. He opened the window and leaned out. He almost thought he heard dance music in the distance above the noise of the sea, and as though suddenly gripped by it, he quickly slammed the window shut and, tearing his cap from the door-hook, sprang down to the hall below. When he had just as quickly reached the front door, the maid asked him if she should wait up for him before locking up; but he simply shook his head as he left the house.

A short time afterwards, preparing the bedrooms for the night, the maid went into the guest's room. She had left her lamp behind on the landing and was only going to put the water jug in the room; however, when the moon outside suddenly poured its strong light down through the broad heavens, she too went to the window and looked out at the waves crowned with silver foam; but she was soon no longer looking at these, for her young far-seeing eyes had picked out a boat being rowed by a single man through the spray towards the island.

* *

Whenever Hans Kirch, or the young couple, went to the Harmony Society to gather further information about that uncanny rumour, they found themselves disappointed; no one dropped so much as a hint about it; it was the same as before, as though Heinz Kirch had never existed.

Not until next morning did they learn that he had gone out soon after they had that evening, and so far had not returned; the maid, when questioned, informed them of her suspicions which might well not have been far from the truth. When the absentee returned home shortly before midday with a bright red face, Hans Kirch, who met him in the hall, turned his back on him and went quickly to his room. Frau Lina, whom he met on the stairs, looked at him reproachfully and questioningly; she paused for a moment as though she wanted to speak to him; but – who was this man? – She changed her mind and went past him without speaking.

After the midday meal, taken in silence, Heinz sat down on the sofa in the corner of the young couple's room upstairs. Frau Lina busied herself about the room; Heinz, his head supported, fell asleep. When, after a considerable time, he woke up, his sister had gone; instead he saw his father's grey head bending over him, and he still seemed to feel how the sharp eyes had been peering into his face.

For a few moments the two stared at each other, then the son got up and said: 'Let it be, father, I already know you'd prefer me to be Hasselfritz from the poorhouse; it would really please you if I could become someone else.'

Hans Kirch stepped back. 'Who told you that?' he said. 'You can't say I would have said such a thing about you.'

'But your face says it all to me; and our young wife, she shrinks away from my hand as if she had to grasp a toad. Didn't know what was going on at first; but this evening, over there, at the dance, it was being sung from the rooftops.'

Hans Kirch did not reply; the other, however, had stood up and was looking into the lane where gusts of rain were being driven along by the autumn wind. 'But there's one thing I'll ask you to tell me!' he began again, turning and looking grimly at the old man. 'Why, when I was young, did you do that to me with the letter? Why? If it had not been for that, I would definitely have brought my old face home again.'

Hans Kirch gave a start. This subject had not been touched upon since the death of his wife; he himself had buried it deep within himself. He felt in his waistcoat pocket with his fingers and bit a plug from the black roll of chewing tobacco he had pulled from it. 'A letter?' he said at last. 'My son Heinz was not one for writing letters.'

'Maybe, father; but once – once he did write; he posted the letter in Rio, and later, a long time afterwards – the devil might well have had a hand in it – in San Jago, that den of fever, when the letters were given out to the crew they called out: "Here's something for you too." And when the son, trembling with joy, stretched out his hand, at first content only to devour the inscription on the letter with his eyes, he saw it had really come from home, and there was handwriting from home on it as well; but – it was only his own letter, which had come back to him after six months unopened.'

It looked almost as if the old man's eyes were close to tears; but when he saw the defiant look of the young man facing him, his mood suddenly changed. 'Might have had nothing in it worth reading!' he said grudgingly.

A harsh laugh escaped from the younger man's mouth followed by a curse in a foreign language which his father did not understand. 'You might well be right, Hans Adam Kirch; but it was not according to the rules; the young fellow would have prostrated himself before his father at that time; but a thousand miles were between them; and besides – he was racked with fever and had only just left his miserable hospital bed! And then later – what do you think, Hans Kirch? A man disowned by his father doesn't ask what the cargo is below decks on his next ship, whether it's sacks of coffee or black ivory, that's to say black people, just as long as there are doubloons to be earned; and he never asks where the devil is taking them and where the new ones are coming from!'

The tone in which these words were spoken sounded so wild and alien that Hans Kirch instinctively asked himself: 'Is this your Heinz, whom the choirmaster always used to place in the front row for the "Amen", or is he actually the boy from the poorhouse who's only after your money?' Again he searched the other's face; the scar, across his brow and one eye, glowed burning red. 'Where did you get that?' he said, thinking of his conversation with the pastor. 'Were you in a fight with pirates?'

A desperate laugh escaped from the younger man's mouth. 'Pirates?' he said. 'Believe me, Hans Kirch, there are some good fellows amongst pirates! But that's enough. It's too long a story, about the people I've been with!'

The old man looked at him, startled. 'What did you say?' he asked, so quietly that it seemed no one else was to hear.

But before an answer could follow, heavy steps were heard on the stairs outside; the door opened and, led by Frau Lina, Aunt Jule entered the room. While she stood puffing and leaning on her walking stick with both hands, Heinz slipped quietly past her out through the door.

'Has he gone?' she said, pointing after him with her stick.

'Who do you mean?' asked Hans Kirch, looking at his sister in a none too friendly way.

'Who do I mean? The one you've had in your house for the last two weeks, of course!'

'What is it you want this time, Jule? You don't usually make me a surprise visit.'

'Yes, well, Hans,' and she nodded to the young wife to fetch her a chair, then sat down upon it, 'you didn't deserve it; but I'm not like that,

Hans; I've come to apologise to you; I must admit that Fritz Reimers probably lied, or if he didn't, the other one did!'

'Lied about what?' asked Hans Kirch, sounding tired.

'About what? You shouldn't let yourself be taken in so! You think you've recaptured your bird; but just take a good look and see if it's really the right one!'

'You've come with that tittle-tattle too, have you? Why shouldn't he really be my son?' He said this crossly, but as though he wanted to hear it.

Frau Jule had settled in a determined posture. 'Why, Hans? When he came to my house with Lina on Wednesday afternoon, we were already having our third cup of coffee and still he hadn't once said "Aunt" to me! – "Why," I asked, "don't you ever call me Aunt?" – "Well, Aunt," he said, "you never finished talking!" See Hans, he lied from his very first word to me; no one can ever say that of me, I always let a person have his say! And when I held him closer to me and felt his face with my hand and looked at him with my miserable eyes – well, Hans, his nose could never have come from either east or west!'

Her brother sat opposite her with his head bowed; he had never noticed it, how his Heinz's nose was set on his face. 'But,' he said – the conversation that had just taken place flashed through his mind, but the words seemed to come with difficulty – 'that letter he wrote; we talked about it; he received it back himself in San Jago!'

The buxom woman laughed so heartily that the stick fell out of her hands. 'The story of that letter, Hans! Of course, it's been well raked up in the last two weeks; he could have had his fill of it from any beggar boy for a copper! But he should have explained to you why the real Heinz stayed away from you all those years. Don't let him pull the wool over your eyes, Hans! Why didn't he want to come with you when you fetched him from Hamburg? Was it really so bad to come back into the fold? – I want to tell you something, and this is it: he couldn't decide soon enough on the rascally trick!'

Hans Adam had raised his grey head, but had not interrupted; he had listened almost eagerly to everything his sister had said.

'And then,' the latter continued, 'Lina has spoken about it.' – But suddenly she stood up and felt towards the window with her walking-stick which Lina had dutifully picked up for her; the voices of two men could be heard outside in lively conversation. 'Oh, Lina,' said Aunt Jule, 'I can hear, one of them is the Councillor of Justice, run and ask him to come up here for a moment!'

The Councillor of Justice was the old district physician; at a time when there were few honorary titles in these parts, all elderly physicians held this title.

Hans Kirch had no idea what his sister wanted with this man; but he waited patiently, and soon the old gentleman entered the room with the young woman. 'My, my,' he said, 'Aunt Jule and Herr Kirch together? Where's the patient then?'

'Here,' said Aunt Jule, pointing to her brother, 'he's got cataracts in both eyes!'

The Councillor laughed. 'You're joking, dear lady. I wouldn't mind having our friend's sharp eyes myself.'

'Get on with it, Jule,' said Hans Kirch, 'why beat about the bush!'

But the stout woman would not be put off. 'I'm speaking figuratively, Councillor,' she explained emphatically. 'But cast your mind back and remember how you were once called to this house, twenty years ago. Lina, she's now a grown woman, she was wailing about the house because her brother Heinz, in a boyish fancy, had tattooed a fine anchor on his forearm, and had quite injured himself.'

Hans Kirch suddenly became alert; for the conversation at the first evening meal after Heinz's return, which he had disregarded at the time, now came back to him loud and clear.

But the old doctor shook his head. 'I can't remember it; I've attended to so many boys in my time.'

'Indeed, Councillor,' said Aunt Jule, 'but you're familiar with boyish fancies like that today in our town. The question simply is, and we'd like to know the answer from you: could an anchor like that disappear without a trace over twenty years?'

'Over twenty years?' responded the Councillor of Justice without hesitation. 'Indeed it could, quite easily!'

Now Hans Kirch joined in the conversation. 'You're thinking of how it's done now, doctor, with blue India ink; no, the boy had it done at the time in the old permanent way; pricked deep with a needle and ingrained with indelible pigment.'

The old doctor rubbed his brow. 'Yes, yes; I remember now. Hm! No, that should be quite impossible; it goes as deep as the cutis; old Hinrich Jakobs is still going about with his anchor today.'

Aunt Jule nodded in approval. Frau Lina stood up, her hand on the arm of the chair, pale and trembling beside her.

'But,' said Hans Kirch, his voice faltering as it struggled from his throat, 'aren't there illnesses? In foreign parts, in those hot countries?'

The doctor thought for a moment, then shook his head firmly. 'No, no; that is not conceivable . . . and smallpox would have scarred his arm.'

There was a pause while Frau Jule put on her knitted gloves. 'Well, Hans,' she said, 'I must be off home; but it's your choice now: an anchor or smallpox scars! What's your new Heinz got to offer then? Lina hasn't been able to see either of them; take a look for yourself if your sight is still sound!'

Soon afterwards Hans Kirch walked up the street to his warehouse; his hands were folded behind his back, his head bowed even lower than usual on his chest. Frau Lina had also left the house, following after her father. When she entered the gloomy lower floor of the warehouse, she saw him standing in the middle of it, as though he needed first to remember why he had gone there. Because of the noise of the shovelling of corn coming from the upper floor he might well have failed to hear her come in; he almost pushed her away as he saw her so suddenly in front of him. 'You, Lina! What do you want here?'

The young woman, trembling, wiped her face with her handkerchief. 'Nothing, father,' she said, 'but Christian is down at the harbour, and I felt so bad alone in the house with him – with that stranger! I'm afraid. Oh, it's terrible, father!'

During these words Hans Kirch had lowered his head again; then, as though out of an abyss, he raised his eyes to his daughter's and looked into them long and steadily. 'Yes, yes, Lina,' he at last said hastily. 'Thank God it is a stranger!'

Quickly he turned, and the daughter heard him climbing the stairs to the top floor.

* *

An overcast evening had followed this day; no star was visible; dank mists lay over the sea. The harbour was unusually full of ships, mostly cutters and schooners, but a few three-masted square-rigged sailing ships were also among them, together with the steamship which docked here each week. A deep peace lay over everything, and even along the harbour quay only a single man strolled, to all appearances without specific purpose. He stopped in front of one of the two barques, on whose deck a boy was still working at the capstan; he shouted a 'good evening', and almost without thinking asked the name of the ship and its cargo. As details were being given, a head emerged out of the cabin, appeared to scrutinise the person standing ashore for a moment, then spat far out into the water and dived below decks again. Ship and captain were not from here; the man ashore strolled on further; from the Warder opposite came the occasional shriek of a bird; from the island only a faint gleam of light from the beacons penetrated through the fog. When he came to the place where the houses neared the water, a babble of voices reached his ears and caused him to stop. From one of the houses a red light shone out into the night; he recognised it well, even though his foot had not yet crossed its threshold; the light came from the lantern of the harbour tavern. The house had a low reputation; only foreign sailors and the sons of leaseholding shipmasters went there; he had heard all about it. And now the noise broke out again, this time with a woman's shrieks added to it. A grim smile spread across the man's face; the light of the red lantern and the wild sounds behind the curtained windows might have awakened all kinds of things in his memory which it did no good to recall. He walked towards the house, however, and just as he heard the striking of the town bell he entered the low-ceilinged but spacious bar room.

A number of old and young seamen sat at a long table; a group of them, which the landlord appeared to have joined, was playing with dirty cards; a woman beyond the flower of her youth, with pale, worn-out face and a line of sorrow round her still beautiful mouth, entered with a number of steaming glasses and distributed them without a word among the guests. As she came to a man with small eyes greedily protruding from his large-boned face, she pushed the glass in front of him with obvious haste; but he laughed and tried to hold her by the skirt. 'Well, Ma'am, have you still not changed your mind? I'm a polite man, I assure you! But I know all about women: black or white, they're all the same!'

'Leave me alone,' said the woman, 'pay for your glass and let me go!'

But the other was of a different opinion; he grabbed hold of her and pulled her suddenly towards him, so that the glass standing in front of him overturned and its contents poured over them both. 'Look, pretty Missis!' he shouted, without noticing the upset, and nodded with his head of red hair towards a companion sitting opposite, whose flaxen hair fell down over a pale, drink-bloated face. 'Look – Jochum there, with his silly old face, has nothing against it! Drink up, Jochum, I'll buy you another!'

The man he had spoken to emptied his glass in one swig with a foolish smile, then pushed it forward to be refilled.

For a moment the woman's hands, with which she had been trying to release herself from the strong embrace, were still, and as her eyes fell on the pale drunkard it was as though loathing and contempt made her temporarily forget everything else.

But her tormentor only pulled her more firmly to him. 'See here, my beauty! I should have thought it wouldn't be such a bad swap! But that's not the whole of it! Take care I don't gossip out of school!' And as she resisted again, he nodded to a handsome lad with brown locks who sat at the lower end of the table. 'Heh, you tiddler,' he shouted, 'think I don't know who left the red lamp yesterday two hours after we did and crept below decks?'

The poor woman's face blushed bright red; she no longer defended herself, she simply looked round for help. But no one lifted a hand; the young handsome lad only smiled quietly and stared into his glass.

From an empty corner of the room the last guest to arrive had studied the whole scene with indifferent eyes up to now; and when he raised his fist and slammed it down on the table in front of him, it seemed to be from a former habit of being more than just a spectator at such moments. 'A glass for me too!' he shouted, and it almost sounded as though he were looking for a fight.

All those opposite sprang from their seats. 'Who is he? Does he want to have a taste of our Bowie knives? Throw him out! God damn it – who does he think he is?'

'Just a glass!' the other said quietly. 'Don't let me disturb you! There's room for us all in here I think!'

The others eventually agreed with this and sat down again at their table; but the woman had seized the opportunity to break free and now went over to the new guest's table. 'What'll it be?' she asked politely; but when he told her she seemed almost not to hear; surprised, he watched her vacant eyes fixed on him as she remained standing in front of him.

'Do you know me?' he said, quickly tossing his head back so that the light from the ceiling lamp fell onto his face.

The woman took a deep breath, and the glasses she held in her hand audibly jarred against one another. 'I'm sorry,' she said nervously, 'I'll fetch it straight away.'

He gazed after her as she went out though a side-door; the tone of the few words she had spoken to him had been quite different from what he had previously heard from her; he slowly raised his arm and supported his head on it; it was as though all his thoughts were very far away. It should have eventually occurred to him that he had still not received his order; but he gave no thought to it. Suddenly, while the card game at the other table changed to dice, he got up. Had the attention of the other guests been on him instead of the new game, he would certainly not have escaped their derision; for the tall strongly built man visibly trembled as he stood there with his hands braced on the table.

But it was only for a brief moment; then he left the room by the same door through which the waitress had gone out. A dark passage led him into a large kitchen which was barely lit by a lamp hanging on the wall. Hurriedly he entered, his keen eyes searching the sparse room before him; and there she stood, the one he was looking for; as if drained of strength, with the empty glasses still in her joined hands, she was leaning against the wall by the fireplace. A brief moment, then he went up to her. 'Wieb!' he cried out. 'Wieb, little Wieb!'

It was a rough voice that uttered these words and now fell silent, as though it had given them its last breath.

A rose-red glow now swept over the woman's pallid face, and as the glasses crashed to the ground, a cry rose from her breast; who could have said whether it was sorrow or joy. 'Heinz!' she cried. 'Heinz, it's you; oh, they said it wasn't.'

A dark smile hovered about the man's mouth. 'Yes, Wieb; I've known for some time; I should never have come back. And even you – everything was so long ago – I didn't want to see you again, to hear from you, Wieb; I gritted my teeth when I wanted to say your name. But – last night – there was a fair again over there – I stole a boat just as I did when I was a boy; I had to, I couldn't do anything else; I looked for you at every stall, on every dance floor; I was a fool, I thought old Möddersch was still alive; oh, dear little Wieb, I thought only of you; I didn't know myself what I was thinking!' His voice trembled, his arms stretched wide open towards her.

But she did not throw herself into them; only her eyes looked sadly at him. 'Oh, Heinz!' she cried. 'It's you! But I – I'm no longer the same! – You've come too late, Heinz!'

Then he pulled her towards him and let her go again and lifted both his arms. 'No, Wieb, and these are no longer the innocent hands that used to steal the red apples for you; *by Jove*, it takes it out of you, it does, seventeen years among these people!'

She had sunk to her knees beside the fireplace. 'Heinz,' she murmured, 'Oh, Heinz, those old times!'

As if embarrassed, he remained standing beside her; but then he bent down and took hold of one of her hands, and she accepted it in silence.

'Wieb,' he said softly, 'let's wait and see if we can find each other again, you and I!'

She said nothing; but he felt a movement of her hand, as though it were painful, in his.

Sounds of wild commotion came from the bar; glasses clashed, there was the sound of a punch. 'Little Wieb,' he whispered again, 'can't we go far away from all these vile people?'

She had let her head rest against the stone fireplace and was moaning painfully. The shuffling of feet was heard in the passage, and as Heinz turned, a drunkard stood in the doorway; it was the same man with the bloated vulgar face whom he had already noticed among the other seamen. He held onto the door-post, and his eyes appeared to be staring about the dim room without seeing. 'Where's the grog got to then?' he stammered. 'Six new glasses. That red-headed Jakob's cursing for his grog.'

The drunkard went away again; they heard the door to the bar close behind him.

'Who was that?' asked Heinz.

Wieb struggled to her feet. 'My husband,' she said. 'He sails to England as a seaman; I work for my stepfather here as a bar-maid.'

Heinz did not respond; but his hand searched his hair-covered chest, and appeared to pull something forcibly from his neck. 'Look,' he said tonelessly, holding up a small ring from which hung the ends of a broken cord, 'our children's game, still here! If it had been gold, it wouldn't have stayed with me so long. But besides that – I don't know, was it because of you? It was probably just superstition, because it was the only thing left of home.'

Wieb stood opposite him and he saw her lips move.

'What are you saying?' he asked.

But she did not answer; her eyes only seemed to plead for pity. Then she turned and busied herself in doing what she had been asked to do, mixing the hot drink. She paused only once in her work, when the light sound of metal on the stone floor struck her ears. But she knew, there was no need for her to turn round; what else was he to do with the ring now?

Heinz had seated himself in a wooden chair and was looking quietly at her across the room; she had poked the fire and the flames flared up and cast a red glow over them both. When she had gone out, he remained sitting there; at last he got up and went into the passage that led to the bar. 'A glass of grog, a strong one!' he called out when Wieb came towards him from the bar door; then he sat down again, alone at his table. Soon Wieb reappeared and put the glass down before him, and once more he looked up at her. 'Wieb, dear little Wieb!' he murmured when she had gone again; then he drank, and when the glass was empty he shouted for another, and when she quietly brought it he let her put it before him without looking up.

Amid the noise of the other table no further attention was paid to the solitary guest. One hour of the night struck after the other, one glass after the other he drank; only occasionally, as through a fog, he saw the sad beautiful face of the woman who was lost to him, until at last he followed the others out, and in the late morning woke with a terrible head in his bed.

* *

It was no longer a secret in the Kirch family where Heinz had spent the previous night this time. The midday meal, as on the day before, had been taken in silence; now, in the afternoon, Hans Adam Kirch sat in his office doing the accounts. Among the other ships in the harbour was his own ship and its cargo of coal from England. It was being unloaded today, something Hans Adam never usually missed. But this time he had sent his son-in-law; he had something more important to do. He was calculating, he was keen to know, what more this son could possibly cost him, whom he had so rashly brought home, or – if it was not his son – this person. In a rapid hand he dipped his quill and wrote down his figures; son or not, he was quite certain things must now come to an end. But of course – and his pen halted for a moment – he wouldn't leave easily for nothing; and – if it were really Heinz, he shouldn't send his son away with a pittance. He had even thought of a once for all payment for the lawful proportion of his inheritance; but how was a valid receipt to be obtained? For it had to be done securely, so that he would not come back again. He threw down the quill, and the sound that died away behind his teeth sounded almost like a laugh: but it wasn't his Heinz! The Councillor of Justice, he really understood the matter, and old Hinrich Jakobs still carried his anchor at eighty!

Hans Kirch reached for a leather bag which lay nearby; he slowly opened it and withdrew a number of low-denomination treasury notes from it. After he had spread them out in front of him, then put some of them back, and after some hesitation still more of them, into the leather bag, he stuffed the remainder into a ready envelope; he had carefully considered the moderate sum.

Now he was ready; but he remained sitting there with his jaw sagging, his idle hands gripping the table. Suddenly he jumped up, his grey eyes opened wide: 'Hans! Hans!' the call had come; here in the empty room, where, as he now noticed, the twilight already lay in every corner. But he reflected; it was only his own thoughts passing through his mind; it was not now but many years before that this voice had called him. And yet, as though he were reluctantly obeying someone outside himself, his hands opened the leather bag once more and hesitantly took a number of the larger-denomination notes from it. But with every single note that Hans Adam now added to the earlier calculated small sum, his resentment mounted against the one who was to sell his future inheritance of house and home to his father for cash; for what should have served the furtherance of long-laid plans for life he was now to throw away, just to remove the last wreckage of them!

When Heinz, an hour or so later after a stroll through the town, made his way upstairs, Hans Adam appeared at the same moment from the door to his room below and followed him so rapidly that they both entered the son's room almost together. The maid, who was working on the landing, quickly stood up, hands on hips; she was well aware that all was not right between father and son, and behind the closed door an angry conversation now seemed to ensue. – But no, she had been mistaken, it was only the old man's voice she heard; and louder and louder and more threatening it sounded, although no answer followed; she tried in vain to understand something of the content of the conversation; she heard the shutters banging inside the room in the wind, and it felt to her as though the ever more angrily expressed words in there were being sent out into the dark night. Then at last it was quiet; but at the same time the maid was struck by the opening bedroom door – she sprang with a cry to one side, saw her feared employer with dishevelled hair and wild flashing eyes stumble down the stairs, and heard the office door torn open and slammed shut again.

Not long afterwards, Heinz too stepped out of his room; when he met his sister in the hall downstairs he clasped both her hands with only just less than violence and squeezed them so fiercely that she looked up at him in amazement; as she was going to speak to him, however, he was already outside in the lane. Neither did he appear for the evening meal; but when the town bell rang, he was climbing the stairs again and making for his bedroom.

In the small hours of the next morning Heinz stood fully clothed upstairs by the open window; the sharp air swept over him, but it appeared to do him good; almost with reverence, he looked down on everything which, in the last traces of night, lay spread out before him. The broader waters between the Warder and the island opposite gleamed like pale steel, while the bluish-red early morning light already played on the narrower stretch of water between the Warder and the mainland shore. Heinz studied it all; but he did not stand there for long; soon he walked to the table on which the envelope with the reluctantly counted-out treasury notes still lay in the same place where Hans Kirch had left it the evening before.

A bitter smile played about his lips as he pulled out the contents, and then, after putting aside a few of the smaller notes for himself, returned the remainder to their place. With a pencil which he found on the table he noted down the small sum he had taken out beneath the total listed on the envelope; then, when he had put it aside, he picked the pencil up once again and wrote underneath in English: *Thanks for the alms and farewell for ever.* He did not himself know why he had not written it in German.

Quietly, so as not to wake the sleeping house, he picked up his luggage from the floor; more quietly still, in the hall below, he unlocked the door to the street outside and left the house.

In a nearby lane a lad with a one-horse carriage halted; into this he climbed and left the town in it. When they had reached the top of the range of hills from where the town can be seen for the last time, he turned round and waved his cap three times. The carriage then went out into the wide world at a trot.

* *

But one of the Kirch household had been awake with him nevertheless. Hans Kirch had already been sitting up in his bed long before daybreak; with every stroke of the tower bell he had listened more intently for a first stirring upstairs. After a long while he thought he heard a window shutter open up there; but it became quiet again, and the minutes lengthened and would not pass. They passed, however, and at last he heard the gentle creaking of a door, someone coming down the stairs to the hall below, and now – he heard it clearly, the key turning in the front door lock. He wanted to jump out of bed; but no, he did not want to; with arms braced he remained sitting, while in the street outside a man's heavy footsteps could be heard, gradually fading away until they became inaudible in the distance.

When the remainder of the house gradually stirred, he got up and sat down to the breakfast that was prepared for him, as every morning, in his office. Then he reached for his hat – as an old shipmaster he still had no need for a walking-stick – and, without having seen the other occupants of the house, went down to the harbour, where he found his son-in-law already busy directing the continued unloading of his ship. He appeared not to consider it necessary to tell him about the recent course of events, sending him to the coal sheds and giving him jobs to do in the town while he remained here in his place. Taciturn and angry he issued his instructions; it proved difficult to do anything right for him that day, and whoever spoke to him generally received no answer; but before long his mood wore off; everyone knew him well.

Shortly before midday he was again in his room. He had instinctively closed the door behind him; but he had hardly sat down in his armchair when Frau Lina's voice outside urgently requested entry. Ill-temperedly he stood up and opened it. 'What do you want?' he asked, as his daughter entered the room.

'Don't be cross with me, father,' she pleaded, 'but Heinz has gone, his luggage too; oh, he'll never come back!'

He turned his head away. 'I know that, Lina; there's no need for floods of tears.'

'You know, father?' she repeated, turning rigid as she looked at him.

Hans Kirch grew angry. 'Is that all you wanted? The farce's over; we settled everything between us yesterday.'

But Frau Lina just shook her head gravely. 'I found this up in his room,' she said, and passed him the envelope with the brief words of farewell and the hardly touched contents. 'Oh, father, but it was him! It's been him all along!'

Hans Kirch took it and read the words written on it; he tried to remain calm, but his hands shook so that the notes fell out of the open envelope onto the floor.

He had just picked them up with Lina's help when there was a knock at the door, and without waiting for a response a pale-looking woman entered, her anxious eyes darting from father to daughter.

'Wieb!' cried Frau Lina, and took a step backwards.

Wieb struggled for breath. 'I'm sorry!' she mumbled. 'I had to; Heinz has gone. You probably don't know yet; but the coachman was saying, he won't be coming back, ever!'

'What's that to do with you?' Hans Kirch interrupted her.

A cry of despair rose in her breast, such as to make Lina gaze involuntarily and with great pity at this face that had once been so lovely. But Wieb had been given renewed strength. 'Listen to me!' she cried. 'Out of mercy for your own child! You think it wasn't him; but I know that it was no one else! This,' and she pulled the string with the small ring from her pocket, 'it doesn't matter now if I tell you – I gave it to him when we were hardly more than children; so that he would not forget me! And he even brought it back with him, and yesterday he threw it into the dust in front of my eyes.'

A laugh, which sounded like mockery, interrupted her. Hans Kirch looked at her with staring eyes. 'Well, Wieb, if he was your Heinz, nothing much ever came of it.'

But she was not listening; she had thrown herself down before him. 'Hans Kirch!' she cried and grasped both the old man's hands and shook them. 'Your Heinz, don't you hear? He's left in sorrow, he's never coming back! Perhaps – O God, have mercy on us all! Perhaps there's still time!'

Lina had now also thrown herself down beside her; she was no longer afraid of uniting herself with the poor woman. 'Father,' she said, stroking the sunken cheeks of the hardened man who now let it all simply wash over him, 'you shall not go alone this time, I'll come with you; he's bound to be in Hamburg now; oh, I'll not rest until I've found him, until we hold him here in our arms again! Then we will make it better, we will have patience with him; oh, we didn't have it, father! And don't say you're not as sad as we are, your pale face can't lie! Just say the word, father, tell me to fetch the coach, I'll run for it myself this minute, we've no more time to lose!' And sobbing loudly, she threw her head against her father's chest.

Wieb had stood up and gone quietly to the door, her fear-filled eyes fixed on them both.

But Hans Kirch sat like a lifeless portrait; the resentment pent up in him for so many years would not let go of him; for now for the first time, following this reunion with the homecomer, there was no more hope for him in the bleak future. 'Go!' he said finally, and his voice sounded as hard as before. 'Whoever it was that slept under my roof this time can call himself what he likes; *my* Heinz left me seventeen years ago.'

* *

To the eyes of outsiders Hans Kirch even now might have appeared to go about his various activities in the usual way; in reality, however, he had more and more handed over the reins to the junior partner of the firm. And long ago he had resigned even from the college of deputies, much to the silent relief of some of its peace-loving members; he no longer felt the urge to intervene in the running of the small world that revolved around him.

From the first pungent breaths of spring he would often be seen sitting in front of his house, being an old shipmaster, without any head covering in spite of his now almost completely grey hair. One morning an even greyer-haired man came down the street and, on reaching him, without ado sat down beside him. The man was a previous manager of the poorhouse with whom, as a councillor, he had once had much to do; later the man had held a similar post in another district, but had now returned to spend his retirement benefit in his home town. It appeared not to deter him that his former superior's expression was not in the least welcoming; he wanted simply to chat, and did so the more expansively the less he was interrupted; and he now came to a subject which seemed more inexhaustible than any other. Hans Kirch was unlucky with people with greyer hair than his own; when they should have been talking about Heinz, they would speak about themselves, and when they could have been speaking about everything else, they would speak about Heinz. He grew restless and sought to be dismissive with brusque words; but the talkative old man did not seem to notice it. 'Yes, yes,' he continued, happily carried along by his stream of words. 'My God! Hasselfritz and Heinz. When I think of both those boys, how they once branded a large anchor on their arms! Your Heinz, so I've heard, had to be seen by the doctor; but Hasselfritz I cured myself with a hazel- switch.'

He laughed joyfully over his word-play; but Hans Kirch suddenly stood up and looked down at him in open-mouthed fury. 'If you want to go on jabbering, Fritz Peters,' he said, 'find yourself another seat; there's a spanking new one over there by the young doctor's!'

He went into the house and paced up and down his room; his head sank lower and lower on his chest, but he gradually raised it again. What had he actually learned just now? That Hasselfritz, too, had had to have his anchor? What else? – As to who it was who had lodged with him from one Sunday to the next or a few days more, there was no need for others to enlighten him.

And this day, too, passed by, and others followed, taking their regular course. A child was born on the upper floor; the grandfather asked if it was a boy; it was a girl, and he spoke no more about it. But what help would it have been to him if it had been a future Christian, or even a Hans Martens! The noise alone that now prevailed at night in the young couple's bedroom above his head disturbed him.

One evening, as it was already autumn – it was just a year since his son's departure – Hans Kirch as usual had entered his bedroom next to the courtyard on the stroke of ten. It was the season of equinoctial storms, and the full force of the weather could be heard on this side of the house; now roaring in the uppermost aerial strata, now descending to rage against the small window-panes. As on every evening Hans Kirch had taken out his silver pocket-watch to wind it up; but he remained standing with the key in his hand, listening out for something in the wild night.

The beams and rafters in the new roof creaked as though they would part from their joints; but he did not hear them, his thoughts had been driven outside with the storm. 'South-west!' he murmured to himself, putting the watch-key away in his pocket and hanging the watch un-wound on a hook above his bed. Whoever was at sea now had no time to sleep; but he had not been to sea for a long time; he wanted to sleep as he had done through many a storm here; always storms came at the equinox, he had heard them many times.

But this night, it seemed, there was something else besides; hours had passed and still he lay awake on his pillows. He seemed to hear a rocky coastal stretch of the Mediterranean hundreds of miles away, which he had once sailed in his youth; and when his eyes had at last closed he immediately forced himself to keep awake; for he had quite clearly seen a ship, a full-rigged sailing ship with broken masts, being tossed about among towering waves. He tried to rouse himself fully, but his eyes closed again, and he recognised the ship once more; clearly he saw the figurehead between the bowsprit and the stem post, a huge white Fortuna, now plunging into the foaming sea, now rising proudly from it again, as though wanting to hold ship and crew above the water. Then suddenly a crash made him start, and he found himself sitting upright in bed.

All around him was now quiet, he could hear nothing; he tried to remember if the storm had still been raging a short while ago; then he had the feeling that he was not alone in the room; he rested both hands on the sides of the bed and opened his eyes wide. And – there it was, there in the corner stood his Heinz; he could not see the face, for the head was bowed, and the hair, dripping with water, hung down over the brow; but he recognised him just the same – how, he did not know or ask himself. Water even dripped from the clothes and the arms that hung down; it continued to flow and formed a wide stream which ran towards his bed.

Hans Kirch wanted to call out, but he sat as though paralysed with his arms braced; at last a loud cry broke from his chest, and immediately he also heard crashing sounds above him in the young couple's bedroom, and again he heard the storm furiously shaking the timbers of his house.

Soon afterwards his son-in-law entered the room with a light to find him sunk in his pillows. 'We heard you shouting,' he asked; 'what is wrong, father?'

The old man looked straight towards the corner. 'He's dead,' he said, 'far from here.'

'Who's dead, father? Who do mean? Do you mean your Heinz?'

The old man nodded. 'The water,' he said, 'move away, you're standing in the middle of the water!'

The younger man lowered the light towards the floor. 'There's no water here, father. You've had a bad dream.'

'You're no seaman, Christian; what do you know about it!' said the old man fiercely. 'But I know about it – this is how our dead return.'

'Shall I fetch Lina for you, father?' asked Christian Martens.

'No, no, she ought to stay with her child. Just go, leave me alone!'

His son-in-law left with the light and Hans Kirch again sat upright in his bed in the dark; shaking, he stretched his arm towards the corner where his Heinz had just been standing; he wanted to see him once more, but looked in vain into the impenetrable darkness.

It was already late morning when Frau Lina entered the office downstairs to find her father's breakfast untouched; when she went into his bedroom he was still lying in his bed; he could not get up – he had had a stroke, though on one side only and not affecting his speech. He asked for his old doctor, and his daughter herself ran to the Councillor's house and was soon standing with him at her father's side.

It was really not so bad, the ill effects would soon pass, was the prognosis. But Hans Kirch was hardly listening; his thoughts were more on the events of the previous night than on his illness; Heinz had contacted him, Heinz was dead, and the dead person had all the rights that Hans had ceased to grant him when he had been alive. When Frau Lina wanted to talk him out of it he eagerly appealed to the Councillor, who, he said, had been to many a seaman's house over the years.

The Councillor tried to calm him. 'Certainly,' he added, 'we doctors know of circumstances in which dreams themselves leave the mind in broad daylight and appear as reality before people's eyes.'

Hans Kirch angrily turned towards him. 'That's too academic for me, doctor. What happened with old Rickert's son that time?'

The doctor felt the sick man's pulse. 'You're right, but wrong too,' he said thoughtfully. 'That was the elder son; the younger one, who was said to have made contact too, sails his father's ship to this day.'

Hans Kirch fell silent; he knew better than anyone else what had happened the previous night far from here.

* *

It turned out just as the doctor had predicted. After some weeks the sick man could leave his bed and gradually his room too, and even the house; but now he needed to use a walking-stick like his sister, which he had previously spurned. Of his earlier hot temper only a pitiful impatience seemed to remain; but if anger ever overcame him as in former times, he would break down exhausted afterwards.

When summer came he wanted to get out of the town, and Frau Lina accompanied him many times along the high coastal path round the bay from where he could see not only the islands but also eastwards across the open water. As the shore sloped and fell sharply down towards the beach in many places, no one dared to leave him alone here, and when his daughter had no time she arranged for one of the workers or some other reliable person to be at his side.

Autumn followed summer, and it was the second anniversary of Heinz's brief stay in the family home. Hans Kirch sat on a sandy ledge of the steep shore and let the afternoon sun shine on his grey head as he held his hands folded on his walking-stick in front of him; his eyes stared out over the smooth surface of the sea. Next to him stood a woman, with an air of indifference similar to his, holding the old man's hat in a hand hanging limp by her side. She appeared scarcely over thirty; it would have taken an eye sharper than most to see the traces of a charm ruined long ago in this face. She seemed to hear none of what the old shipmaster, motionless, was saying to himself; in just a whisper, as though he were confiding to the empty breeze; but gradually his words grew louder. 'Heinz, Heinz!' he called out. 'What has become of Heinz

Kirch?' Then he moved his head slowly again. 'It really makes no difference, for no one knows him any more.'

As the woman beside him sighed, he turned and looked up at her. She leaned her pale face down towards him, and he searched for her hand. 'No, no, Wieb, you – you knew him, and that's why' – and he nodded confidentially to her – 'you will stay with me, as long as I live, and afterwards as well – I have written that firmly into my will; it was for the best that your good-for-nothing husband drank himself to death.'

As she did not answer, he turned his head away again and his eyes followed a gull that flew out from the shore across the water. 'And there,' he began again, and his voice sounded quite cheerful now as he pointed with his stick towards the Warder, 'that's where he rowed you about in those days? And did they shout at you from the ship?' When she nodded silently to him, he laughed quietly to himself. But soon he lapsed back into talking to himself while his eyes stared at the vast emptiness in front of him. 'Only in eternity, Heinz! Only in eternity!' he cried, suddenly breaking into tears; then trembling, he stretched both arms up to the sky.

But this time his loudly spoken words received an answer. 'What have we mortals to do with eternity?' said a hoarse voice beside him. It was a down-and-out carpenter whom they called the 'social democrat' in the town; he believed he had found a flaw in his own Christian faith and now, in the manner of inferior people, argued defiantly on the subject to others.

With a rapid movement which appeared to go well beyond the strength of the broken man, Hans Kirch had turned to face the speaker, who was standing with folded arms. 'Don't you know me, Jürgen Hans?' he shouted, all his poor body trembling. 'I'm Hans Kirch, who disowned his son – twice! Do you hear that, Jürgen Hans? Twice I disowned my Heinz, and that's why I have something to do with eternity!'

The other had stepped up close to him. 'I'm sorry to hear that, Herr Kirch,' he said, each word dryly dispensed, 'eternity is in the heads of old women!'

Feverish anger flashed in the old man's eyes. 'Swine!' he screamed, and a stroke of the walking-stick suddenly whistled past the other's head.

The carpenter sprang to one side, then let out a scornful laugh and strolled on his way down to the town.

But the old man's strength was exhausted; the walking-stick dropped from his hand and rolled down the slope in front of him, and he would have tumbled after it had not the woman quickly bent down and caught him in her arms.

Kneeling beside him, gentle and unstirring, she cradled the grey head in her arms, for Hans Kirch had fallen asleep. – The sunset lay over the sea, a light wind had sprung up, and the waves broke louder on the shore below. Still she remained in her uncomfortable position; not until the stars were already shining did he open his eyes and look up at her. 'He is dead,' he said, 'I know for certain now; but – in eternity, there I will recognise my Heinz again.'

'Yes,' she said softly, 'in eternity.'

Carefully, supported by her, he lifted himself up, and when she had laid his arm round her neck and her arm round his waist, they walked slowly back to the town. The further they went, the heavier became her burden; occasionally they had to stop, and then Hans Kirch looked at the stars, which had shone on him on board his swift cutter on many an autumn night, and said: 'It's all right now', and they walked slowly on. And not only from the stars, but also from the blue eyes of the poor woman, there shone a soft ray of light; no longer of the kind that had drawn a wild boy's head to her young breast one spring evening, but a ray of woman's all-compassionate love which contains all solace in life.

* *

Over the following years, mostly on quiet afternoons and when the sun was about to set, Hans Kirch could still be seen with his constant companion on the path along the shore; during the autumn equinox he refused to be kept at home even during a north-east gale. Then they buried him in the churchyard of his home town at the side of his gentle wife.

The business that he founded lies in the best of hands; people already speak of 'wealthy' Christian Martens, and the town council won't be able to resist Hans Adam's daughter's husband; an heir was born some time ago and already walks to the rector class with his satchel; – but what has become of Heinz Kirch?

Notes

IN THE PREPARATION of these notes the translators have been greatly indebted to the following: Dieter Lohmeier's notes and commentary on *Immensee* in the four-volume edition of the collected works of Theodor Storm used as source text (see Translators' Preface), and Karl Ernst Laage's notes and commentary on *Eine Halligfahrt* and *Hans und Heinz Kirch* in the same edition; commentaries on all three Novellen by Peter Goldammer in *Theodor Storm. Sämtliche Werke in vier Bänden* edited by him (Aufbau-Verlag, Berlin, 8th ed. 1995); information and notes in editions of *Immensee* edited by J. M. Ritchie (Harrap, London, 1969) and by Ingwert Paulsen (Husum Druck- und Verlagsgesellschaft, Husum, 1991); notes and commentaries on *Immensee* in Frederick Betz, *Erläuterungen und Dokumente* (Philipp Reclam, Stuttgart, 1984); references to Prussianisation and *Eine Halligfahrt* in David A. Jackson, *Theodor Storm. Life and Works of a Democratic Humanitarian* (Berg Publishers, Oxford, 1992), pp. 129–58, 185–7; notes and commentaries on *Hans und Heinz Kirch* in Heike A. Doane, *Erläuterungen und Dokumente* (Philipp Reclam, Stuttgart, 1985); and information and sources provided by Otto Rohkohl, *Neue Chronik von Heiligenhafen* (Verlag Eggers, Heiligenhafen, 1989), Wilhelm Jensen, *Heiligenhafen das Ostseebad im Winkel* (Wullenwever-Druckverlag, Lübeck, 1949) and Fr. Böttger, *650 Jahre Stadt, 700 Jahre Kirche, Heiligenhafen* (Verlag Eggers, Heiligenhafen, 1995).

Immensee

Page 39: *The scent of a violet rises from these pages* . . . 'Aus diesen Blättern steigt der Duft des Veilchens . . .' A poem written by Storm shortly before Christmas 1856 for the illustrated fifth edition of *Immensee* (1857). Storm wrote to a friend at the time that 'this violet is no poetic fiction; it grew near Husum on the Schobüll heath . . . its colour was inconspicuous compared with the deep-blue of the garden variety, but had the strong aromatic scent of the heath. It is also true, as far as I know, that apart from myself it has not been observed by anyone else' (Storm to Friedrich Eggers, 20 December 1856) (see map on pages 68–9). In an earlier letter to Paul Heyse (8 May 1855) Storm draws attention to the atmosphere of love that pervades the work. The first version of the poem began: 'From these pictures rises . . . [Aus diesen Bildern steigt . . .]', referring to the illustrations by his friend the artist and journalist Ludwig Pietsch (1824–1911).

Page 39: *a parlour.* The Schleswig-Holstein *Pesel* or best room in the house. Here a living or dining room on the ground floor of a house.

Page 40: *As he sat there. . . he was back in his youth.* A passage that bears many similarities to one found in Eduard Mörike's two-volume novel *Maler Nolten* (*Nolten the Painter,* 1832), in which a moonbeam travels across a room, finally falling on a portrait of a girl. Storm added Eduard Mörike (1804–75) to his list of lyric mentors during his second period of study in Kiel (1839–42). *Maler Nolten* and its poems made a deep impression on him.

Page 40: *Her name was Elisabeth.* See Introduction, page 17.

Page 40: *walked along the bank.* Storm uses the word *Wall* here rather than *Deich,* possibly to disguise the setting. It could, however, refer to an inland, or former sea dyke, known locally as a 'sleeping' dyke. Such dykes were created by further land reclamation on their seaward sides. 'Sleeping' dykes can often be found many miles inland in North Friesland and divide one polder from another (see fourth and ninth notes to page 71).

Page 40: *wild mallow.* The European marsh mallow is used medicinally and was formerly used in the confection marshmallow.

Page 41: *'Once upon a time there lived three spinners –'.* The tale *Märchen von den drei Spinnfrauen* ('The Three Spinners') originated from the collection of fairy-tales (*Kinder- und Hausmärchen,* 2 vols, 1812–14) compiled by the Brothers Jacob and Wilhelm Grimm. Storm had published a version of it in K. L. Biernatzki's *Volksbuch auf das Jahr 1846.* A beautiful girl, pressed by a rich suitor to spin vast amounts of flax for him before their wedding, fulfils these demands only with the aid of three good fairies, disguised as ugly old women, each deformed in some way by spinning. Their appearance at the wedding brings home to the suitor how his bride's beauty might be destroyed were he to insist on her continued spinning, and so he has the spinning wheel destroyed.

Page 41: *the story of the poor man who was thrown into the lions' den.* Daniel 6 : 16–28.

Page 42: *small vellum-bound book . . . his first poem.* According to Gertrud Storm in her biography of her father, Storm's first poem was written in July 1833 'in a small book' (Gertrud Storm. *Theodor Storm. Ein Bild seines Lebens,* Berlin, 1912/13, repr. 1991, p. 132).

Page 42: *he wrote the stories down precisely as he had heard them himself.* Storm was an avid collector of the folktales, myths and legends of his native Schleswig-Holstein, many of which appear in his Novellen. His collection was eventually included and published in Karl Müllenhoff's *Sagen, Märchen und Lieder der Herzogtümer Schleswig, Holstein und Lauenburg* (Kiel, 1845).

Page 43: *to continue his studies elsewhere*. Young women in mid-nineteenth-century Germany were denied any secondary or higher education, generally having to wait to be 'rescued' by a wealthy suitor. Boys, in contrast, were expected to complete their grammar-school education and to undertake university studies and/or concentrate on their careers.

Page 47: *the queen of the forest land*. In the first version of *Immensee* which appeared in K. L. Biernatzki's *Volksbuch auf das Jahr 1850 für die Herzogtümer Schleswig, Holstein und Lauenburg*, Storm gave this poem the title 'Als wir uns im Walde verirret haben' ('When we lost our way in the forest').

Page 47: *fellow-students . . . Ratskeller*. Rathauskeller. A large pillared cellar or basement beneath a town hall (Rathaus) converted for the purposes of eating and drinking. A *Ratskeller* can be found in most large German towns and cities; here the city is probably Kiel where Storm attended university from 1837 to 1842.

Page 47: *a zither-player, a girl with fine gypsy-like features*. Not the zither as generally known today. The girl's instrument was more often described as a small harp which she would lay on a table or on her lap. A girl playing such an instrument was known at the time as a 'harp girl' (*Harfenmädchen*). Such wandering girl musicians were a common feature of nineteenth-century inn and street life. Storm uses the then alternative description *Zithermädchen*. In a letter to Helen Clark, the first English translator of the Novelle, Storm wrote: 'I don't mean a "gypsy girl", but rather simply a girl whose facial features remind one of a gypsy.'

Page 47: *Junker-like appearance*. A Junker was a member of an exclusive Prussian aristocratic party. Given the author's known dislike for the Prussian nobility – as expressed, for example, in a letter to Hartmuth Brinkmann of 18 January 1864: 'The nobility [...] is the poison in the veins of the nation' – the description here of 'Junker-like' can be read only in the pejorative sense.

Page 48: '*Today, just today . . . perish alone.*' The 'Song of the Harp Girl' ('Lied des Harfenmädchens'). First printed in the second version of *Immensee* which formed part of a collection called *Sommergeschichten und Lieder* (*Summer Stories and Songs*, 1851). A hint of the origin of this song is to be found in a letter of Storm's to Bertrand Sichel dated 17 February 1886: 'I can give an assurance respecting my lyric verse that most lines fell out of the air, as it were, without any noticeable mental activity on my part; among other things, as I clearly remember, "Song of the Harp Girl" in *Immensee*, while I journeyed from Husum to Tondern alone in a coach through the empty landscape in evil autumn sleety weather.'

Page 48: *the Christ-child*. The infant Jesus is particularly associated with Christmas in the imagination of German children as the giver of gifts. 'Gifts' from the Christ-child were distributed to children on Christmas Eve.

Page 48: *brown biscuits*. Hard, treacle-coloured spicy biscuits (*Plätzchen*), the baking of which was a widespread custom at Christmas in North Germany in Storm's time.

Page 49: *the linnet you gave me*. The linnet is a traditional symbol of love (see note to page 51).

Page 50: *the second part of Christmas Eve had begun*. The early part of the German Christmas Eve is the public part, with the 'processions of children' going from door to door singing carols. Now the streets are quieter, for the later part of the day towards evening, as it grows dark, is the family ceremony from which strangers are excluded: it is the time for gift-giving. Storm's two poems titled 'Weihnachtsabend' ('Christmas Eve' of 1843 and 1852) capture scenes similar to the ones here described.

Page 51: *botanist's vasculum*. Among the educated middle-class families in nineteenth-century Germany the collecting-case for plants and other natural objects was considered an essential item of equipment for the young. Storm himself was a keen amateur botanist and prided himself on it; his detailed knowledge of local flora and fauna was extensive, and this, together with his knowledge of the folklore surrounding them, provided him with valuable material for his Novellen. He often introduced plant and bird species to convey a specific message to a knowledgeable reader (see notes to pages 49, 61, 62, 63, 65 and 75).

Page 53: *the mail-coach*. Until the coming of the railways the mail-coach was one of the main forms of transport into and out of the North German west-coast region. In Storm's home town of Husum the first train arrived in 1854 with the opening of the Tönning-Husum-Flensburg railway (see map on pages 68–9), some five years after the first version of *Immensee* was written.

Page 53: *St Mary's clock*. The church in Storm's home town of Husum is the Marienkirche. This and other allusions and descriptions throughout *Immensee* are taken by some to indicate that Storm had Husum partly in mind when writing the Novelle.

Page 55: *the right way to Immensee*. Literally 'Bees' Lake'. The question of any real-life topography in connection with this Novelle remains controversial, some commentators suggesting a mountainous setting in Southern Germany, others the Imisee in Switzerland, others still the Immenhof estate not far from Storm's home town of Husum.

Page 55: *Not half a pipe of tobacco*. In the nineteenth century a journey was often measured by watchless travellers in units of time taken to smoke a pipe of tobacco.

Page 56: *God greet you. 'Gott grüß dich!'* or *'Grüß Gott!'* A salutation especially common in Southern Germany, Austria and parts of Switzerland.

Page 57: *That long-legged Egyptian*. The stork, a summer visitor in many parts of Europe from Egypt, places its nest – usually a huge pile of sticks – on rooftops and chimneys. This one may be stealing pea-sticks for its nest.

Page 57: *espaliered peach and apricot trees*. A common method of cultivating fruit in Germany.

Page 57: *That's the distillery*. A rural potato or corn schnapps distillery.

Page 58: *he had collected verse and songs current among the people*. See note to page 42.

Page 59: *Tyrolean Alpine songs*. The *Schnaderhüpferl*, short extempore songs common in the Bavarian and Tyrolean Alps at harvest time: merry bantering rhymes usually sung to the accompaniment of the zither, the singer composing them on the spur of the moment in answer to another.

Page 60: *They're not written . . . as if we had all had a common share in them*. These words are frequently taken to be Storm's own poetic creed. He was first and foremost a gifted poet, and he seems here to be describing the creative attitude of a writer whose 'craft of fiction grew out of his lyric verse' (see Introduction, page 13 and note to page 48).

Page 60: *'I stood high up in the mountains . . .'* Opening line of the old folk-song 'Die Nonne' ('The Nun') from the collection of German folk-songs *Des Knaben Wunderhorn* (*The Boy's Magic Horn*, 1805–8) gathered by Achim von Arnim (1781–1831) and Clemens Brentano (1778–1842). It tells the story of a beautiful but poor young maiden who, unable to marry a young count, retires to a convent. Storm later included this folk-song in his anthology of German poetry *Hausbuch aus deutschen Dichtern seit Claudius* (Hamburg, 1869/70).

Page 60: *Elisabeth's alto voice . . . Reinhardt's tenor*. Storm's first wife Constanze sang alto and would often accompany her husband's tenor voice in the singing of the 'The Nun' (see previous note).

Page 61: *'My mother wished it so . . . heath!'* Written by Storm in 1849. The poem arose from a social occasion he attended at which he learned of a marriage arranged by a mother between her young daughter and a wealthy older man.

Page 61: *a nightingale sang*. In folk belief the nightingale, a symbol of love and longing, is sometimes associated with the cuckoo: to hear the nightingale before the cuckoo foretells success in love (see note to page 51).

Page 62: *a white water-lily*. Symbol of the presence of a loved one; also an emblem of virgin purity. The rope-like leaf-stalks of the plant stretch to the bed of the pond or lake.

Page 62: *the lily lay as before, distant and alone upon the dark depths*. In a letter dated 2 April 1885 to Gertrud Eckermann, a friend from Hademarschen, Storm wrote that while studying in Berlin in 1838 he himself had swum out into the River Havel from one of its islands to examine a water-lily, only to be caught up in its rope-like stalks from which he quickly extricated himself and returned to the shore.

Page 63: *he heard the call of a cuckoo*. The hearing of a cuckoo has an age-old association in folk belief with ill or good fortune, prospects of marriage, prosperity and many other aspects of future life (see note to page 51).

Page 64: *a woman's beautiful hands which rest at night on a broken heart*. An echo of these words is to be found in a later poem by Storm, 'Frauenhand' ('A Woman's Hand'), first published in 1852, said to have been written for Dorothea Jensen who later became his second wife:

> Die Hand, an der mein Auge hängt,
> Zeigt jenen feinen Zug der Schmerzen,
> Und daß in schlummerloser Nacht
> Sie lag auf einem kranken Herzen.

Page 65: *the first lark climbed into the air rejoicing*. A touch of irony, the lark here being regarded as a symbol of good luck or happiness in folk belief. The lark is a traditional symbol of love (see note to page 51).

Journey to a Hallig

Page 71: *vast forests of oak along our coast*. The coastal region of North Friesland, Schleswig-Holstein. Forests of oak covered the region between 5500 and 800 BC and stretched far beyond the coastline known today. Beech gradually replaced oak and remains the prevailing tree in the region.

Page 71: *the tidal flats*. Known locally as the Wattenmeer: the area of sand and mudflats in the North Sea exposed for many hours at low tide between the North Friesian Islands and the coastline of Schleswig-Holstein. The Wattenmeer with its islands and Halligen (un-dyked islands) covers some 800 square miles. It is one of the largest continuous areas of mud flats in the world (see map on pages 68–9).

Page 71: *their struggle with the north-west storms.* Storms from the north-west are especially feared in North Friesland. Many chronicled accounts of the greatest storms in the region give the wind direction as north-west.

Page 71: *our dykes.* The flat-ridged earth dykes along the west coast of North Friesland in Schleswig-Holstein. Based on Dutch designs to protect the land from storm tides from the North Sea, they were about sixteen feet in height in the eighteenth and nineteenth centuries; they are much higher than this today.

Page 71: *we look . . . as if into an eternity.* The west coast of Schleswig is exceptionally flat. Seen from the top of the dykes the apparently limitless North Sea tidal flats extend far to the horizon in the west, and the marshlands many miles inland to the east. The sky is a dominant feature of the scene, like a huge all-enveloping canopy with its edges stretching down to below the onlooker's feet. The feeling of 'looking into an eternity' is very real indeed.

Page 71: *a hallig.* One of a number of small islands (Halligen) in the North Sea tidal flats unprotected by a dyke; some are only a few feet above sea level. Today as in Storm's time they are crowned either by a single isolated house standing on an artificial earthwork (*Warft, Werft*) or by a complex of houses on one or more earthworks (*Warften, Werften*).

Page 71: *and there's Holland too!* In Low German in the original. One of a number of Low German sayings collected and published by Storm in Biernatzki's *Volksbuch auf das Jahr 1844* (*Folk Annual for the Year 1844*). At Kiel University (1832–42) and after his return to Husum, Storm avidly collected folktales, superstitions, legends and sayings of Schleswig-Holstein (see note to page 42). Low German is one of five local languages spoken in North Friesland: High and Low German, Danish, Sønderjysk and Friesian; the latter itself has seven dialects including Hallig-Friesian, a dialect common on the islands.

Page 71: *I have just come home.* Possible reference to Storm's return to Husum in March 1864 after his exile as a political refugee in Potsdam and Heiligenstadt.

Page 71: *polders.* The North Friesian polder (area of fertile marshland reclaimed from the sea by dyking), known as a *Koog* or *Kog*, joint product of river and sea but almost wholly man-made, is extremely rich pasture land, and excellent for cattle grazing.

Page 71: *fens.* Tracts of marshland used mainly for animal pasture, enclosed by deep drainage ditches.

Page 71: *starlings . . . those winged friends of cattle.* Before going to their roosts, starlings feed in fields, foraging where the feet of cattle stir up insects. The pests they remove from the soil help to offset the damage these birds do elsewhere.

Page 72: *the river which ran into the sea from the town.* The Hever channel, a broad and deep watercourse which runs from the town of Husum out into the Wattenmeer. This was, and remains, the main shipping lane into the town (see map on pages 68–9).

Page 72: *the newly-laid straw covering.* Rye, wheat straw or reed used to be used on the North Friesian coast to protect the toe (leading seaward edge) of the dyke against ice and winter storms. It was laid on the dyke to cover it to slightly above the high-water line, then secured by straw-rope. The rope was first stretched over the laid straw, then at regular intervals pushed several inches, staple-like, into the clay. The finished covering had the appearance of carefully woven, thick matting.

Page 72: *The Frau Geheimrätin.* Privy Councillor's wife or widow.

Page 73: *large neighbouring island behind us.* The island of Nordstrand in the Wattenmeer. One of the three largest islands in the area, today occupying some 20 square miles (see map on pages 68–9).

Page 73: *'Rungholt!'* The old parish of Rungholt on the former large island of Alt-Nordstrand. Rungholt, together with its small prosperous harbour and a population of around 1500 people, and 29 other parishes in the region, was swept away in the Marcellus Flood of 16 January 1362: 7,600 people were said to have been drowned. It was believed at the time that it had been destroyed because of the sins of its people (see note to page 74). The large island of Alt-Nordstrand was itself almost completely washed away in the great storm of 11 October 1634. The actual remains of Rungholt – including pottery, dykes, sluices, animal and human bones – confirming the old legends about the parish, were not discovered until 1921. Documents further confirming Rungholt's earlier existence were later also discovered in the Hamburg State archives. The location of the old parish of Rungholt is now known to centre around the present-day Hallig Südfall situated in an area known as Rungholt Sand, a sandbank still shown on present-day maps (see map on pages 68–9).

According to legend the bell of the Rungholt church can still be heard ringing on a very quiet day, being rung by the swift currents deep below the water. It is said that every seven years on 24 June, Midsummer-night (*Johannisnacht*), Rungholt rises out of the water in all its former splendour.

Page 73: *according to Seneca.* Reference to a passage in the 99th letter of Seneca's 'Moral Letters' to Lucilius: 'To us belongs the time that has passed, and nothing is a more certain place than that which has been.' Storm used the theme 'the land of certainty in the past' in the opening line of his poem 'Constanze' which he quoted in a letter to his daughter Lisbeth in 1871. The poem is named after his first wife who died in 1865.

Page 73: *In King Abel's time.* King Abel, Duke of Schleswig, King of Denmark 1250–52. Arising from an attempt to raise taxes, he is believed to have been killed by an axe after a battle on the 'Königskamp' (King's Field) near Oldenswort. He was also suspected of murdering his brother, Erik IV of Denmark. Legend has it that because of the murder his soul could not rest, and that at midnight his dark ghost would rise from the grave and ride through the air on a grey horse accompanied by fiery dogs. It was further said that a large flock of gulls settled at the place where Erik was murdered and cried continuously: 'Erik! Erik!' Erik's body was eventually recovered from the marshes and buried in Schleswig cathedral, but the gulls flew off and nested by King Abel's island castle (Abelsburg). The castle is thought to have long sunk in the mud, but the gulls to this day occupy the island and are said to cry: 'Erik! Erik!'. King Abel's body was first buried in Schleswig cathedral, then eventually reburied near the island of Gottorf, a place known today as Königsgrab (King's Grave). The King Abel legends belong to those collected by Storm and Theodor Mommsen and published in Biernatzki's *Volksbuch auf das Jahr 1844*.

Page 73: *"You can't touch us now, Wild Hans!"* In Low German in the original: 'Trotz nu, blanke Hans!' German seafarers and coastal dwellers refer to the North Sea as 'blanke Hans', rather as English seafarers use the name Davy Jones to denote the 'spirit of the sea'. The saying 'Trotz nu, blanke Hans', however, originates historically from Anton Heimreich's *Nordfresische Chronik* for the year 1662, some 300 years after Rungholt's destruction (see above note to page 73). The words are said to be those uttered by dyke-builders on completion of a new dyke. Driving their spades into the finished dyke they would then utter the challenge to the wild North Sea to try and destroy it (see following note).

Page 74: *The men of Rungholt – at least, according to the religious chroniclers.* Early chronicles were written mostly by priests; the interpretation of events was therefore generally in terms of God's retribution for evil done. The reference here is probably to the chroniclers Anton Heimreich, Pastor of Nordstrandischmoor (an island in the Wattenmeer), compiler of a *Nordfresische Chronik* (1668), an old volume of which was in the possession of Theodor Storm's family in Husum, and to Johann Melchior Krafft, author of *Zwey-Hundert-Jährigen Husumische Kirchen- und Schul-Historie* (Hamburg, 1723). The legend of 'the men of Rungholt' and their 'sinful' behaviour prior to the great Storm of 1362 was known to Storm from Anton Heimreich's *Chronik*, as well as from Karl Müllenhoff's *Sagen, Märchen und Lieder der Herzogthümer Schleswig, Holstein und Lauenberg* (Kiel, 1845, no. 173). The Müllenhoff version of the legend began: 'In Runghold on Nordstrand there once lived rich people; they built massive dykes and when they stood on them, they said: "Trotz nu, Blanke Hans!".' A case of courage before a fall.

Page 74: *'Not heard 'em in my lifetime'*. Spoken in Low German. Storm's use of Plattdeutsch in his Novellen is limited and mostly confined to coloration and character definition, although it was widely spoken throughout the region, as it is today. Storm was Low German by descent and by nature and spoke Plattdeutsch freely.

Page 74: *And we sailed on over Rungholt*. A nine-verse ballad 'Trutz Blanke Hans' (1883) by Detlef von Liliencron (see also note to page 73) echoes the scene here described by Storm:

Heut bin ich über Rungholt gefahren,	I have sailed over Rungholt town today,
die Stadt ging unter vor fünfhundert Jahren.	five hundred years ago it was washed away.
Noch schlagen die Wellen da wild und empört,	The waves still pound there, wild and harsh,
wie damals, als sie die Marschen zerstört.	just as before, when they destroyed the marsh.
Die Maschine des Dampfers schütterte, stöhnte,	The steamship's engines shake and creak,
aus den Wassern rief es unheimlich und höhnte:	From the sea comes a weird and mocking shriek:
'Trutz, Blanke Hans' . . .	'Trutz , Blanke Hans' . . .

Page 75: *my friend Aemil*. Storm is reflecting here on his youngest brother, Dr Aemil Storm (1833–97).

Page 75 : *a hallig of old North Friesland which had been rent into these smaller islands by the great flood of five hundred years ago*. Hallig Süderoog in the Wattenmeer (see map on pages 68–9). One of the farthest-lying of the small halligen in the region. Once part of the larger island of Alt-Nordstrand, it was finally separated from it during the great storm, the Marcellus Flood, of 16 January 1362 (see note to page 73). The separation, however, had already begun centuries earlier when it had been part of a much larger area of the mainland. Because of the hallig's important location near the Hever channel, the main shipping lane into the coastal town of Husum, it is often mentioned in old chronicles. As early as 1650 it is recorded as possessing a beacon to mark the channel for shipping. In the summer of 1873 Storm identifies the hallig in a letter to the writer Ludwig Pietsch: 'The precise location is [Hallig] "Süderoog". I was there once, four years ago.' In a letter dated 9 February 1884 to his daughter Elsabe he writes:

'Read my "Journey to a Hallig" [. . .] there I have described Süderoog and
Paulsen's earthwork.' Paul Andreas Paulsen (1814–91) was the hallig's
inhabitant at the time; his ancestors, under an hereditary lease, had inhabited
the hallig with its now single large earthwork (see note to page 75 below) from
1608 until 1871, when the Paulsen family, the last private owners of the hallig,
finally bought it.

Page 75: *herring gulls.* Gulls feature frequently in seafarers' superstitions, along
with the albatross (cf. Coleridge, *The Rime of the Ancient Mariner*, 1798), as omens
and reincarnations of drowned sailors or fishermen. They are therefore shot
only with the greatest reluctance. There is evidence that these beliefs are still
very much alive among sailors today. Birds play a large symbolic part in Storm's
works in which over eighty species have been identified (see note to page 51).

Page 75: *on the high earthwork.* The North Sea coast of Germany has many
examples of small settlements on round earthworks, originally natural, but
with many artificial additions and known locally as *Werften.* Various sizes of
earthworks are to be found on the halligen and marshlands and they vary in
height up to about fifteen feet. In earlier times, before the building of dykes,
they were the only protection against the sea. Late medieval maps of Hallig
Süderoog show that originally there were two earthworks on it. It is supposed
that after the great storm of 1634 the other was used to broaden and heighten
the present one.

Page 75: *the large hallig-house with the steeply pitched straw-thatched roof.* The typical
North Friesian house is the long, low, thatched Utland house divided in the
middle by a hall that separates the living quarters from the main work areas of
threshing floor, barn and stables. Their style reflects the flat landscape and their
construction, along an east-west axis, offers the least resistance to the prevailing
winds. The much larger 'hallig-house', however, as here described on Hallig
Süderoog, is constructed in the form of a quadrangle (*Vierkanthof*) with a large
central courtyard (*Lichthof*). The large oak supporting timbers for such a house
and its roof are sunk deeply into the body of the earthwork to offer maximum
resistance against storms. Wooden pegs were also used throughout the house's
construction instead of metal ones, which would rust in such a harsh climate.
In former times, the large earthwork on Süderoog accommodated further
houses on an area of land which was used in Storm's time to keep animals
during high water and for storage of items salvaged from stranded ships. The
large hallig-house on Hallig Süderoog today, standing on its isolated earthwork
with its trees and bushes, is among the most beautiful island houses in the
region.

Page 75: *the 'Cousin'*. The term 'Cousin' (*Vetter, Cousine*) included a much wider and less precise usage in Storm's time than today (hence his use of inverted commas to indicate this wider use).

Page 75: *its taciturn occupants*. Life on a North Sea hallig was a very isolated and lonely one. The occupants of these small islands were often cut off from the mainland and other neighbouring islands for long periods of time, particularly in winter: postal and other services at the time were minimal. The Prussian occupation of the Duchy of Schleswig in 1864 was soon followed by regular postal and other services to the islands, but for Hallig Süderoog the future postal service, when it came, was via the nine-mile-long Wattenweg, an often dangerous route across the tidal flats taken by the postmen when tides permitted.

Page 75: *'The cogs of state machinery . . . being prodded in the coat-tails'*. Storm here gives vent to his own bitterness; he had himself suffered under Prussian bureaucracy in recent times. Prussia's annexation of both the duchies of Schleswig and Holstein in 1866 resulted in their speedy assimilation after 1867 into the structures of the Prussian monarchy (see Introduction, page 25). The common Schleswig-Holstein practice of combining judicial, administrative and policing functions in one post, in one person, was incompatible with the Prussian system. Civil servants, like Storm, were therefore required to opt for either a judicial or an administrative career. Storm, then holding the post of *Landvogt*, a post combining the duties of Judge and Chief Constable, had to settle in 1868 for the lesser post of *Amtsrichter*, District Court Judge, at a much reduced salary.

Page 76: *during my later absence from the homeland*. A possible reference to Storm's own exile from North Friesland between 1852 and 1864 arising from personal conflicts with the Danish authorities. In a letter to Ludwig Pietsch in the summer of 1873, Storm wrote: 'I am the old man.'

Page 76: *the so-called Pesel*. The best room in a North Friesian household, reserved mainly for visitors and special occasions.

Page 76: *the powerful face of Beethoven on the familiar massive bust*. The bust is probably that by Franz Klein (1812).

Page 77: *to carry her across the blue Aegean Sea* . The sparrow was one of the birds sacred to Aphrodite, the Greek goddess who sprang from the sea-foam off the island of Cythera. In an ode by the Greek poetess Sappho, Aphrodite's carriage is described as being drawn by a pair of sparrows.

Page 77: *the front of the house faced south*. The working areas of a hallig-house, the barn, workshops and stalls, are generally located to face west into the prevailing wind and sea, while the living areas face south and east for protection and the sun.

Page 77: *What indeed were not stranded goods here!* Seawards from Hallig Süderoog lie three large sandbanks, 'Japsand', 'Norderoog-Sand' and 'Süderoog-Sand', which mark the boundary between the tidal flats and the rapidly increasing depth of the North Sea (see map on pages 68–9). Local records from the beginning of the nineteenth century show the names and dates of many ships that foundered on the Süderoog sandbank, including vessels from Sweden, England, Holland, Germany and Spain, all of which carried a variety of cargoes. Attached to the then hereditary lease of Hallig Süderoog was the stewardship of the Süderoog sandbank, involving the provision of help to ships' crews stranded there, and the storage, for later auction, of wreckage and cargoes. It is possible that the ship 'to the west' had grounded on this very bank. Above the doorway to the house on Hallig Süderoog there still hang today the carved and richly decorated wooden figures that once adorned the stern of the Spanish barque *Ulpiano* which foundered here in December 1870, a few months before Storm began to write this Novelle in spring 1871.

Page 77: *Hesperus.* Published in 1795, this novel, with its intimate expression of emotion and sensitive landscape description, established the reputation of its author Jean Paul (1763–1825). On 26 June 1882 Storm wrote in his diary: 'A propos of my Novelle *Eine Halligfahrt,* I now own my Cousin's edition of Jean Paul.'

Page 78: *'Frau Cousine!'.* A respectful form of address at the time (see also note to page 75).

Page 79: *raging mountains of water.* High seas and spring tides, and the occasional severe storm, remained – and remain – in the memories of most people of the halligen and islands throughout their lives. The great storm of the night of 3 February 1825 was one Storm frequently remembered from boyhood. It was just after a full moon during a spring tide. The sea rose many feet above normal along the west coast of Schleswig to a height that is one of the highest recorded in the region. Seventy-four people and hundreds of livestock were drowned on the halligen. Storm was later to recall his feelings and fears in his poem 'Sturmnacht' ('Night of the Storm').

Page 79: *hang by their strings . . . their wooden arms.* A possible comparison between members of the new Prussian administration set up in Schleswig-Holstein and Hoffmannesque string puppets. In Storm's eyes the Prussian annexation in 1867 violated the basic human right of self-determination. Supposed liberators became oppressors. In his view, Prussian brute force had triumphed over right (letter to H. and L. Brinkmann, 21 January 1868). The introduction of the Prussian bureaucratic system and the influx of Prussian civil servants generated great friction in the duchies.

Page 79: *their rankings from the court register.* The state or court register (*Staatskalender*) of the genealogical trees of the nobility also contained the names and ranking, by number, of each member. Storm, through the old man, is here citing his personal distaste for those who publicly paraded their rank and status without which they were nothing. Storm's poem 'Vom Staatskalender' ('From the Court Register', 1845) highlights the importance of the social status associated with one's 'number' or 'ranking'.

Page 80: *Tönningen, the largest town in the district of Eiderstedt.* The present-day coastal town of Tönning in Eiderstedt at the mouth of the River Eider some twelve miles south-west of Husum (see map on pages 68–9). It was heavily besieged and destroyed during the Northern Wars (1700–21), first by the Danes in 1700, then by the Swedes in 1713.

Page 80: *the neighbouring parish of Kathrinenheerd.* The present-day parish of Katharinenheerd which lies five miles north-west of Tönning (see map on pages 68–9).

Page 80: *'To good health in our old age!'* In Low German in the original: 'Dat et uns wull ga up unse ole Dage!' The legend of Martje Flors, a farmer's daughter in Katharinenheerd, first appeared in Karl Müllenhoff's *Sagen, Märchen und Lieder der Herzogthümer Schleswig, Holstein und Lauenburg.* Storm's words correspond very closely to those of the published original which ends: 'And from that time on in Eiderstedt, landlords and guests seldom met without remembering the girl and her toast, and everyone knows the story when it is "to Martje Flor's health!"'

Page 81: *a small pond enclosed within a high privet hedge.* The *Fething*, a deep funnel-shaped reservoir, built to collect rainwater for the animals on a hallig, is still in common use today on remote islands not linked to the mainland by pipeline. Drinking water for the inhabitants was generally obtained by rainwater collected from the roofs of the buildings, filtered and then stored in large tanks. Early twentieth-century photographs of the reservoir on Hallig Süderoog show a picturesque garden-setting for the wide deep pond (*Fethinggarten*), surrounded by an expanse of dense trees, bushes, many kinds of beautiful flowers and vegetable plots. Garden and pond lie to the south-west of the house. Here, to enhance the setting, Storm creates a garden wonderland from a basic necessity.

Page 81: *the north-west winds.* The wind direction mostly associated with severe storms in the region. Such strong, cold, salt-laden winds would scorch the leaves of a tree and restrict its growth.

Page 82: *the various rooms of the large quadrangular house.* Storm's account of the rooms in the large hallig-house matches the layout of extant old house plans. The 'kind of carpenter's shop' (today a living room) lay in the south-east corner of the house, the stalls occupied almost the whole of the east side of it, and the huge barn its north side. The living room (*Pesel*) in which coffee was served faced south.

Page 82: *blocks for a sailing boat.* Wooden or metal cases in which one or more sheaves (revolving wheels) are fitted: used in association with ropes for various purposes in a boat or ship, either to increase the mechanical power applied to them or to lead them to convenient positions for handling.

Page 82: *the livestock were out on the hallig grazing.* The inhabitants of remote islands needed to be self-sufficient, and the keeping of livestock was essential. Eight cows, five calves, eighty mother ewes, thirty rams and eighty lambs were recorded for Hallig Süderoog in 1862. Horses were not kept.

Page 82: *All Saints' Day.* A religious festival celebrated on 1 November, occurring during a period noted in North Friesian chronicles as a time of the worst storms.

Page 83: *deep watercourses, which covered the whole hallig like a web.* Watercourses, often deep, fast-flowing and quite wide, are a general feature of halligen and islands, as they are across the entire North Sea tidal flats. They provide the main waterways for the incoming and outgoing tides (see map on pages 68–9).

Page 84: *smaller dark birds with stork-like bills.* The oystercatcher, the bird that characterizes the North Sea tidal flats, takes the place of the stork as the bringer of children among the beliefs and customs of the halligen.

Page 85: *So says the poet.* A stanza from the poem 'Das Paar' ('The Couple') by C. Reinhold (pseudonym for Reinhold Köstlin, 1813-56).

> Nur ein Hauch darf beben,
> Blitzen nur ein Blick;
> Und die Engel weben
> Fertig ein Geschick.

Page 85: *my grey Hecker hat . . . my moustache.* A three-cornered hat with a feather after the German revolutionary republican politician Friedrich Hecker (1811–81), leader of radical forces demanding that the 1848 revolution establish a republican form of government in Germany. After a popular rising was quickly crushed by troops, Hecker fled to Switzerland and the United States. The Hecker hat and the moustache were the 'uniform' of democrats in 1848.

Storm here appears to be reflecting on his own earlier personal conflicts as a lawyer with the Danish authorities over his democratic principles, which eventually led to his own political 'exile' in Prussia in 1852. The original text, after the word 'prosper', included the words 'among his conservative fellow countrymen'.

Page 87: *it was a young seal.* The large sandbanks that lie seawards from Hallig Süderoog (see map on pages 68–9), are the home and breeding grounds of many seals. On still days, seals can be heard from far away.

Page 87: *the boat's goblin.* North Sea legends have it that as long as the goblin, the *Klabotermann,* is on board, the vessel will be safe, but once it leaves, the vessel's destruction is assured. The goblin was considered to be 'the invisible patron saint of mariners who prevented good and respectable mariners from meeting with disaster, and who looked after everything himself, as much the actual running of the vessel as its safe passage' (Heinrich Heine, *Reisebilder* (*Travel Sketches*, 1826-31)).

Page 88: *the town.* Husum.

Page 88: *a lark was still singing.* See note to page 65.

Page 89: *Cremona violin.* From the town of Cremona in northern Italy, celebrated in the mid-sixteenth to early eighteenth centuries for its violin-makers, including the Stradivari, Amati and Guarneri families.

Page 89: *he found there, as he expressed it, 'the necessary rest from life'.* An echo of Storm's own strong affection since boyhood for the heathland that lay near his home. His poem 'Über die Heide' ('Over the Heath', 1875) written on a journey across it, which was later set to music by Brahms, reflects this attachment:

Über die Heide	*Over the Heath*
Über die Heide hallet mein Schritt;	Over the heath my footsteps resound;
Dumpf aus der Erde wandert es mit.	Pounding beside me from out of the ground.
Herbst ist gekommen. Frühling ist weit –	Autumn has come, and spring taken flight –
Gab es denn einmal selige Zeit?	Did they exist, those days of delight?
Brauende Nebel geisten umher,	Round me the gathering vapours rise,
Schwarz ist das Kraut und der Himmel so leer.	Dark is the heather and empty the skies.
Wär' ich hier nur nicht gegangen im Mai!	Would I had come here, and walked in May!
Leben und Liebe – wie flog es vorbei!	Life and love – they have both flown away!

Page 90: *into the hall.* The *Saal* was a very large, often ornately decorated room for receptions and social occasions found in a manor house or castle. The room

described here, with its gallery of ancestral portraits, is suggestive of the large *Rittersaal* in Husum castle, the seat of administration for the district. Storm was a frequent visitor to the castle and a friend of its then occupant, the Prussian *Landrat* Ludwig Graf zu Reventlow and his family. From 1873 Storm, as *Amtsrichter*, was to have his own office in the castle which was the setting for some of his works.

Page 91: *Geheimrat.* Privy Councillor.

Page 91: *Adolf, our music director.* An allusion to Adolph Möller (1841–87), Husum music teacher and musical advisor to Storm's choral society. He taught Storm's daughters and gave a concert in Husum on 17 January 1871 in which he performed the Largo and Minuet from Beethoven's Piano Sonata op. 10 in D major. Storm wrote an account of this concert which appeared in the *Husumer Wochenblatt* the following day.

Page 91: *the great new composer.* Robert Schumann (1810–56).

Page 92: *Kapellmeister Johannes Kreisler.* The musician and eccentric composer of genius in E. T. A. Hoffmann's *Kater Murr (Murr the Tom-Cat*, 1819–21). In the figure of Kreisler, Hoffmann incorporates his own passionate devotion to music, which delivers mankind from the tragedy of human life. In this un-finished work Kreisler, after mortally wounding a would-be assassin, flees to a monastery where he is temporarily happy composing and performing church music.

Page 92: *We knew each other well.* The relationship between Storm and Adolf Möller was somewhat strained through Möller's alcoholism. Both Möller and Hans Storm, Storm's eldest son, also an alcoholic (see Introduction, page 28), would often be found drinking excessively together late at night in the town's *Ratskeller* (see note to page 47).

Page 92: *Nöck by the waterfall.* Reference to the Nordic saga that August Kopisch (1799–1853) adopted as the subject for his poem 'Der Nöck', in which children call to Nöck singing by a waterfall: 'O Nöck, what use is that singing of yours? / You still can't go to Heaven.'

Page 92: *You know this, my muse . . . a long, long time.* A similar dialogue with his muse occurs in another work of Storm's written at about this time, in which, after declaring he can no longer write as before, he suddenly catches sight of her in his garden beneath a tree – an eternally youthful goddess with gold-blonde hair, whose eyes he cannot withstand and whom he asks to 'strike the grey hairs from his temples' and to help him write again (*Zerstreute Kapitel*, 'Heimkehr'). Storm was frequently anxious about the loss of his muse. For some time after the death of his first wife, Constanze, in May 1865, he was convinced that his muse had left him. 'If only I could write something respectable again,' he wrote to his son Hans in autumn 1867, 'but where is my muse? She sleeps the sleep of the dead! I shall never again write anything that enraptures a human heart!'

Page 93: *And if you had all spoken the truth – let us be!* A possible personal reference to Husum's close-knit society's reaction towards Storm's own well-known attractions to much younger women (see Introduction, page 17 and last note to page 94). An older man's affair with a teenager is also treated in Storm's later Novelle *Waldwinkel* (1874).

Page 93: *what would life be if there were no roses!* Roses were Constanze's especially favourite flowers. 'Your beloved roses', writes Storm in his dedication to *Immensee* (1850), a work he dedicated to her. The symbolism is evident.

The themes of loneliness and transience pervade many of Storm's works, and the puzzle of death his correspondence; all taking on a particular significance for him after Constanze's death in May 1865. In a letter dated 3 June 1865 to Eduard Mörike (1804–75) he wrote: 'Loneliness and the torturing riddle of death are the two dreadful things with which I have now entered on a silent, untiring struggle.' And to his friend Gottfried Keller (1819–90) in December 1879: ' . . . now I fear that the ghost of transience in life, which sits in every corner for me, and creeps up every stair, could crush me very easily.'

Page 93: *second sight.* Storm's daughter Gertrud was of the opinion that her father 'definitely believed in apparitions and second sight, as indeed do almost all of us coast-dwellers' (Gertrud Storm, *Vergilbte Blätter aus der grauen Stadt*, Leipzig, 1922, p. 46) (see also note to page 152).

Page 93: *Never possessed, yet lost.* 'Im eigenen Herzen geboren, / Nie besessen, dennoch verloren.' The maxim of Storm's poem 'Junge Liebe' ('Young Love').

Page 94: *a harvested field.* Symbol of old age.

Page 94: *in the look of death, in that last moment when all spirits of this world leave you.* A likely reflection of the descriptions of Constanze's death that Storm gave in correspondence. In one such letter, to Ludwig Pietsch on 25 May 1865, he wrote: 'Her groaning as death approached was hard and lasted long, but finally it became as soft as the buzzing of bees; then suddenly [. . .] a wonderful transfiguration passed over her face: a gentle blue gleam flitted over her dying eyes, and then there was peace.'

Page 94: *No ribbon.* A possible reference to the end of Goethe's *The Sorrows of Young Werther* (1774), in which Werther, in his suicide note, requests that the ribbon given to him by his beloved Lotte be buried with him after his death.

Page 94: *Who was this Eveline . . .?* After Constanze's death in 1865 it is believed that Storm, close to fifty, thought of marrying a younger, musically talented woman, Pauline Petersen, with whom he worked in his choral society. The depiction of the hero's affection for the young Eveline in this story may possibly owe something to these feelings. There is also a striking resemblance between Storm's 'Eveline' and 'Evelina' in Heine's *Reisebilder* ('Die Nordsee'):

> I love the sea, like my soul.
>
> Often inside me is the feeling that the sea is actually my soul; and as in the sea there are hidden aquatic plants, which only at the moment of their flowering float to its surface, and at the moment of their withering sink below its surface again: so floating up from the very depths of my soul, there come at times also wonderful pictures of fragrant and radiant flowers that then disappear again – 'Evelina!'

Hans and Heinz Kirch

Page 97: *a small town whose squat church tower.* The Baltic town of Heiligenhafen in the north of East Holstein. The 'squat church tower' refers to the town church, the Heiligenhafener Stadtkirche, built by Duke Adolph IV in 1260, which can still be seen today. The tower, some 92 feet high, is of Danish construction and was built in 1636/7 after the original high steeple, which served as an important landmark for sailors, was destroyed by lightning in 1591. In a letter dated September 1882 to Margarethe Mörike, wife of the writer Eduard Mörike (1804–75), Storm wrote that 'from this story you will receive a fairly true picture of Lisbeth's town.' Lisbeth, Storm's daughter, was married to Pastor Gustav Haase in Heiligenhafen at the time. A memorial to Storm stands by the church today.

Page 97: *a few cable-lengths.* The cable-length was a unit of measure equal to 608 feet. In nineteenth-century marine charts it was equal to 100 fathoms or one-tenth of a sea mile.

Page 97: *the Warder.* Known locally as the Graswarder. A long narrow sandbank lying parallel to the coast opposite Heiligenhafen, an inner sea being formed between it and the town's harbour. It is the natural result of a complex interaction of tide and sand over many centuries (see map on page 96). *Warder* is Low German for island.

Notes

Page 97: *shore birds and waterfowl*. The Graswarder is the habitat of many species of birds, particularly gulls which gather there in their thousands. Today the small island is a bird sanctuary.

Page 97: *the island opposite . . . the shore of the strait*. The large island of Fehmarn and its strait (Fehmarnscher Sund) which lie between the north coast of East Holstein and Denmark (see map on page 96).

Page 97: *two lighthouses . . . cast a shimmer of light over the dark sea towards the near shore*. In a letter to the writer Paul Heyse (1830–1914) dated 23 July 1883, Storm describes a similar scene he observed during a visit to Heiligenhafen to see his daughter Lisbeth and son-in-law Pastor Gustav Haase: 'I was staying there myself then for some eight days with our children at the Heiligenhafen parsonage, in the town of "Hans and Heinz Kirch", where we often sat in a boat out at sea in real summer weather, once well into the night, while from the distant island the lighthouses shimmered, and near and far excited the smooth surface of the water with sparkling lanterns, and the birds from the Warder occasionally emitted their calls.'

Page 97: *roughly paved steps lead . . . to the small houses*. In Heiligenhafen steps led from the road directly to the front of the properties. Waste water from the houses was carried away down to the harbour via gullies running on both sides of the cambered cobbled roads. Such steps often spanned these gullies.

Page 97: *complete remoteness . . . across the long chain of hills*. The hills stretched from Seekamp and Lütjenbrode in the east, ending on the west coast as high cliffs (see map on page 96). The town of Heiligenhafen was very much isolated from the rest of the mainland, not only because of the steep hills cutting off the town but also because of the extremely poor roads at the time. Road transport was infrequent and journeys were often hazardous: mail-coaches frequently turned over and it was not uncommon for passengers to arrive with injuries. Even at the time of Storm's visits to the town, as late as 1881, the journey was described as 'most uncomfortable'. There were no real improvements until late in the second half of the nineteenth century, particularly with the coming of the railway (see note to page 117).

Page 97: *the so-called town bell*. A 'secular clock', the Kökschenglocke, in a belfry on the roof of the former town hall in the centre of the market-place in Heiligenhafen (see cover illustration). The bell, originally a fire bell, is believed to have assured the townsfolk of the presence of the fire watch and reminded them to dampen down their fires before retiring to bed. Few people owned clocks at that time. Because of this, particularly for the servants of the community, the bell was saved when the building was pulled down in 1878 and reinstalled on another building in the town; it was in use until 1960 when it was taken down and placed in the town's museum.

Page 97: *woe betide any servants . . . who ignored its call.* In contrast to the church clock, the town bell, in addition to its fire watch purposes, regulated the daily life of the town. Within the Novelle it serves as a symbol for the strictly ordered nature of the town's life. The Heiligenhafen town chronicle includes a verse in Low German to match the rhythm and purpose of the clock:

Go to Bett!	Off to bed!
Slop recht nett!	Off to sleep!
Up to Tied!	Early to rise!
Ut mit Fried!	In blessèd peace!
Bur vöran!	The farmer leads!
Knecht achteran!	The hands follow!
Arbeit in Hüll!	Much work today!
Segen in Füll!	Abundance tomorrow!
Go to Bett!	Off to bed!
Slop recht nett!	Off to sleep!

Page 97: *wide stone-walled steps.* The walls of these imposing stairways to the houses in Heiligenhafen were often decorated with reliefs and a bench-seat was frequently set into the side of them.

Page 97: *up to the last decade.* Up to 1871.

Page 97: *only a few of them studied the sciences.* A reference to Heiligenhafen's isolation from mainstream scientific development and thought. Mid-nineteenth-century Europe was noteworthy not only for a considerable number of important scientific discoveries, but also for the foundation of modern science which especially in Germany became identified with learned academies and universities. Science was of particular interest to many educated Germans following the publication of Darwin's *Origin of Species* in 1859; its influence was then probably greater in Germany than anywhere else in Europe.

Page 97: *Bürgermeister.* Mayors.

Page 97: *there would seldom be a local man.* The town records of Heiligenhafen for the beginning of the nineteenth century show that Bürgermeister came from other parts of the region. The town chronicles also show that Bürgermeister around the time of the author's association with the town in 1881 were still being chosen from outside and moving on from Heiligenhafen to take up similar or associated posts in other towns. The Bürgermeister at the time of

Storm's researches in 1881 moved on to Hamburg, in the following year to become the director of its Work- and Poorhouse.

Page 97: *rector class*. The *Rektorschule*. The school system in Heiligenhafen during the early and mid nineteenth century provided a preparatory school, a girls' school and a boys' school, the last consisting of two classes, the upper of which was a 'rector class' (*Rektorklasse*). The rector had to teach not only English and French, but also when requested to provide private tuition in Latin and Greek. The principle of state education independent of Protestant as well as Catholic influence was established in Schleswig-Holstein under Prussian rule in 1872. Storm's son-in-law, Gustav Haase, was pastor (*Hauptpastor*) in Heiligenhafen from 1866 to 1885. It is possible that Storm obtained many details of local schooling from him.

Page 98: *'Shipmaster!' Schiffer*, the most prominent citizens in the town (Heiligenhafen). They were both ship-owners and shipmasters. By the mid-nineteenth-century there were some twenty-three *Schiffer* in Heiligenhafen.

Page 98: *Ship's boy*. A boy apprenticed to learn sea-duties, but generally appointed as a servant.

Page 98: *senator*. A municipal officer ranking next to the Bürgermeister; generally the head of a prominent and property-owning family in the community. From 1854 onwards, three senators (*Ratsherrn*) were appointed to the Heiligenhafen town council; prior to that date only two had been appointed (see note to page 109).

Page 98: *church built by a duke*. See first note to page 97.

Page 98: *Shipmasters' Gallery*. The Schifferstuhl, a gallery in the town church reserved for members of the seafarers' guild. Only captains and ship-owners who had passed the helmsman's or mate's examination were eligible for membership and could sit up in the gallery for church services, but an exception was made in the case of the early ship-owners in the town who had progressed to be prominent and respected merchants. A place in the Shipmasters' Gallery had to be paid for, and the seating was arranged according to rank and status. The Schifferstuhl at the time in which the story is set was the only place in the church to have upholstered seating. It is said locally that the idea for *Hans and Heinz Kirch* first occurred to Theodor Storm when he was sitting up in the Schifferstuhl during one of his visits to the church, an honour bestowed upon him by the town.

Page 98: *barque in full rigging*. A three-masted vessel with only fore-and-aft sails on her mizzen-mast. The model was of the 34-gun Swedish warship *Samson* built in 1632 in Västervik. There were originally two models of ships hanging in the Shipmasters' Gallery, but the whereabouts of the second remains unknown.

Page 98: *helmsman's examination*. The German *Steuermannsexamen*, equivalent to the mate's examination or 'ticket' in the British merchant marine. Such examinations had to be passed before the rank of captain or shipmaster was attained.

Page 98: *Hans Adam Kirch*. During a visit to Heiligenhafen in September/ October 1881 Storm learned the moving story of the trader and *Schiffer* Johann Brandt (1801–78) and his son Christian (see Introduction, page 28). Many events in the lives of Johann and Christian Brandt closely resemble those in the lives of Hans and Heinz Kirch. Johann Brandt's gravestone is still to be found in the Heiligenhafen cemetery. It is believed that the names Hans and Heinz Kirch derived from Storm's study of Heinrich Scholtz's Chronicle of the Town of Heiligenhafen (1743) which he discovered in the house of his son-in-law, Pastor Gustav Haase, in Heiligenhafen. In it are the Low German names of the senators Hans Karck (1557) and Hinrich (Heinz) Karcke (1570). 'Karck' is Low German for 'Kirch'.

Page 98: *leaseholding shipmaster*. A *Setzschiffer* was shipmaster who was neither owner nor joint owner of the ship he was commanding.

Page 98: *a cutter*. A small single-masted, fore-and-aft-rigged sailing vessel.

Page 98: *produce of the region, corn and flour*. Corn and flour were important exports from Heiligenhafen in the second half of the nineteenth century. The town was located in one of the richest corn-growing regions (Kreis Oldenburg) in Schleswig-Holstein. Seven windmills alone operated in the town; together with the church tower, they could be seen for many miles around. It was such an unusual number in one location that Heiligenhafen was known as 'the seven mills town'.

Page 98: *the bays*. The numerous narrow sandy bays of the Warder on its mainland side (see map on page 96).

Page 99: *a 'play-bird' as he put it*. A *Spielvogel* – sailor's expression for someone who goes to sea for pleasure, not to work.

Page 101: *his sister was born . . . could not be helped*. A reflection of the low status that women still had in Germany. As in Victorian England, the subordinate place of women in nineteenth-century German society was an essential part of its very fabric and functioning. Women were still excluded from higher education, business, the professions and politics, their role in society being perceived by church and state to be solely family-centred, to provide the husband with a proper domestic atmosphere, and to provide moral guidance for the family. The very idea of equality was considered to be against God's ordering of the sexes (see also note to page 43).

Page 101: *his neighbour, the pastor, whose garden extended from the front of the house to the street.* The elegant house of the trader and *Schiffer* Johann Brandt and his son Christian, on whose relationship the story is based (see note to page 98), stood at the corner of the Thulboden and the Poststraße in Heiligenhafen which was next to the parsonage's very large garden.

Page 102: *day-boarders.* Pupils who in return for payment were also provided with their meals by the pastor.

Page 102: *a lesson about these creatures.* Gertrud Storm, in her biography of her father, recalls that in her father's grammar school (*Gelehrtenschule*) in Husum, which he attended before going to Lübeck, two hours per week were set aside in the weekly timetable to the study of 'strange amphibians, fish and insects'. (Gertrud Storm, *Theodor Storm. Ein Bild seines* Lebens, Berlin, 1912/13, repr. 1991, p. 90).

Page 104: *over on the island.* The island of Fehmarn (see note to page 97).

Page 104: *'Möddersch'.* A Low German pet-name for aunt or for an old female relative.

Page 104: *St Michael's Fair.* An autumn fair held on 29 September, the feast-day of St Michael. Storm had many fond memories of fairs from his boyhood in Husum and such an occasion is described in an earlier Novelle, *Auf der Universität* (*At University*, 1862): 'The lamps on the roundabout were already lit; the music of the barrel-organs, laughter and a medley of voices drifted over to me, and between times the jingle of the foils on the iron ring-holders. I stopped and gazed through the lime-trees . . . at this animated scene. The merry-go-round was going at full tilt, with seats and horses all occupied. Male and female, young and old, were milling about round it . . .'

Page 104: *gingerbreads. Kuchenherzen,* heart-shaped gingerbreads that are still sold today at fairs in Germany.

Page 104: *three six-pfennig pieces.* Small copper coins known as *Sechslinge* worth about half a German Schilling.

Page 104: *eight shillings.* Small North German coins valid until the end of the nineteenth century.

Page 104: *schooner built at the local yard.* Topsail and three-masted schooners were built in the 'local yard' in Heiligenhafen during the latter part of the nineteenth century.

Page 105: *shipped corn to England . . . returned with cargoes of coal.* Before Heiligenhafen was connected to the inland rail network towards the turn of the century, two- and three-masted schooners frequently brought, among other cargoes, coal from England via Newcastle and Cardiff. Commercial shipping from Heiligenhafen ventured as far afield as the Far East, East Asia and Australia, imported cargoes including cotton, coffee beans, mineral coal and rice, and exported, corn, flour, peas, cheese, butter and pottery (see note to page 126).

Page 105: *'play-bird'.* See note to page 99.

Page 105: *blue peakless sailor's cap.* The caps worn by merchant seamen at the time generally conformed to the particular style adopted by the shipping company for which they worked. Most caps displayed a loose ribbon attached to the rear of the cap, the ship's or owner's name appearing on a band at its front.

Page 106: *the marble bust of . . . a commander of three of His Majesty's ships.* Moritz Hartmann (1656–95), son of the local rector, became an officer in the Danish marine before entering maritime service with the Venetian Republic in 1685. In recognition of his bravery against the Turks he was decorated by the doge with the Republic's highest honour, the Cross of St Mark. The marble baroque memorial displaying the bust of Hartmann flanked by draperies, cherubs, warriors' spears and anchors, and placed in the Heiligenhafen town church at the dying request of his brother, may be seen today on the wall by the entrance to the nave; it was in the Schifferstuhl's direct line of sight.

Page 106: *Hamburg-registered ship . . . to the China Sea.* By 1850 Hamburg had become continental Europe's leading trading centre and the second largest port in Europe after London. Ships flying the Hamburg flag had opened the world to its city's merchants.

Page 107: *Kuff.* An eighteenth- and nineteenth-century, two-masted coastal cargo ship employed on the Dutch and Belgian coasts, also on north-west German coasts from the early nineteenth century. The last Kuffs were built on the River Weser in 1895.

Page 109: *thoughts and inclinations.* A reference to Genesis 6:5. 'When the Lord saw that man had done much evil on earth and that his thoughts and inclinations were always evil, he was sorry that he had made man on earth, and he was grieved at heart' (New English Bible).

Page 109: *college of deputies.* The administrative structure of the town of Heiligenhafen at the time in which the story is set consisted of the Bürgermeister, the council (*Magistrat*), formed by the Bürgermeister himself and three senators (*Ratsherrn*), and the college of deputies (*Deputierten-Kollegium*), chaired by a leading member. Only those of independent means, and who owned property in the town, were eligible for a seat on the council. The right to be elected to the council was restricted chiefly to business-owners. The Prussians changed the civic titles of senators and deputies after their annexation of the duchies of Schleswig and Holstein in 1867 (see last note to page 117).

Page 109: *tail of the giant fish.* A killer whale. It was said to have been caught in a storm in 1742 and its tail hung by the door of the old Heiligenhafen town hall that once stood in the middle of the market-place. The whale was recorded as being some 28 feet long, 12 feet wide and with eyes wider than a hand, its tail measuring 8 feet across. A fish's tail still hangs above the door to the present-day town hall, but is smaller and made of wood.

Page 113: *the Fourth Commandment.* 'Honour your father and your mother' (Exodus 20:12; NEB).

Page 113: *the Commandment in which . . . all the others are included.* A possible reference to Leviticus 19:18: 'You shall not seek revenge, or cherish anger against your kinsfolk; you shall love your neighbour as a man like yourself . . . ' (NEB).

Page 115: *she had taken an order to the distillery.* Local chronicles record two distilleries in Heiligenhafen for the year 1872, supplying some thirteen local public houses with beer and wine.

Page 115: *Little good was said about the new enterprise . . . the burning red lamp.* Red lanterns have indicated brothels since the late nineteenth century, and the 'sailors' tavern' here could well have had a double meaning.

Page 117: *a new house had been built in the market-place for a young merchant.* A possible reference to a new house, the present town hall, built in the market-place in Heiligenhafen in 1881/82 for the wealthy mill, distillery and ship-owner, Senator J. P. Massmann.

Page 117: *telegraph wires.* The first telegraph office was set up in Heiligenhafen in 1874, followed by a telephone exchange in 1900 (the telegraph was first introduced into Germany in the late 1840s and the telephone about 1880). These events brought radical change to the life of small towns such as Heiligenhafen.

Page 117: *'Imperial Post Office'.* The postal service in Schleswig-Holstein after it became part of the German Empire in 1871 under Wilhelm I (1797–1888), King of Prussia (1861–88) and German Emperor.

Page 117: *when the north-west wind veered to the east-north-east, the high tide washed the walls of the distillery.* The distillery is the 'last house' at the 'end of the town' which, being in a bay, would generally be sheltered from the tidal effects of the north-west winds (see map on page 96). A strong wind from the east-north-east, however, would blow directly into the bay. The Baltic sea has very little tide by North Sea standards.

Page 117: *the end of the railway was still some miles away inland behind the chain of hills.* By 1866 the German railway network had reached only as far as Neustadt on the Baltic coast, some 20 miles from Heiligenhafen; the further link between Neustadt and Oldenburg was not completed until September 1881. It was not until 1898, however, that the first special twin-tendered train from Oldenburg covered the final 12 miles of railway along the coast and arrived at Heiligenhafen's newly-built station amid great pomp and ceremony. The German railway network expanded significantly between 1840 and 1880; the narrative statement that 'the end of the railway was still some miles away inland behind the chain of hills' serves to emphasise the town's isolation from the rest of Germany. The triad of railway, steam-ship and telegraph were strong symbols of progress in the nineteenth century.

Page 117: *even though Senators had been transformed into 'Aldermen' and Deputies into 'Town Councillors'.* In 1867 the former Danish duchies of Schleswig and Holstein were annexed to the Prussia-dominated North German Confederation (Norddeutscher Bund). The stresses and conflicts involved in these events are central to the life and works of Theodor Storm, who here levels indirect criticism at the unnecessary changes to local government administration by the Prussian authorities. The title of *Senator* was changed to *Stadtrat* and the title of *Deputierten* to *Stadtverordneten*: the primary functions of the posts, however, remained unchanged (see note to page 109).

Page 120: *the Harmony Society, as was well-known, admitted only respectable citizens.* The institution known as the *Harmoniegesellschaft* played a central role in German nineteenth-century industrial society. It was among the first purely social institutions in Germany established in large cities like Hamburg and Berlin towards the end of the eighteenth century, and spreading to the smaller towns early in the nineteenth. Its proclaimed aims, similar to those of other like institutions, included the 'acquisition of general scholarly knowledge' and the 'provision of social communication'. A Harmony Society was established in Storm's home town of Husum in 1827. These new societies were supposed to give people a place and a stake in the new industrial social order. Respectability featured strongly among the virtues of middle-class society of the time.

Page 120: *a solid gold chain on a brown velvet waistcoat.* Watches had once been ornaments of the rich, but by the 1850s millions of men could proudly display a watch chain across their chests. Owning a watch was a sign of autonomy since it implied a kind of power over time that dependent people could not enjoy, but it also suggested the owner's voluntary conformity to the authority of schedules and timetables. To be on time, to save time, and to spend it wisely were all important virtues of the *Bürgertum*.

Page 120: *a regular game of 'Sixty-Six'*. A German card game for two to four players, the winner being the one who first reaches a score of sixty-six.

Page 121: *Thaler*. A silver coin in use as late as 1876 when it was replaced by the Reichsmark following the foundation of the German Empire in 1871.

Page 121: *Johannisstraße*. Storm has in mind here a road of similar name (Johannisbollwerk) by the harbour in Hamburg near the St Pauli landing stage.

Page 122: *it's the tail of a killer whale*. See note to page 109.

Page 122: *'And they trade, said he, quite a lot; they've two boats, said he, and a yacht!'*. From a plattdeutsch hiking song (1850) about Heiligenhafen, the whale and its tail which Storm carefully noted in his diary in October 1881.

Hilligenhaven, seggt se, is man lütt,	Heiligenhafen, they say, is rather small,
un an'ne Radhus, seggt se, hangt en Bütt,	A plaice, they say, adorns its town hall,
un de Schiffohrt drievt se dor mit Macht,	At the seafaring trade they work quite a lot,
hebbt twe Böd, seggt se, un en Jacht.	They've even, it's said, two boats and a yacht!

The song has twenty-five stanzas, the seventeenth of which, quoted above, is inscribed on a plaque which can still be seen today beneath the wooden tail hanging above the entrance to the town hall (see note to page 109).

Page 125: *'Very well!'* In English in the original. Heinz is frequently made to utter foreign words and expressions to underline his seafaring life.

Page 125: *'Demonio! . . . – basta y basta!'* Spanish: 'Devil' . . . 'enough is enough'.

Page 126: *off-loading of hard coal*. Anthracite. After the establishment of the German Empire in 1871, imports into Heiligenhafen harbour outstripped exports. By the end of the century imports of hard coal exceeded 3000 tonnes per annum (see note to page 105).

Page 127: *by Jove*. In English in the original.

Page 129: *marble bust of the old commander*. See note to page 106.

Page 129: *Todos diabolos*. Spanish: 'To the devil with it'.

Page 130: *a boy from the poorhouse*. A new poorhouse was built in Heiligenhafen in

1840 with twenty-four rooms, a sickbay and a mortuary. The town's population was then some 1800. In 1853 the poorhouse was enlarged and converted into a home, or refuge, for the poor. The local chronicle records that some '6.2 acres of farmland and 4.9 acres of meadowland were also provided so that four cows and two pigs could be kept.' From 1853 until 1895 the home was managed by a Christian Friedrich Hasse whom the chronicle records as 'an extremely competent man'.

Page 131: *that blond Dithmarscher.* From the district of Dithmarschen on the west coast of Schleswig-Holstein.

Page 132: *Heinz, . . . not yet ready to present to the Society.* Many of the societies or associations (*Vereine*) formed in nineteenth-century Germany were intended to be exclusive places where the more affluent citizens, local businessmen, officials and professional men met to talk among 'their own kind'; many were simply societies for the cultivation of respectability and good taste. Their levels of subscription and entry requirements ensured their exclusiveness. The Harmony Societies catered mainly for those of the middle classes, while those like the Casino catered for the upper classes (see also note to page 120).

Page 132: *over the island opposite.* The island of Fehmarn (see fifth note to page 97).

Page 134: *San Jago.* Santiago, the largest of the Cape Verde Islands off the coast of former Portuguese West Africa. The islands featured prominently in the slave trade until its abolition there in 1876.

Page 135: *black ivory . . . that's to say black people.* 'Black ivory' was a term denoting African slaves which emphasised their high value. The slave trade was an integral part of a developed 'Atlantic economy' which reached its apogee in the last thirty years of the eighteenth century.

Page 135: *doubloons.* Spanish and Spanish American gold coins in circulation between the sixteenth and nineteenth centuries. One of the world's commercial currencies at the time.

Page 137: *Councillor of Justice. Justizrat* was a title in Germany normally given to professors of law and high law officials and the like, but not used in this sense here. In England an equivalent title was (and is) Queen's Counsel.

Page 139: *The harbour was unusually full of ships [. . .] together with the steamship which docked here each week.* At the peak of the sailing ship era, in the second half of the nineteenth century, the harbour in Heiligenhafen was generally filled with local and foreign vessels, notably three- to five-masted square-riggers. The town was the home port to some 56 sailing ships. The steamship *Zephir*, from 1860 onwards, plied once a week between Heiligenhafen, Kiel, Fehmarn and Denmark. From 1862 the steamship *Neustadt* sailed from Lübeck to Kiel, docking at Neustadt, Burgstaaken and Heiligenhafen on the way. One such vessel could have been in Storm's mind.

Page 139: *Ship and captain were not from here.* Foreign vessels frequently visited the small harbour of Heiligenhafen. In the 1870s, at the height of the town's trading activities, as many as 700 ships might visit the harbour in a year, among them three-masted schooners from Sweden. Danish ships were often used to export the town's pottery.

Page 141: *'God damn it!'* 'Goddam' in the original.

Page 142: ' . . . *by Jove.'* In English in the original.

Page 143: *'Where's the grog got to then?'* 'Old Grog' was the nickname of Edward Vernon (1684–1757), the British admiral who ordered that diluted rum be served to his sailors. There is a monument to Admiral Vernon near the harbour in Heiligenhafen.

Page 143: *sails to England as a seaman.* See note to page 105.

Page 146: *the broader waters between the Warder and the island opposite.* The Fehmarn strait (Fehmarnscher Sund) (see map on page 96).

Page 146: *Thanks for the alms and farewell for ever.* In English in the original.

Page 149: *retirement benefit.* Before Bismarck's 'Old Age and Disability Insurance' (1889) Germany lacked state-controlled provision of old-age pensions or similar assistance. Nevertheless various kinds of payments were made to persons in old age before this date, derived as much from local, town or regional (*Länder*) sources as from private ones.

Page 150: *it was a girl, and he spoke no more about it.* See note to page 101.

Page 150: *equinoctial storms.* Severe storms occurring at the time of the spring and autumn equinoxes.

Page 150: *silver pocket-watch . . . with the key.* The winding crown of a pocket watch, winding the mainspring, was not introduced until around 1840; before this time pocket watches were wound with a key.

Page 151: *storms came at the equinox, he had heard them many times.* A severe storm struck the town of Heiligenhafen on 13 November 1872; 42 families lost their homes and the water rose some twelve feet above its normal level; a fully laden ship was swept over the Warder and onto the town's shore. The author himself was no stranger to such severe storms in his home town of Husum on the Schleswig coast. The severe storm that occurred there on 3 February 1825 left a lasting impression on the then eight-year-old's mind (see note to page 79). He described the terrors of such storms in his Novellen *Carsten Curator* (1878) and

Der Schimmelreiter [trs. *The Dykemaster*] (1888), and the poem 'Sturmnacht' ('Night of the Storm').

Page 151: *stem post*. The stem is the foremost piece uniting the bows of a ship; its lower end joins the keel, and the bowsprit rests upon its upper end. Hence the expression 'from stem to stern', from one end of a ship to the other.

Page 151: *a huge white Fortuna*. Fortuna, the Roman goddess of destiny or chance, had the power to lift up lowly mortals and cast down the mighty. Her symbols in art were a ship's rudder and a cornucopia. As the patron saint of sailors, she was frequently carved as a ship's figurehead, painted white, and shown holding a cornucopia in her right hand. Sailing ships were often named after her.

Page 152: *'He's dead,' he said, 'far from here.'* According to age-old popular belief a member of the family or other close person makes contact at the time of his/her death, such an appearance being witnessed through the spiritual phenomenon known as 'second sight'. Seafarers in particular believed they were able, by second sight, to detect from a distance the circumstances surrounding a misfortune. Like other North Friesians, Storm did not repudiate the possibility of second sight, and the unvarnished narrative manner of his earlier ghost stories, *Am Kamin* (*By the Fire*, 1862), shows how real to him was the underlying presence of inexplicable forces influencing the fate of human beings. He wrote to Gottfried Keller on 4 August 1882, having described a visit to his son Ernst in a supposedly haunted house: 'In a particular case my attitude to these matters is indeed doubting or even incredulous, but on the other hand, in general very open-minded: I don't believe in either the un- or the supernatural, but I do think that natural phenomena that are inaccessible to everyday perceptions are as yet far from being recognised.' (P. Goldammer, (ed.), *Der Briefwechsel zwischen Theodor Storm und Gottfried Keller*, Berlin, 1960, p. 119) (see also note to page 93).

Page 153: *he could see . . . the islands*. The islands of the Warder and Fehmarn to the north-east (see map on page 96).

Page 154: *'social democrat'*. The German Social Democratic Party, founded in 1875, suffered prolonged hostility from the ruling parties and classes who saw its growth in the cities and industrial areas as a threat to the unity of the new Reich. With their revolutionary agenda of religion as a private matter, and with their leaning towards a materialistic (Marxist) view of the world, the Social Democrats in their early period were suspected of distancing themselves from Christian belief. Whether Storm is here adopting the sentiments of the ruling class of his time regarding the 'godless revolutionaries' is open to interpretation.

Also in Angel Classics

THEODOR STORM
The Dykemaster (*Der Schimmelreiter*)
Translated by Denis Jackson
0 946162 54 9 (paperback)

One of the most celebrated narratives in German literature – the story of a visionary young creator of a new form of dyke at odds with a short-sighted and self-seeking community, set on the eerie west coast of Schleswig-Holstein, with its hallucinatory tidal flats, hushed polders, and terrifying North Sea. The translator's introduction and end notes provide intimate commentary on the topographical, historical and biographical background to the tale.

'Translations of the high standard of this one are more than ever in demand.' – Mary Garland, editor of *The Oxford Companion to German Literature* (third edition, 1997)

THEODOR FONTANE
Effi Briest
Translated by Hugh Rorrison and Helen Chambers
0 946162 44 1 (paperback)

A brilliant new translation of Fontane's story of adultery in Bismarck's Prussia – the outstanding nineteenth-century German novel – which was the basis of a Radio 4 *Classic Serial* adaptation (1998) and is also being used for the script of a feature film of *Effi Briest* now in development.

'Accurate as no previous translation has been . . . you can hear Fontane himself in it and understand for the first time, if you have no German, why this is a novel to draw tears.' – D. Sexton, *The Guardian*

'The Rorrison/Chambers version brings *Effi Briest* vividly to life in a way that previous versions have not.' – Hermione Lee, *Sunday Times*

'Only now is the English-speaking reader in a position to enjoy the novel as it really is.' – A. Bance, *Times Literary Supplement*

THEODOR FONTANE
Cécile
Translated by Stanley Radcliffe
0 946162 42 5 (cased)   0 946162 43 3 (paperback)

The first-ever English translation of the second in Fontane's series of 'Berlin' novels. At a fashionable spa in the Harz Mountains an affair develops between an itinerant civil engineer and the delicate, mysterious wife of a retired army officer – to explode in the bustling capital of a newly unified Germany.

'*Cécile* is written with wit and a controlled fury and Radcliffe's elegant translation does it superb justice.' – M. Ratcliffe, *The Observer*

SIX GERMAN ROMANTIC TALES
Translated by Ronald Taylor
0 946162 17 4 (paperback)

Heinrich von Kleist: 'The Earthquake in Chile'; 'The Betrothal on Santo Domingo';
Ludwig Tieck: 'Eckbert the Fair', 'The Runenberg'; E.T.A. Hoffmann: 'Don Giovanni',
'The Jesuit Chapel in G.'

'All the varieties of the German Romantic movement are here: magical, musical, political
and aesthetic . . . Excellent translations.' – S. Plaice, *Times Literary Supplement*

ARTHUR SCHNITZLER
Selected Short Fiction
Translated by J. M. Q. Davies
0 946162 49 2 (paperback)

The balanced selection of Schnitzler's short fiction that has long been needed: thirteen
novellas and short stories – a number of them translated into English for the first time –
ranging from brief comic tales to substantial novellas like 'Lieutenant Gustl', 'Fräulein
Else' and 'The Duellist's Second', and displaying Schnitzler's intuitive understanding of
the human psyche that was admired by his Viennese contemporary Sigmund Freud.

'. . . collectively these stories show the fingerprints of a master hand.' – B. Fallon, *The Irish
Times*

VSEVOLOD GARSHIN
From the Reminiscences of Private Ivanov *and other stories*
Translated by Peter Henry, Liv Tudge and others
0 946162 08 5 (cased)   0 946162 09 3 (paperback)

Russia's outstanding new writer of fiction between Dostoyevsky and the mature
Chekhov, Garshin gave voice to the disturbed conscience of an era that knew the horrors
of modern war, the squalors of rapid industrialisation, and a politically explosive
situation. This extensive selection contains nearly all Garshin's published novellas and
short stories – among them, some of the best Russian war stories and densely semiotic
narratives like 'The Red Flower' and 'The Signal'.

'Garshin's supreme gift is an acute moral intelligence steadied by the economy of his style
. . . he anticipates Babel; and it is legitimate to hear in the spare articulation of his prose
the rhythm of Pushkin.' – H. Gifford, *Times Literary Supplement*

HENRYK SIENKIEWICZ
Charcoal Sketches *and other tales*
Translated by Adam Zamoyski (author of The Polish Way*)*
0 946162 31 X (cased)   0 946162 32 8 (paperback)

The best short fiction by the author of *Quo vadis* – three novellas with contemporary
nineteenth-century backgrounds. The title-story is a headlong satire on Polish provincial
life under tsarist rule. In 'Bartek the Conqueror' a Polish hero of the Franco-Prussian
War finds he is no match for the Germans in the postwar peace. 'On the Bright Shore' is

a deliciously observed study of manners and morals among the expatriate Polish gentry on the French Riviera in the 1890s.

'Zamoyski's sprightly new translations demonstrate that the passage of a century cannot disguise the wit or lessen the bite of these three novellas.' – *Publishers Weekly*

PIERRE CORNEILLE
Horace
Translated by Alan Brownjohn
0 946162 57 3 (paperback)

This powerful drama, which helped launch French classical tragedy, lays bare the sinister nature of patriotism.

'Corneille's rhyming alexandrines have been superbly translated into a flexible blank verse which captures the nuances of meaning . . .' – Maya Slater, *Times Literary Supplement*

HEINRICH HEINE
Deutschland
Translated by T. J. Reed; bilingual edition
0 946162 58 1 (paperback)

The wittiest work of Europe's wittiest poet.

'a fine example of superior political poetry. This translation triumphantly conveys the satirical power, ironic tone and humorous accessibility.' – Anita Bunyan, *Jewish Chronicle*

FERNANDO PESSOA
The Surprise of Being
Translated by James Greene and Clara de Azevedo Mafra; bilingual edition
0 946162 24 7 (paperback)

Twenty-five of the haunting poems written by Portugal's greatest modern poet in his own name – the most confounding of his personae.

'Indispensable.' – J. Pilling, *PN Review*

For a complete list please write to Angel Books, 3 Kelross Road, London N5 2QS